Abigail hated

'Photography has [...]
more people than [...]

'Oh, I can think of one or two others, off-hand,' said Carl with a devilishly lazy smile, and now Abigail's cheeks shot with scarlet. She decided to bring this disturbing discussion to a rapid conclusion.

'Are you lost, perhaps, or do you often make a practice of bowling up people's drives in order to abuse them?'

Dear Reader

After tackling Victorian Devon, Sarah Westleigh was inspired to try her hand at a Regency, and A MOST EXCEPTIONAL QUEST is the result. Who is the 'John Smith' who lost his memory fighting in the Peninsular War, and why does Davinia so resent having to help him? Marion Carr's WHISPERING SHADOWS also involves a quest, which reaches back from 1907 to medieval Italy as Carl and Abigail try to resolve their differences and find a fortune — two fascinating mysteries for you to solve!

The Editor

Marion Carr spent many years in the Lake District where she brought up two daughters and various animals. She has been a teacher, bookseller and smallholder, but now lives in Cornwall with her husband and two dogs. She loves researching through travel, old books, and talking to people.

Recent titles by the same author:

HESTER
OUTRAGEOUS FORTUNE

WHISPERING SHADOWS

Marion Carr

First published in Great Britain 1993
by Mills & Boon Limited

© Marion Carr 1993

Australian copyright 1993
Philippine copyright 1993
This edition 1993

ISBN 0 263 78058 9

Masquerade is a trademark published by
Mills & Boon Limited, Eton House,
18–24 Paradise Road, Richmond, Surrey, TW9 1SR.

Set in 10 on 12 pt Linotron Times
04-9308-74358

Typeset in Great Britain by Centracet, Cambridge
Made and printed in Great Britain

CHAPTER ONE

ABIGAIL CARTER clicked her tongue with exasperation as she peered through the viewfinder of her new folding pocket Kodak at the wavering image of her sister.

'Will you please stop fidgeting, Polly? How shall I ever get a good photograph if you will keep prinking and preening at your hair? You are quite the vainest person I know.'

Polly wriggled some more so that the wide neck of her summer dress slipped further down her bare arms where she had pulled it in an attempt to show off the sloping white curve of her shoulders. She consoled herself that if her sixteen-year-old chest did not quite match Abigail's fine bosom at least the cascade of golden curls that floated so delectably in the soft summer breeze was infinitely superior to her older sister's chestnut locks, which was a perfectly boring colour in Polly's estimation.

Unimpressed by this display of youthful beauty, Abigail gave out a great sigh, marched over to her sister, and pulled the cream spotted net unceremoniously upwards in an attempt to restore decorum. Allowing Polly to wear this most revealing of gowns had clearly been a mistake. But then most of Abigail's efforts to control her wayward sister met with similar lack of success. Why her parents had thought she could succeed where they had failed, heaven alone knew.

Abigail had always been well aware that she would require employment of some sort. Her father did well enough, she supposed, in his ironmongery shop, for their standard of living had always been good and her mama most particular about whom her two young daughters consorted with, a task easier to impose upon the more sensible Abigail than the recalcitrant Polly. And at gone twenty-five there was little hope now of marriage snaring her, not that Abigail cared one way or the other. She felt perfectly well able to take care of herself and was far more interested in her beloved photography than any young man she had ever seen come tapping on her father's door. No, she had been willing enough to accept the post of companion to Mrs Emilia Goodenough, an elderly lady of private means, at least until something more exciting turned up. Particularly since the lady already had one household servant so there was no question of Abigail being coerced into emptying ash cans or washing out linens. But to be expected to take Polly along with her had come as something of a blow.

Abigail wanted, most desperately, to travel, and was constantly scanning the small advertisements of the local newspaper for the right opportunity to present itself. But what would become of Polly then?

The object of Abigail's study now gave a loudly exaggerated sigh and smoothed out the sash of her dress with pettish fingers. 'My back is positively *aching* from sitting so long. I thought this was supposed to be a modern camera which took simple snapshots at the press of a button. I have been sitting here *forever*.'

'It does,' said Abigail rather sharply, taking her eye from the viewfinder to fix it sternly upon the sitter. 'But the light must be just right and the subject must undertake to keep still. Now, are you ready?'

Polly gave a little wriggle and then a surprised hiccup

of laughter, but Abigail did not notice as she had turned her attention to studying a suspiciously mobile grey cloud that threatened to block the sun out at any moment. Polly could be great fun, and an absolute dear if one was depressed or unwell or whatever. Her heart, as they said, was in the right place despite her frivolous nature, childlike vanity and downright wilfulness at times. And the child knew, of course, that however grumpy Abigail might sound, and however much she might scold Polly, there was never any doubt but that she loved her.

'Keep absolutely still. Hold your breath.' Abigail was likewise holding hers. Having carefully framed her delightfully pretty sister in exactly the right pose, the sunshine glinting perfectly on her silver fair hair, even the tilt of Polly's head beguilingly sweet and appealing, the blue eyes open and trusting, Abigail was anxious to capture the image for all time on this most magic of cameras. 'Hold it. . .' And as Abigail's finger sank the button and the shutter blinked slowly across the aperture the pretty pink and cream picture vanished, replaced by a dark head, round glittering eyes and a leering gargoyle grin. So startled was Abigail by this monstrous vision that she very nearly dropped the precious camera upon the stone driveway. 'What on earth. . .?

'Sorry. Did I make you jump?' The interloper was laughingly stripping off huge goggles and gauntlet driving gloves. No wonder he had unnerved her, peering into the lens of her camera in that get-up. What effrontery, and she would tell him so, at once.

Had Abigail been able at that juncture to think of some quick rejoinder she would have made it. But her mind was filled with only red-hot fury and her tongue stilled by a freezing paralysis the moment the mask was torn away. Far from being that of a gargoyle, the smile on the face before her was positively beatific. Slightly crooked, admittedly, with a touch of sardonic humour at the corner, but wide and apparently genuine beneath a classically straight nose and assessing dark eyes with a swoop of soot-black lashes that flicked lazily up at the tips. Not wishing him to see how he had startled her, Abigail met his gaze candidly, with frank and open speculation, not dropping her own eyes nor even a curtsy, as might have been appropriate for a young woman in her humble station before what was evidently a gentleman of some means come calling upon her employer. But the new century was seven years old and such niceties did not appeal to Abigail.

The smile deepened as he became aware of her scrutiny, penetrating right to the heart of her, a heart that was behaving in an exceedingly odd way were she to pay credence to it, which of course she did not. A large olive-skinned hand was being thrust out towards her.

'Carl Montegne. At your service.'

She ignored it. Did he imagine that his handsome charm would excuse him for spoiling her picture? The fact that she had any number of unexposed shots still to use on her roll of film was, in Abigail's opinion, quite beside the point. They had waited through ten long days of rain for this sun. It had taken half the afternoon to get Polly to the point of being satisfied with her appearance, after half a dozen changes of gown and even more of hairstyle, not to mention the agony of making her sit still, and this, this *idiot* had come along and stuck his head in front of the lens and ruined it. Abigail proceeded to tell him so in no uncertain terms. He listened, with surprising patience, for some moments before interjecting.

'Shall I withdraw while you pose again, Miss — er — Polly, is it?' he asked, with a winning smile.

'Oh, bother all that,' said she, her own blue eyes positively twinkling with impish delight. 'I'm vastly tired of being looked at,' she mourned outlandishly.

A deep-throated chuckle that had an alarming effect upon Abigail's equilibrium, and from the look of it upon Polly's too, rumbled forth. 'You surprise me. I thought pretty young misses never tired of being looked at. Isn't that why they take photographs of each other, so that we gentlemen may admire them further, at our leisure?'

This was too much for Abigail. Had she not been so very sensible and mature she would have stamped her booted foot and enjoyed the sensation.

'Really, I do not take photographs for gentlemen, or *otherwise*, to ogle,' she said in shocked tones. 'How dare you suggest such a thing?'

Carl Montegne had the audacity to laugh. 'I wasn't suggesting anything of the kind. I do assure you that I have never, in my life, ogled, though I'll admit on occasions to being sorely tempted.'

Polly burst into peals of laughter and even Abigail, struggling with her dignity, felt a nervous twitch at the corners of her mouth. But not for one moment would she let it slip. This interloper must be dealt with, and that right smartly. 'I am pleased to hear it,' she said, rather stuffily. 'There are enough peeping Toms taking advantage of the camera lens.'

'Indeed.' Brown eyes glowed and, leaning back against his gleaming automobile, Carl Montegne crossed his arms against a remarkably broad chest as if

settling down for a leisurely discussion. 'I believe some
have been known to photograph unsuspecting ladies in
their bathing dress. What cads. But what would you
consider to be the camera's greatest asset, Miss —
er. . .um — what was the name again?'

'I didn't give it.' Abigail drew herself up to her not
inconsiderable height. Even then it was far short of his,
but she had no intention of being intimidated. 'The eye
of the camera records truth.'

'Not art?'

She hesitated fractionally. 'Yes, art in a sense, I
suppose, but more direct. Art gives an interpretation;
photography records things as they actually are and
thereby instructs. It is more science than art, and
history too.'

But he was shaking his head. 'The camera is a
dangerous instrument. It purports to tell the truth, but
can in fact publicise fakes. See how you pose young
Polly here. Forgive me, but though I am certain she is
always perfectly delightful to look at I wonder if she is
quite so angelic as she appears.'

Polly gave a splutter of laughter that was almost
vulgar and Abigail's soft cheeks suffused with pink.
Not for one moment would she admit as much to this
odious cocksure young man who appeared to have a
passion for practical jokes that clearly overcame
common decency. 'I accept that painters of portraits
are now finding themselves in straits, but photography
tells me so much more about the real person, if it is
well executed.'

'Rubbish,' he said, rather rudely. 'Are you saying
that Titian's *Venus* or Leonardo da Vinci's *Mona Lisa*
are less truthful because they are painted? Absolute
heresy.'

Abigail was embarrassed. 'That was not what I meant and you know it. Besides,' she scoffed, 'there were no cameras in fifteenth-century Italy.'

'You surprise me.' His voice held a hint of mockery. 'Perhaps it is just as well or the Fathers might have settled for sticking sepia prints all over the Sistine Chapel instead of asking Michelangelo to paint the *Last Judgement*.'

There was a small silence as Abigail sought a way out of this intellectual trap he had laid for her, perhaps deliberately. She was infuriated to find none, for he had quite blatantly shifted the emphasis of her own argument to score a cheap point. She decided relentlessly to pursue her own. 'You know full well I was not talking of Great Art with a capital A. I am talking of family portraits of *ordinary* people with whom perhaps you are not acquainted, being so lofty.'

'Ouch,' he said, but Abigail was not to be distracted by humour. Though her own keen sense of it was usually her saving grace, preventing her taking life or herself too seriously, this man had somehow rubbed her up the wrong way, first by not really caring that he had spoiled her picture and secondly by scoring some very valid points at her expense. She hated, above all, to be bested.

'I'll own that perhaps we pay too much attention to photographing people at play rather than recording the realities of work, but photography has brought more pleasure to more people than any other single hobby.'

'Oh, I can think of one or two others, offhand,' said he with a devilishly lazy smile, and now Abigail's cheeks shot with scarlet. He had gone too far and the worst of it was that she found this roguish sense of mischief really rather appealing. She decided to bring this disturbing discussion to a rapid conclusion.

She looked beyond him at the long sleek lines of green automobile. 'Are you lost, perhaps, or do you often make a practice of bowling up people's drives in order to abuse them?'

Carl Montegne gave a snort of laughter. He decided he liked this spirited young woman, despite her rather negative attitude towards art. He wondered what she would look like if she released that long curtain of chestnut hair from the dull brown ribbon that so sensibly bound it, and whether that tight, disapproving mouth ever softened and how it would taste in a kiss. Not that he could ever imagine her allowing such a thing, so very proper was she. And yet, somewhere in the depths of those entrancing amber eyes, had he detected an answering gleam of mischief? It might be a possibility worth pursuing.

'I did hope to see my aunt,' he continued, glancing about him as if she might materialise at any moment from behind the rose bushes. 'Is she about, do you know? Or is she still engaged on her exhausting inventory?'

Polly's half-smothered snort of laughter this time threatened almost to choke her and indeed the fit of coughing that ensued took some time to abate and required much slapping on the back from her less than patient sister. Though, far from being annoyed, Abigail was almost glad of the diversion, for she had felt a treacherous bubble of laughter explode in her own throat. The fact was that Mrs Goodenough, the aunt of this rude man, and her employer, had indeed done little else since Abigail and Polly arrived but make out endless lists of the contents of each and every drawer.

'One never knows when one may be called,' she had soberly replied when Abigail had gently queried this practice. 'It is our duty to leave our affairs as tidily as possible for those who come after.'

'But what if you should lose something or move it from one drawer to another in the interim?' Abigail had asked, laying down her pen to relax her tired fingers for a moment.

'Order is the key to a happy life,' the old lady had replied starkly. 'And we simply must not lose anything, must we? I very much believe in a place for everything and everything in its place.'

'Yes, but it could be years before. . .' Abigail had halted, aghast by what she had been about to say. It simply was not done in her eyes to speak of the death, however long distant, of an employer. But Emilia Goodenough was made of sterner stuff and had only chortled with glee at the apparent breach of good manners on the part of her young companion.

'I sincerely hope it is,' she had said crisply. 'I am fit enough. What the modern idiom likes to call a fine figure of a woman, I believe. Nevertheless I like to be organised. And if changes are made in the coming years it is not beyond our wit or capabilities to remake the lists, eh?'

'Oh, indeed, yes,' Abigail had hastily agreed, inwardly mortified at the prospect of spending years compiling and re-compiling lists of linen handkerchiefs and counterpanes. The prospect was made worse by the vast number of chests and wardrobes in the large rambling house, a white seaside villa well served with balconies, iron fretwork and attics. Would Mrs Goodenough's descendants care whether each chest and cupboard carried its due quota of goods according to its enclosed inventory? Presumbly they would, else why do it?

'As my late husband used to say as we made camp in the African bush and he was looking for his after dinner cigars, "Where would we be without Goody's lists?" What a card he was.' And her grey eyes had softened momentarily and she had blinked rather rapidly before seizing the handles ready for assault on the next drawer. 'And it's such fun tidying the damn things out, eh? Never know what we might find.'

In that moment Abigail had seen that it was loneliness which actually drove her to this over-zealous task, and not a desire to pacify greedy relatives at all. For a woman who had spent the majority of her life travelling the world with her adventurer husband, retirement in a Devon seaside town must be anathema. But the whole pantomime did result in the most awful complications. Nothing could be moved, worn, washed, read or even eaten without first consulting and adjusting the appropriate list.

'Pray offer your apologies, Polly,' urged Abigail now, not wishing to seem totally without honour, but Carl Montegne merely waved a hand.

'No need to on my behalf. It's been driving me demented for years. Why she doesn't just sell up and move into a smart little apartment on the sea front I shall never understand.'

'She likes space. And would be lost without her things.'

'Unless she had some greater purposes to her life.'

'That goes without saying.'

Brown eyes were speculative. 'Not necessarily. I take it you are the latest in what has turned out to be a dismally long line of companions. If you have the patience, and take the trouble to understand her, Goody can be a fascinating lady. It would seem that you are already halfway there. I take my hat off to you, Miss. . . Ah, now, you really must not be coy any further about your name. I'm sure it cannot be so dreadful.'

Abigail gasped. 'Why do you always assume the worst?' she complained.

'Because he's a rogue of the first quarter who loves nothing better than to tease the life out of God-fearing folk,' came a booming voice from the open door of the house behind Abigail. 'Carl, you young fox, come and hug me.' And to Abigail's vast astonishment and Polly's delight he did just that. He even lifted the bulky little lady off her feet and swung her round till she squealed like a girl. Abigail felt an unexpected tug of jealousy as her errant mind wondered what it would feel like to be held in those strong arms and brush her cheek against the warmth of his. As a result she was forced to cloak tell-tale eyes with the deep swath of her dark lashes in case he should read her wayward thoughts.

'If you'll let me get my breath,' gasped Emilia Goodenough, 'I'll introduce you. Abigail, meet my nephew, Carl Montegne, a real miscreant if ever there was one. Abigail Carter. And you are not to plague her, Carl, for she's a saint and I'll not have you scare her off as you did the others.'

'A calumnious lie. Would I do such a thing to my favourite aunt?' Carl teased. 'You were well rid of that last one you hired since she chose to help herself to your silver. As for Miss Carter, why, I have already made her feel welcome, and she has taken a picture of me with her camera, have you not?' He asked the question with such a blithe innocence in his tone, his brows quirking upwards with impish enquiry, that Abigail's composure finally cracked and she laughed out loud.

'Ah, splendid,' said the old lady. 'I see we are all going to get along quite famously. Do come in and we'll see what the girl can find for us to nibble and you can tell me what it is you want from me this time.'

'Good lord, don't make me out to be a scrounger as well. I am surely not that.'

Emilia looked contrite, and, reaching up, patted his tanned cheek. 'No, my dear, of course you are not; don't get on your high horse. It is only that you so often come by with some impossible scheme or other to restore the family fortunes, to which I am expected to give my blessing at the very least. So what is it this time?'

Carl Montegne gave an engaging grin that quite took Abigail's breath away and she at once vowed to guard against his undoubted charms. Emilia had no need of such resolution and smiled up at him as if the sun rose and set upon his dark, curly head. He tucked her hand in the crook of his arm, brown eyes alight with enthusiasm.

'I am determined, Goody, to give it one last try. Somewhere in that huge *castello* the secret lies hidden. All we have to do is find it and our fortune is made.'

'What are you babbling about? Oh, do come in. It's almost four and I'm parched. Can't think without my regular cups of tea, and the girl will have set it out all ready.'

Carl Montegne escorted the small, bustling figure of his aunt along the passage from the front door and through to the conservatory at the back of the capacious house where a very ample tea of muffins, scones and saffron cake had been set out upon a large cast-iron table.

Abigail and Polly followed at a respectful distance, the former wondering if perhaps it would be more polite to forgo tea today in order to leave the two of them in peace. But Emilia was already waving them to seats with an impatient hand and obediently they took them. China teacups were handed out by the girl, who would not in fact ever see sixty again but had been so dubbed ever since that long-ago day when she had been just that, a young girl starting work for Emilia's parents. Now the lean face was marred with wrinkles and the hair was iron-grey, what you could see of it beneath the most unflattering cap she always wore pulled low down over her forehead. And if she had had any other name, Abigail suspected she must long since have forgotten it.

When everyone was happily sipping at the scalding liquid, scones loaded with cream, or muffins cut up ready to nibble without losing the butter, Emilia nodded to her nephew and settled into her wing-back chair. 'Go on, I am quite ready for more. Tell me all. What secret do you seek?'

Carl abandoned his cup and saucer with a thankful clatter. 'The alabaster figurine?' Abigail noted that Emilia appeared quite unmoved by this news.

He was on his feet, pacing the tiled floor of the conservatory with barely concealed excitement.

'This time I have a feeling. I'm sure this time I shall strike lucky. And with more money to finance the expedition, I can spend longer looking. You will come, Goody, won't you?'

And now Emilia did look astonished, and she put

the muffin slowly back upon its plate, a small glint of matching excitement lighting her grey eyes. 'Come with you?'

He was standing before her chair, seizing the arms to lean over her, wide mouth firm and no longer smiling, a glittering sparkle in narrowed eyes. 'To Italy, of course. Florence, deep in the Tuscan hillside. How about it? Leave all of this. Put your damned inventories away. Forget English muffins, the constant rain and even your endless stream of solemn-faced companions, and come with me to find the sun and adventure. What do you say? Isn't that what you love? Excitement? Travel? *Danger*?'

It was what Abigail would love, and she stared at the two of them, a picture of perfect accord as the one gazed upon the other, freeze-framed forever in her mind. To nephew and aunt nothing existed beyond themselves and whatever it was that forged this dream. Abigail's heart had leapt at that one word, 'Italy', but then her spirit had sunk to the gloomy depths of her stomach as she had found herself dismissed together with the muffins and the rain. She had always known she was of no account, but to have it quite so clearly stated left her weak with the pain of it. If she could have slipped invisibly from the room at that point she would have done so, but so afraid was she of calling attention to herself that she sat as one frozen, hardly daring even to breathe. Polly, however, was not so socially sensitive and she let out a little squeal of excitement which brought both faces swivelling round to look at her, slight puzzlement mingling with the rapture as if they did not quite remember who she was.

'How terribly marvellous. Isn't Florence flooded or has a church leaning or falling down or something?'

There was the most dreadful pause. But instead of answering her, Carl Montegne looked straight at Abigail. 'Do you teach your sister nothing? Not that she could learn much from someone who prefers photographs to true art.'

The gibe stung despite the lightness of the tone which offered it and Emilia scolding that he must not be unkind to little Polly for if her education was lacking it was her fault, Emilia's, not poor Abigail's, for she had undertaken the task of improving it herself.

'It is Venice, not Florence, my dear, whose streets are flooded,' she explained. 'And the tower of Pisa which leans, though I assure you it will not fall down; I am quite certain of it. No one would allow such a thing. And yes, it is all marvellously exciting. Tell me what you plan, Carl. I am all ears.'

And as Carl Montegne settled back in his seat and began to recount a tale of such fascination and mystery that would kindle a flame of interest in any heart, Abigail did not wonder at the stirring in her own. Watching him, more carefully than she realised, she noted every nuance of expression, the flicker of eyelash, the twitch of brow, the wry humour that often lifted the corner of the wide, full mouth. She marvelled at the resolution writ plain in the way he held the square jaw firm. She saw the mission glow from out those polished mahogany eyes and could not fail to appreciate the certainty of power he felt to command his own destiny. All these were revealed in his expression, the way he held the attention of his audience and the fluidity and purpose of his movements, even to the way he ticked off problems on his long fingers and as swiftly set those same problems aside as of no consequence.

Abigail sat listening, stunned with misery, and to her dismay realised that it was not simply for the loss of the opportunity to visit Italy, but also for the loss of getting to know this fascinating man.

CHAPTER TWO

As ABIGAIL plaited her fingers in numb misery, Carl Montegne took the opportunity to study her with greater care. Without question there was strength in the full mouth and a latent sensuality not yet in full bloom. Though the eyes were hooded now with a down-drawn sweep of dark brown lashes, he remembered their startling brilliance, the glorious glint of gold in the amber depths. There was passion in those eyes, and daring, quite at odds with the practical, everyday image of their owner. Her figure, what he could see of it in the plain grey stuff dress that did nothing to flatter, was fine, almost regal, a neatly cut waist beneath a bosom any woman, and man, would be proud to own, in their respective manners. And there was about her the assurance of a woman who had found herself, albeit one with yet unfulfilled dreams.

It occurred to him that Miss Abigail Carter might not be entirely what she appeared. For all he knew she might be the very worst kind of calculating fortune hunter, the kind who preyed on old ladies. Why else should such a woman choose to act as companion to an eccentric with an obsession for lists? However dear Emilia might be to him, she had little to offer the likes of Miss Carter in these, the twilight of her years. Perhaps he was being unnecessarily suspicious, but he decided to probe further. As was his wont he came straight to the point.

'Forgive me for enquiring, for it may not be considered any of my business, but how is it that you, Aunt Goody, are commissioned with the task of improving pretty Polly's education?'

Polly herself giggled at this but it was Abigail, eyes suspiciously bright, who jumped in with the answer before Mrs Goodenough had time to draw breath. 'Our mama is indisposed at the present time and Papa quite fully occupied in his business. They both felt that Polly would benefit from a period away from home, but she is young and still needs careful guidance. Mrs Goodenough kindly offered her services in exchange for mine.'

'I see.' He watched her with an intentness that he saw discomfited her, saw, in fact, rather more than she had intended by her carefully chosen words. So young Polly was a problem, and had been offloaded on to the sensible elder sister, and, it seemed, his aunt. An inconvenience, to say the least.

Since his exciting discovery, he had been unable to restrain his impatience for this much longed for trip to Italy, and had no intention of having it spoiled by a peck of giggling females. Though he had to admit there were certain temptations in Miss Carter's case. She looked at him now, with that wide-eyed amber gaze, and he found himself unable to break away for a surprisingly long moment. The result left him somewhat shaken. It became suddenly imperative to rid himself of her presence with all speed. She was a complication he could well do without. Not until he'd restored family honour and fortune would he be free to consider a woman as anything but a passing fancy, a category which did not include Miss Abigail Carter and her kind. And this mission he had set himself could very well take a lifetime.

Yet he knew, from past experience, that his aunt was nothing if not loyal to her staff, and would not willingly abandon these girls. 'Perhaps a finishing school of some description might be more appropriate,' he suggested, as if attempting to be helpful. 'Which would give you the opportunity for — shall we say? — a more exciting position. I'm sure my aunt could help produce one for you, perhaps abroad, if that would appeal?'

Abigail looked lost for words. But not for long. 'And where do you imagine we find the funds necessary for such an extravagant enterprise? I do not think, Mr Montegne, that you and I occupy the same world, certainly not the same economic plane.'

'Oh, hush, we can discuss all of that later,' put in Emilia Goodenough, refreshed from her tea and sensing a storm brewing. 'I'd much rather you continue with the family story. I confess I forget the details and I'm sure dear Abigail would find it equally fascinating to learn how you came to be searching for this so elusive figurine, Carl.'

Carl Montegne drew dark brows together to form a veritable crag over black-brown pools of disapproval. Abigail merely clenched her teeth beneath a smile of cool composure, of which she was an expert.

'Very well, Aunt.' He really had no option but to comply.

'Oh, how very exciting this all is,' interjected Polly, clapping her hands together. 'Why, Abigail might even be able to help you in your quest, Mr Montegne. She is exceeding clever with clues and things and always solves the Sherlock Holmes mysteries before the end, you know.'

'You surprise me,' said he in a voice meant to show he was quite unmoved by such credentials.

'And she does have her camera, and a pair of fine binoculars.'

'What every good detective needs.'

'Polly, do *hush*.' Abigail felt herself flushing from somewhere around her neat neckline right up to her rosy cheeks. The effect was not unbecoming, had she but known it.

'Very well,' said Montegne with thoughtful reluctance, his glance straying up to the chestnut hair which had somehow broken free from its binding and was sliding tantalisingly across one cheek. 'The story begins with a pair of lovers.'

'Ooh, as all good stories should.'

'*Polly.*'

Carl Montegne leaned forward in his chair to rest his elbows on his knees, tapping his fingertips impatiently together as he began his tale. His gaze remained fixed upon Abigail however.

'In fifteenth-century Italy there lived a young girl, Elisabetta Sylvante, who was to be forcibly married to a Count Ercole Paolo. He was to have been her sister's husband, but she tragically died. It was quite common in those times for a substitute to be made. Presumably vast sums of money were involved so apparently the count cared little which sister brought the dowry so long as he received it.'

'Naturally,' muttered Abigail, half under her breath, but subsided into silence as her interruption brought forth a frown.

'Elisabetta, not surprisingly, was dismayed by this turn of events. She had other plans, being in love with Prince Giovanni di Montegelo. The Count proved to be a tyrant and on her wedding-day the young Elisabetta fled to her former lover, who at once married her despite his family's disapproval. But since she was not of royal blood it could only be a morganatic marriage and his family completely ignored her existence. Nevertheless, the pair were said to be blissfully happy and quickly produced two children, a boy and a girl, both of whom thrived.'

At this point Carl Montegne got to his feet and walked swiftly over to the window, hands thrust deep in pockets, a restlessness in his pacing. 'The Count, of course, had been none too pleased by this turn of events and set out to reclaim his bride, without success. Having failed, he swore never to rest until he had regained his lost honour, damaged by her defection. And so a vicious vendetta was born.'

Montegne fell silent at this point and not even Polly spoke, as the three of them sat enthralled, Abigail unable to tear her eyes from the breadth of the shoulders blotting out the view from the window. Even as she watched, Carl Montegne turned, his eyes almost automatically going to hers. For a moment she thought he smiled at her, but it was no more than a trick of the light. She sensed the growing excitement in his voice as he continued his tale.

'Giovanni was a man of his time, greatly interested in art, literature and culture. He helped enthusiastically with the education of both his children with equal favour, and gained a not inconsiderable reputation as an artist and sculptor himself. But in due course he was duty bound to take a princess as a royal bride for the sake of his throne and his family, and Elisabetta became bitterly jealous as she watched his affection for his young bride grow.'

'I am not surprised. How fickle men are,' Abigail burst out, unable to restrain herself.

'He never promised her a *royal* marriage, and he still loved Elisabetta even though he was forced to do his duty,' argued Carl Montegne with quiet reason. Abigail sniffed her disbelief.

'If he had truly loved her he would never have married the princess, not even to please his family.'

The black brows rose again, commanding an answer to the question he now softly asked. 'So you think Giovanni should have ignored the honour of his family, the duty of his rank and the needs of his people for the sake of love?'

Abigail quailed slightly beneath the onslaught of his gaze, and beneath the sardonic tone that concluded this unanswerable question. 'N-no, I mean yes. *If* he loved Elisabetta he shouldn't have cared one jot about power. He should have been willing to sacrifice all.'

'Even the people of his country? Have they no rights?'

The insufferable man had caught her out again. 'Oh, blow, you know full well what I mean.'

'That *love* is all. I'm afraid I don't.'

Neither did Abigail as her romantic notions were made to look just that, romantic nonsense. She bit her lower lip tightly and vowed not to speak again.

With a small — one might even say satisfied — smile, Carl Montegne continued. 'War broke out between the two families and Giovanni knew that he must go to fight for his land. Some instinct told him that he would not return and he fashioned two figurines in the shape of Mercury, messenger to the gods. He gave one to each of his wives for he said that he loved them both in different ways but admitted that one held a special place in his heart. To her he had given a figurine with a message of great riches, while the other was of

sentimental value only. He told them each that since
the figurines were identical, save for this one hidden
secret, only the woman who loved him the least would
discover it.'

'How very intriguing,' said Emilia. 'And in order to
find the family fortune you must first solve the puzzle.
But where to begin?'

Carl Montegne gave the ghost of a smile. 'That has
always been the problem. Little is known of the
remainder of Elisabetta's life except that her prince did
not return and the Paolo and di Montegelo vendetta
continued mercilessly down the years. As you will have
guessed, Miss Carter, my own name, Montegne, comes
from the Italian di Montegelo.'

'And now you believe you can find that figurine?'
put in Emilia excitedly.

'I do. And you and I, dear Aunt, will go and collect
it, for only then can the fortunes of the house of di
Montegelo, destroyed over the years by the Paolos, be
restored to their proper glory. Will you come?'

Abigail couldn't remember ever feeling so vexed in
all her life. He would take his aunt, and even the
ancient girl, but she, along with the muffins and the
rain, would be left at home. Of all the places she had
dreamed of visiting, Italy had been the one country she
most longed to see. She had read of the lovely city of
Florence with its glory of domes and steeples, churches
filled with the wonders of the Renaissance, the deep
green forests that ran down to the River Arno which
threaded its way beneath bridges of medieval splendour
to the heart of the city. Florence, Rome, Venice,
Tuscany, the very names themselves wove a magic into
her heart. Loved by writers and artists throughout
history, how could they not? Had not Shelley written

his ode, 'To A Skylark' in Italy? The Brownings had lived and loved and borne a child in their beloved Florence. Byron, Tennyson, even Dickens had written of the romance that was Italy. And it was to be denied her.

'I dare say that is a quest which no one could resist,' she said now, squeezing her fingers so tightly together that they hurt, though no more than the knife lodged in her chest. By her own foolishness she had robbed herself of the opportunity to see all these splendours. Had not Mama so often reproved her for being quarrelsome, for always having to win? And now look where it had got her.

Abigail replayed with ruefully cruel accuracy that so recent meeting when they had at once gone for each other's throats, and winced at the recollection. Why had she not smiled and simpered pleasantly at him, curtsied and shown some respect, offered him tea, for goodness' sake, or even batted her straight brown lashes as Polly had done? But no, such foolishness was not for the eminently plain and sensible Miss Abigail Carter. Her anger now was directed entirely against herself. Was it self-consciousness on her part, or merely a desire for superiority that made her sound so full of herself? Even now she was still at it, postively *bickering* with him for no reason than that she hated to be intimidated, or perhaps because she did not wish him to see how vulnerable she really was. Mama claimed it was an inbuilt sense of self-conscious insecurity which had grown with her height, a nonsense in Abigail's opinion. Yet Carl Montegne far outshadowed not only herself but every other man she had ever met for height, and for a host of other matters best not dwelt upon too deeply.

'And why would you want to drag along an old woman in any case?' Emilia was saying.

Far better than a quarrelsome one, thought Abigail, agonisingly. There was no question but that she had shown the very worst of manners. What would Mama have thought of her? After all, Abigail knew she could easily have taken another photograph if Polly had sat still a moment longer, instead of which she had launched into a veritable tirade. To quarrel with Polly was one thing, to pick a fight with a perfect stranger was quite another. And what a stranger. She swallowed hard on the lump stuck painfully in her throat. Bad enough for her quick temper to make her miss Italy, but to miss seeing it in the company of this enthralling man was more than the human spirit could bear. Perhaps that was why she persisted in quarrelling with him, because she found him so disturbingly attractive. She almost scoffed out loud in disdain at the very idea, but managed to hold her tongue just in time, for it was very likely true.

'Because I enjoy your company.'

'Poppycock. There are any number of women whose company you'd enjoy a whole lot more.'

'Goody, do not underestimate yourself,' laughed Carl. 'But all right, there is more to it than that.'

'Ah. Money? Of course.'

'How can you say such a thing?' He put on a shocked expression, but Abigail wondered if his aunt had struck upon the truth. It did not, however, appear to bother her. Or him.

'Because you are a scamp of the first water and I know you have not two beans to rub together. You would never have got through Oxford without me, now, would you? And who bought that pretty little yacht you love to sail about all over the place?'

Carl pulled a wry face. 'You make me sound an incorrigible rogue. And perhaps in the past I have been just that. But on this occasion you are wrong.' Leaning over, he kissed the old lady's round cheek. 'You must not have noticed, Goody, dear, but I am no longer that scrawny, clumsy student. I am well into my thirty-third year, have worked as a valued member of an eminent City bank for some years now, and have made it my business to save funds for just this very expedition. It is true that even my funds are limited, but I can certainly afford to take the two of us across Europe and spend sufficient time in Italy to put our fortunes on a much sounder footing.'

'You hope.'

He laughed. 'I hope.'

'Why saddle yourself with an old woman?' she persisted.

'You are not old. You need taking out of yourself, away from this dull spot.' He waved a hand at the silent garden, once again shrouded in misty rain. 'You know about travel; you've done enough of it, for goodness' sake, and you love it, you know you do. I couldn't ask for a more experienced and lively companion, so I stand by that. I would like your company.'

'And what must I do to pay for my passage?'

Abigail watched, engrossed by the rapport between the two of them as Carl Montegne very nearly blushed. 'All right, I'll admit it. I intend for us to stay in the family Castello Falenza, for I believe that is where the statuette is hidden. Seems logical, and certainly cheaper than lodgings. But it has not been lived in for a generation or more. You are the ideal candidate, Goody, to make it habitable.'

Emilia Goodenough threw back her neatly clipped

head and chuckled with such vigour that her bronze earbobs danced and jangled against her neck. 'You are indeed an incorrigible rogue if you expect me to right half a century's neglect. Though I love you for it, you don't deserve me, that you don't.'

Carl leaned forward and planted a kiss on her laughing mouth. 'Absolutely right, I don't.'

'And how much do you reckon that will cost me, eh? It'll take more than soap and water, don't you know?'

'It is your organising ability I need. But if you put in any of your funds, I'll pay you back, every penny, as soon——'

'As you come into this dashed fortune, I know.' Emilia sighed. 'I doubt it'll ever happen.' She paused, and her smoke-grey eyes were challenging. 'But I wouldn't miss coming, not for the world. If only for the hell of it.' She shook his hand with a fierce pleasure and then abruptly turned to Abigail. 'What about you, Miss Carter; how do you think you'll take to Italy?'

Abigail was struck dumb for a whole half-minute. '*Me*?' she finally gasped. 'But I thought. . . I mean. . . Surely Mr Montegne said. . .he didn't want——'

'Bosh, I don't give a fig what Mr Montegne wants. Mr Montegne, on this matter at least, will do as he is told. You are my companion, are you not?'

'Y-yes.'

'And didn't I promise your dear mama that I would finish Polly's neglected education?'

'True, but——'

'No buts. Italy will be ideal for rubbing up the rough edges of Polly's education, and your own. Besides, where I goest, you goest. Isn't that what they say?' Her laughter crackled out again, but a quick glance in her nephew's direction told Abigail that he was less entranced by the idea. The scowl upon his brow was positively ferocious. Blind to such niceties, Polly was whooping with excitement.

'Oh, Abby, won't that be divine? I can't wait.'

Carl Montegne was glaring down at the three of them with a thunderous expression on his already dark face. 'Haven't I just explained? Funds are limited. I've saved years for this, taken special leave from the bank. You can hardly expect me to tour Italy, to retrieve my family's honour and fortune, with three women in tow?'

All Abigail's good intentions of not speaking to him directly evaporated at the sound of haughty pride in his voice. 'Four,' she retorted in a voice meant equally to burn.

'Four?'

'Mrs Goodenough will surely wish to bring her maid.'

'Maid?'

'By jove, yes, of course,' agreed Emilia. 'The girl. Can't travel without her. Been with me forever, don't you know?'

Carl Montegne groaned, rolling his eyes heavenward as if for patience. But he knew when he was beaten. Goody was a dear, but every bit as stubborn as he, and, if she had set her mind on taking this plebeian of a gold-digging companion along with her, and her ancient maid, there was absolutely nothing he could do to stop her. From the feverish look in Miss Abigail Carter's amber eyes, and the way she spoke up to him, not a common trait among his more usual women friends, she clearly did not lack courage. But one could never tell. She might very well turn to hysterics, and that he could do without.

'How are you with ghosts, Miss Carter?'

'Ghosts?'

'Long-dead ancestors who walk the stairs at night. Do you think you could cope with such beings?'

He was mocking her again, she could tell. Well, let him. She lifted her chin, buoyed by Mrs Goodenough's support. 'I dare say I could manage, so long as their chains don't clank too loudly,' she said

Polly giggled. Emilia merely raised her brows questioningly, looking rather pleased, and waited silently for her nephew's response. When it came it was just short of ill-mannered.

'Then you'd best start packing. We leave before the week is out.'

The packing was achieved with Mrs Goodenough's usual meticulousness. Safety-pins and malaria tablets, stomach powders and water purifiers. Walking shoes, umbrellas, sunhats, cough pastilles, flea powder and of course the essential Baedeker, all packed in the ubiquitous Gladstone bags, provision for every conceivable problem or catastrophe.

Carl Montegne purchased the necessary Cook's travel tickets and coupons and after a bumpy Channel crossing and an agonisingly slow train journey they made their first halt in Paris.

'I cannot believe we are really here,' whispered Abigail in reverent tones as she leaned out of the window of the room she was to share with Polly, to breathe in the city air as if in some way it would taste different from English air. It was every bit as smoky as London, but she pretended not to notice.

'I suppose we are not allowed to unpack since we are only staying the two nights,' grumbled Polly in morose tones.

'Heavens, no, of course not,' cried Abigail, quickly pulling her head in again. 'The very possibility of repacking all that lot, and checking and possibly rewriting all those lists, appals me.' The sisters caught each other's eye and giggled. 'Now you will be good, Polly, won't you?'

'Of course — when am I anything but?' she scoffed, mildly offended. 'But I do think you should mention to Mrs Goodenough that though you and I have brought every mortal thing we possess we are not equipped to deal with life in the best hotels, as this one seems to be. I vow I shall be too mortified to go down to dinner for I have not a thing to wear.'

Abigail was shocked. 'What a tale. What about the pretty cream evening frock, the one I was photographing you in when we first met. . .when Mr Montegne first startled us with his appearance?'

'Oh, that old thing.' Polly flung herself on to the bed in a pet of ill humour. 'I can't wear that. It is so very childish and quite out of fashion. This is *Paris*.'

Abigail sighed, knowing there was little to be gained by losing patience with Polly, for she was indeed a child, and perhaps always would be. 'We have no money for frou-frou dresses and gewgaws, Polly, so you must learn to make the best of it.'

'Oh, really, Abigail, how terribly old-fashioned you are. Nobody who is anybody wears frou-frou dresses any more. The fashion is all for narrow skirts, draped up at the sides, or even straighter with hidden pleats and slits, showing plenty of ankle.'

'Polly, there is no possibility of my *ever* buying you such a frock, so put the idea right from your mind.'

Polly flounced off the bed, her rosebud mouth set in a most unbecoming pout. 'How *stuffy* you have become, Abigail. Why I agreed to let Ma and Pa send me to stay with you, I do not know.'

'Because you had no choice after you had been thrown out of that exceedingly expensive school they had sent you to. Now let us undress and get to bed. We are both exhausted from the journey and need to be fresh again in the morning for whatever Mrs Goodenough plans.'

Polly's eyes glittered with stubborn determination as she turned her back for Abigail to unfasten the long line of buttons. Her sister was far too polite for her own good in Polly's opinion. As if Mrs Goodenough would want them to go around looking like tramps. The very idea. And Polly had every intention of looking her best on this exciting journey, particularly in front of Carl Montegne.

The three ladies were all seated in Madame Claudine's beautiful and discreet salon, where ready-made gowns aplenty were being brought out for them. She did this with profound apology since it was not the way she liked to do business, but there was no time for even a battery of seamstresses to supply them with their needs quickly enough. Polly could scarcely keep still, so delighted and excited was she.

It had taken no more than a sigh and a whimper at breakfast, accompanied by a tear or two, for Mrs Goodenough to offer to rig them both out at once. Abigail, naturally, had refused, stoutly declaring she had sufficient dresses for any occasion that a humble companion might find herself in.

'Heavens, Miss Carter. Do you not, then, intend to accompany me to dinner?' Emilia had asked. 'You must eat, and I declare Polly is perfectly right in her distress. I should have thought of it myself. At least we are in the proper place to put the matter right, are we not? Where better than Paris, eh, to be rigged out?'

'I wouldn't dream of accepting so much as a hand-kerchief from you, Mrs Goodenough,' insisted Abigail with marginally less conviction. For though she hated the glittering speculation in Montegne's eye as he watched and listened with mocking amusement to her reaction, clearly assuming she was itching to spend his aunt's money, Abigail was human enough to want very much to dress attractively, or at least to be smart. And her best brown velveteen was growing exceeding shiny and worn in places.

'I am sure Miss Carter can be persuaded, if you try hard enough, dear Aunt,' he drawled.

'Mrs Goodenough has quite enough expense,' retorted she.

'And that is another thing,' said that lady, pausing in her carving up of a piece of delectable trout. 'I really cannot spend the next three months being called by that admittedly ridiculous name. For heaven's sake, Abigail, can we agree upon Emilia once and for all?'

'Oh.'

'I shall have no more argument on the subject, or any other. We shall visit Madame Claudine, without delay.' Having made up her mind upon the matter, Emilia returned with relish to her fish.

'Tut, tut, how very devastating for you,' remarked Montegne, half under his breath. And had not her employer been present, Abigail thought she might very well have thrown her breakfast at him.

CHAPTER THREE

FOR Polly there was a candy-striped blue cotton with a pouched bodice and tight lace collar, full sleeves edged with the same cream lace and if not the straight skirt she coveted at least one that fitted narrowly over the hips with sewn-down pleats that flared out about the ankle. It was the perfect dress for a young girl to enjoy a typically idyllic Edwardian summer picnic. And as she swirled and preened herself, adding a straw boater with matching blue ribbon tied about the crown, she dreamed of the admiration she was sure to find in Carl Montegne's eyes.

Even more thrilling was an evening dress in lilac silk net over a pink satin underslip. Figured with embroidered flowers and leaves and fastened with a stiff band of narrow petersham about her tiny waist, it made her feel like a princess, and she stalked about the small salon very much as if she were. To these two were added a sensible day dress and jacket, various accessories in the way of gloves, shoes, bags and chemises and other essential items.

Abigail sat and watched with soft eyes. It was lovely to see Polly so contented for once. She positively glowed and was so pretty that she deserved all these lovely things.

But then it was Abigail's turn and she remained stubbornly tight-lipped throughout. If Abigail could have refused she would have done so, but Emilia had quite got the bit in her teeth, as she said, and would take no more argument.

Independent to a fault, her mother had often told her, and Abigail felt that independence burn raw and fiercely within her breast now. But she offered no opinion on any dress they tried upon her, whether it was apricot moire silk or cream satin, a blue day dress or businesslike costume. She volunteered no requests or suggestions, refused even to look in the mirror, but stood mute and uncooperative, only coming to life when Emilia in her exasperation instructed Madame Claudine to pack the lot and have done with it.

'I wouldn't hear of you being so extravagant,' cried Abigail, distressed that her ploy had had the opposite effect to her intention.

'I vow you are being more childlike than your sister,' returned Emilia, perfectly reasonably. 'And I'll have no more of it. Now, the pair of you can take yourselves off and look at the shops for an hour or so by yourselves. I shall return to the hotel for a rest before tea. See you are back by four o'clock precisely. You know I do hate to be kept waiting for my tea.'

And, not daring to offer any further objections, Abigail grasped Polly by the arm and quickly led her away.

'This is all your fault,' she said. 'How embarrassing. You have made us both look grasping and self-seeking, the very thing I didn't want.'

But Polly was not at all concerned. 'I am sure you would not wish to look dowdy before Mr Montegne, any more than I would. Now do come on, Abby, you wanted to travel, and here we are, in Paris, for goodness' sake, and all you can do is grumble. And I do so wish to look at the famous Galeries Lafayette.'

Meeting those sparkling blue eyes, Abigail weakened. It was exciting to be here in Paris, and perhaps she had behaved rather foolishly. She'd certainly achieved nothing by her stubbornness, and if Mr Montegne had caustic comments to make about her new wardrobe she must simply bear with it. Abigail set aside the slight needling worry that perhaps Polly had a more particular motive for wishing to look so fine. She was a child still, and had always liked to look well. Besides which, the sun was shining, birds were singing, spring was in the air and, as Polly rightly said, this *was* Paris.

'Lafayette it is, then.' And, laughing joyously together, they set off arm in arm down the Boulevard Haussmann, in the direction of the famous department store.

They had a little money of their own to spend and the temptations were so great among the colourful counters packed with delightful extravagances and manned by smiling shop assistants eager to sell that it was exceedingly hard to choose. Abigail bought some ribbons for her hair, not this time in dull brown but cobalt-blue, crimson and a dashing shade of jewel-green. Polly, however, was less easily satisfied. She purchased a silk scarf, a brooch showing the Eiffel Tower, and a lace handkerchief in the shape of a parasol, but despite Abigail's plea for caution was bent on spending the last few coins that burned the bottom of her Dorothy bag.

'Some ladies are wearing cosmetics now, and French perfume. Let us ask to see some,' she whispered.

'Heavens above, no, indeed, you may ask no such thing. What a trial you are, Polly. Come, now, buy this pretty trinket box with the mother-of-pearl lid that you like and then we might have time for a boat trip on the Seine.'

'I'm not sure I have enough money for it.'

Abigail sighed, but drew the strings of her purse open. 'I dare say I can spare a little. But I didn't bring very much money with me today. Wait a moment while I look.' And as she looked she continued, 'You will have to learn to restrain your extravagance, Polly. We've hardly begun our journey. Think of Florence and all you will wish to buy there.'

By the time Abigail had found a sixpence stuck fast in the bottom corner of her reticule and held it out to her sister, Polly had taken her opportunity and fled. It was the most dreadful moment in Abigail's entire life. Her little sister had quite disappeared. Fear rose up and blocked her throat; shafts of hazy scarlet filmed her eyes, blotting out her vision and making the whole crush of people and counters swirl madly before her like a whirligig at a fair.

She spun about, looking this way and that, searching the length of the counter and those adjoining. She asked the rather severe lady behind it if she had seen her sister go, but the woman did not understand and only shrugged her shoulders.

'Polly!' Unmindful now of propriety, Abigail called out her sister's name in desperation as she began to run up and down each aisle, heedless of the glares of shoppers who got in her path. *Where was she*? She thought of abduction, of automobiles running out of control and ploughing poor Polly down in the street, of visiting bandits selecting her as a suitable candidate for the rampant white slave market Abigail had read about in the more sensational Press. All these fantasies and worse slid like thick, nauseous bile through her mind. What was she to do?

Abigail was out in the street now, panic a living weight in her breast. Unchecked tears were spilling from her eyes and she dashed them impatiently away for they impeded her vision even more.

'Miss Carter, whatever is the matter with you? You look quite demented.'

'Oh, Mr Montegne.' She almost fell upon him in her relief, her hands reaching out to clutch at the lapels of his fine worsted overcoat. The sun glinted on the dark sheen of his hair where it was smoothed back like glossy wings behind each ear to curl lazily upon the velvet collar. The dark eyes were almost gentle as he looked down upon her and she felt a shock of recognition so powerful that it made her body shake. It was almost as if this had happened before. But how could it? This was her first time in Paris. *Déjà vu*, wasn't that what they called it? Abigail found herself leaning against him, aware of his arms coming about her waist to support her, making her feel exceedingly safe and protected. The desire to lay her hot cheek against the cool of his so solid chest was almost insurmountable. Valiantly she managed not to succumb.

'It's Polly. I have lost her. She's quite vanished, Mr Montegne; what am I to do? Anything could happen to her alone in this dreadfully wicked city.'

Incredibly he gave a low chuckle. 'I very much doubt it. Mistress Polly has a happy knack, I should think, of being well able to take care of herself. Come, dry your tears, and we will look for her together. Where did you last see her? I expect she is there this very minute, cross at being kept waiting, I shouldn't wonder.'

They made their way back, but no Polly was to be

seen anywhere. He repeated, in fact, the very same
motions which Abigail had already carried out, to no
greater effect. And now it was Carl Montegne's turn to
look worried. More worried, perhaps, than he ought.
Such a very deep frown only aggravated Abigail's own
anxiety. And it made her wonder if he was fonder of
her sister than he owned.

'Where has the minx got to?' he uttered for the
fifteenth time as he strode up and down stairs, combing
one magnificent floor after another, with Abigail scurrying behind to keep up. Since she appeared to be
having difficulty matching his long-legged pace he
grasped hold of her hand, and she was quite unprepared for the electrifying effect this had. The warmth
and strength of his hold was astounding. She felt almost
tiny beside him, and almost cherished.

'You really should have kept better watch over her,
you know,' he said, shattering the illusion.

'*I*?'

'Yes, you. Who else? Are you not supposed to be
your sister's keeper?' he unfairly reminded her. 'Then
for pity's sake why couldn't you do just that?'

Abigail was far too close to breaking down completely to pursue the argument, but did make a valiant
attempt to release herself from his now punishing grip.
She failed, and wasn't sure whether to be glad or sorry.
Never had she felt so far from the sensible image of
herself everyone had come to expect. Abigail felt quite
weak at the knees, not simply from the fright Polly was
giving her, but the masterful, one might almost say
overbearing way in which Carl Montegne was treating
her. Really, she wondered what gave him the right.

'What on earth will your parents have to say to you
if anything should happen to Polly?'

Abigail groaned. The cruelty of the man to even think of such a thing at a time like this was unspeakable.

He questioned every likely shop assistant, called floorwalkers to help in the search, and even interviewed the manager in his office about his security arrangements.

'Are young girls permitted to wander at will in this store? Does no one question the lack of a chaperon?' But all to no avail, since none of them, apart from the manager, spoke much English, and Carl Montegne spoke even less French.

After a further half-hour's fruitless searching, they both collapsed on a bench by the river to catch their breath. 'It is almost four. I suggest we return to the hotel in case she has managed to get back there by her own steam.'

'And if she has not?'

'Then there will be nothing for it but to call out the police.'

Abigail could hear sympathy and concern in his voice now and, unable to help herself, she slumped against him on the seat. The breadth of his shoulder felt exceedingly solid and comforting and, without even looking at her, he moved his arm about her and stroked her hair gently back from her tear-dampened cheek, then squeezed her close as if she were no more than a tiny fluffy kitten needing to be petted. It was a sensation Abigail found so satisfying that she let her eyelids droop closed and hoped it would go on and on.

But guilt still rankled. 'You were quite right; I should have taken better care. She was fussing over some purchase and I was irritated, wanting to take a boat ride on the Seine instead of wasting any more time shopping. Oh, if only I had agreed to take her to the cosmetic counter as she had wanted, instead of which we fell to quarrelling. But she is so young, and I do not approve of paint and powder.'

He moved his head to look down at her, a smile growing at the corners of his wide mouth. 'That is because your skin will never need such artifice.' He smoothed the back of one hand across her cheek and Abigail was beset by a shuddering sensation right down to her toes. It was most alarming. 'Don't be hard upon yourself,' he said, his voice as softly caressing as his hand. 'I am sure young Polly would drive the most diligent parent to distraction.'

Abigail did not at once reply; her mind seemed cushioned from reality and somehow it didn't seem important and certainly not worth arguing over. It seemed perfectly right for her to be sitting here, nestled close in Carl Montegne's arms, his warm breath upon her cheek, the sparkle in his eyes making her feel suddenly, desirably female. What was she thinking of to be thus engaged, and enjoying the sensation, when poor Polly might at this very moment be lying dead at the bottom of the Seine?

She moved, reluctantly, perhaps, but with a brave show of resolution, from the reassuring circle of his arm. 'She has already done so. Dear Mama is quite at the end of her tether. Whatever she asks Polly to do, Polly will insist on doing the exact opposite. Not out of any meanness of personality, you understand, simply girlish high spirits.'

'And a superfluity of vanity perhaps?'

Abigail gave a rueful smile. 'Perhaps. But she is young, as I once was.'

'I cannot imagine you ever having been as wilful as Polly.'

Abigail slanted a challenging glance up at him that was almost coquettish. 'How can you say that when you know nothing about me? Perhaps I was even worse and have learnt better with the onset of maturity.'

He gave a great guffaw of laughter. 'You do not appear terribly mature to me. My aunt is mature, the girl is even more so, but you are yet to reach your prime.' He lowered his voice to a seductively thrumming note. 'A peach yet to bloom. Would that I were around when you do so. Delectable.'

Abigail's heart seemed to stop and then race on at a crackling rate. She got very smartly to her feet, but sat as quickly down again as the pain from her burning soles shot up through her calves. 'Oh, I don't think I can walk another step. I believe I should like to kill my sister if I weren't so afraid that I had already lost her.'

'A natural and fairly common sentiment, I believe. Though I must confess my information is second-hand.'

Abigail looked up at him in open curiosity. 'Do you have no brothers or sisters?'

'None.'

'Parents? Family of any kind?'

'Only Goody.' He grinned. 'What more do I need? She has been mother and father, aunt and uncle to me for as long as I can remember. My parents died in a cholera epidemic in India. I was in school in England at the time, staying with Aunt Goody in the holidays.'

'Oh.' Abigail did not know what else to say. 'I'm sorry.'

He shrugged wide shoulders. 'I never really knew them very well so I could hardly feel grief. Life is strange sometimes, is it not? People with whom one should be close are strangers to you, and yet perfect strangers can seem incredibly close.'

She could not tear her eyes from his face.

'And so you are looking for your roots, not simply a fortune.'

There was a small startled silence. 'You really are most perspicacious.'

'Am I?'

Their eyes still held, searching, questioning, Carl's appearing misty, lost in thought.

'I do wish we could find Polly,' Abigail whispered. 'Then everything would be perfect.'

'Would it?' His voice hushed over her cheek.

'Yes.'

After a long moment they both looked away, she embarrassed, as if she had been caught out in some misdemeanour, while Carl Montegne felt totally mystified by what had undoubtedly passed between them, intrigued by this practical, blushing, caring, spirited, sensible girl with the shining hair and bewitching eyes. He turned his attention to the river. The evening lamps were being lit now, twinkling prettily in the rippling water like live fireflies. Then he was sitting bolt upright, his hand gripping her arm.

'Did you mention a boat trip?'

'Y-yes, why?'

'There is one coming in now, and if I am not mistaken there is little Miss Polly, weeping and wailing and causing something of a fuss, but otherwise perfectly sound in wind and limb.'

Abigail was on her feet in a second, flying down the embankment to a somewhat dilapidated old pleasure boat from which a straggle of tourists disembarked.

'Polly, where have you been?' she cried, annoyance ripe in her voice.

Polly was out of the boat in a second. She was soaked to the skin, hair all over her face and no sign of a hair ribbon. But with scarcely a glance at her older sister, she burst into a fresh paroxysm of tears and flew straight into Carl Montegne's arms. 'Oh, there you are at *last*, come to rescue me.' And, between heartrending sobs, continued, 'I cannot tell you *how* glad I am to see you. Abigail deserted me, and I haven't known where to turn to find her, or you or anyone. You don't *know* how frightened I've been.'

Abigail could do nothing but stare open-mouthed as Carl held the sobbing child in his big, strong arms, smiling quizzically as he stroked the blonde head with a gentling hand.

For once Emilia was not amused by their lateness and Polly was given a good dressing down. Mrs Goodenough also proved quite unmoved by Polly's tale of having taken the boat trip to look for Abigail and having then stood up in the boat when she'd thought she'd seen her sister on the embankment.

'It was not Abigail at all, but then I was so jostled in the crowded boat that I fell in, and had to be hauled out by a far from sympathetic boatman.'

'I do not wonder at it, young lady,' stated Emilia with taut lips. 'You have had us all going quite frantic. And our tea was ruined. Not that it was up to much in any case. No matter, in future you will keep close to Abigail, or myself, do you understand?'

Polly did, but that was not to say that she liked it. An appealing glance up at Mr Montegne from beneath damp lashes produced only a smile of resignation and so she was forced to declare herself sorry and suffer being sent to her room while everyone else dressed for an evening at the opera.

The next day Emilia relented and allowed Polly to accompany them round the Louvre, saying that Polly had suffered punishment enough and no doubt the memory of the dunking would do her some good. Abigail very much doubted it, but held her counsel on the matter.

They spent a few extra days in Paris which gave Abigail the opportunity to use her camera. She snapped all the famous sights, the Place Vendôme, Arc de Triomphe, the Champs-Elysées and the Tuileries Gardens, but she failed utterly to be satisfied with her shot of the Notre-Dame cathedral. She could not get it straight in her lens. However, Abigail made up for that disappointment by photographing the street artists painting their pictures on the walkways and pavements, flower sellers, café owners with their loaded trays and even clever little urchins weaving their nefarious way in and out of the bustling crowds. She was more than satisfied with her interesting record of Paris, and even Carl Montegne declared himself impressed when she had them developed at a small photographic shop close to the Montmartre.

'At least it will help me to remember Paris when we return home,' said Abigail with a sigh.

'Indeed,' said he. 'And I shall remember the *Mona Lisa*.'

Abigail looked sharply at him, saw the teasing light in his dark eyes, and tossed her chin. 'I vow you would drive a saint to distraction. What a snob you are.' So saying, she flounced out of the room, not completely unaware that he watched the swing of her hips with considerable interest.

They took cheap train excursions to Fontainbleau and Versailles where they were particularly impressed with the latter's gardens and its magnificient display of fountains and statues.

'Do you know that visitors to see Louis XVI at his *levée* used to purloin silk tassles, brass taps and even pieces of lead piping from the palace as a souvenir?' Carl told her.

'Heavens, how very inconvenient for him. The first of the dreaded tourists, I suppose,' she giggled. 'I will try to restrain myself and not touch a single thing.'

'Quite right,' he laughingly agreed. 'But then I cannot imagine you ever doing anything quite so vulgar.' His fingers brushed her elbow as he escorted her in to the next room, only for a fraction of a second, but long enough for Abigail to confound herself by blushing.

'Will you carry my shawl, Mr Montegne? I am too hot and quite worn out,' mourned Polly, squeezing in between them, and Abigail wandered off to examine a tapestry, the moment of intimacy over.

When they met up again in the gardens, Polly was hanging on to his arm and they were laughing together at some private joke. Her blonde head was close to his shoulder while his gaze seemed to be fixed upon her rosebud mouth, parted with captivating charm, the tiny white teeth like seed-pearls. Abigail felt again the deep knife-thrust of jealousy and hated herself for it.

Lyons was a pleasant city, used mainly as a terminus by the Cookites, as they were so often called, and the Montegne party was no exception. They stayed only one night and continued the next day bright and early

on the Mediterranean railway, with the promise of the
mountains ahead.

Abigail was quite unprepared for the glory of the
Alps. She gasped in astonishment at the awesome size
of them, their peaks lost in clouds, gazed in wonder at
the tumble of mountain streams, thick pine woods and
jagged rocks. They all gasped and sighed and cried out,
often as much in fear as anything, at the sweep of
landscape below them as the train seemed to ride the
edge of a precipice no wider than a cooking-pot rim.
Several times the train stopped for water and sometimes they had a few moments to climb down from it
and breathe in the sweet, pure air. And all the time
they were drawing closer to Italy, which somehow
seemed the right thing to be doing, as if in some
unknown way it had been predestined.

There first experience of it, however, was sadly
disappointing. Genoa was busy and noisy, filled with
beggars selling dubious Roman coins and artefacts.
Deciding not to linger, they took the coast road
through La Spezia, Viareggio and Lucca, journeying
by diligence, drawn by four sure-footed mules so they
would have a better view of the countryside.

'Pity we couldn't drive the whole way in my automobile,' groaned Carl, easing his cramped limbs.

'Poppycock. This is much more interesting,' declared
Emilia.

It grew yet more interesting, and warmer, the further
south they went. They stopped at a country inn which
was apparently less used to tourists than the long ago
French kings had been, but they were all glad enough
of the rest from the rough, bumpy roads. The beds
were hard and the food indifferent. Yet the innkeeper
and his wife were friendly enough and so they smiled

and made the best of it. Emilia's traveller's pack was breached, and they were all quite ready to sprinkle flea powder about the place, though none of them had much faith in her water-purifying tablets and decided it better to avoid drinking the water altogether.

By morning it became clear that even these precautions had been insufficient, for the girl was ill and quite unable to travel. Abigail volunteered to sit with her.

'No, no, miss, there's no need to do that,' she protested. ''Tis only a bilious attack. I shall stay in bed and be better d'rectly.'

But Abigail would not hear of it, nor would Emilia. The stomach powders were brought forth and the girl took her dose without protest. 'But she should have plenty of fluids,' Abigail pointed out. 'If you would ask the *patron* for boiled water, and see that he does boil it, Emilia, I will undertake to see that it is drunk.'

'Splendid girl,' said Emilia, and, pushing back the sleeves of her gown as if she were about to use fisticuffs upon the man, she strode from the room, declaring that he would boil water or she would do likewise to his head. Left alone, Abigail giggled.

'Take no notice of her; she'm not so fierce as she makes out,' chuckled the girl. 'I shall be up in time for lunch, to be sure.' At which point the only thing that came up was what was left of her breakfast. Wan-faced and exhausted, the poor woman lay back upon her pillows, profuse in her apologies. 'I be holding you all up,' she mourned.

'It doesn't matter,' soothed Abigail. 'There is no hurry.' After a moment's thought she said, 'I really can't call you "the girl" as Mrs Goodenough does. Please, what is your name?'

The pale face broke into a smile. 'Mistress don't

mean naught by it. Matter of fact I quite like it. Makes me feel young again.'

'All the same. . .'

'It's Ida, miss.'

'Please to meet you, Ida.' Abigail smiled at her and Ida smiled back. Abigail combed the iron-grey hair and gently washed the ancient face and work-worn hands. The woman seemed so frail that Abigail thought it a wonder she had managed the journey thus far with no complaint. 'There, does that make you feel better?'

'Oh, it do, miss, you'm real kind.'

'Now try to sleep. I shall be here if you need me.'

Abigail must have fallen asleep too for it was well into the afternoon when she woke with a jump, a hand resting upon her shoulder. 'I'm sorry to startle you, but I've come to relieve you.'

Abigail looked up into mahogany eyes and felt her insides melt. Goodness, was she sickening for something too? 'I'm perfectly all right.'

'You won't be if you don't get some lunch inside you. Polly and Emilia are out walking. I said I would take a turn with the invalid. Go on with you.' He gave her a little push, and, unable to resist the hunger in her stomach, or the kindling smile in his eyes, she complied.

'I won't be long,' she whispered.

'No hurry.' Lowering himself into the chair, Carl Montegne closed his eyes. 'I shall take a doze myself. The lunch was not excellent, but filling. I can't wait to reach the castle. Perhaps we will be able to leave tomorrow.'

'Perhaps.'

As she reached the door he said without opening his eyes, 'It's kind of you to help Ida. Many wouldn't.'

And, uncertain how to reply, Abigail quietly closed the door, reflecting that he at least had known the woman's name.

It was two days before Ida was fit enough to travel, and several more weary miles, with all of them beginning to feel thoroughly jaded, before the much longed for *castello* came finally into view.

'There it is.' Carl's excitement was intense and they all laughed as he leaped down from the carriage they had hired and began to run along the rutted track.

'Why bother? We'll beat you,' cried Emilia. And so they did, but Carl evidently enjoyed the run, for he was not far behind them and came up laughing, hardly out of breath as they pulled up at a great oaken door.

'Golly, how exciting this is,' cried Polly, jumping down in a flurry of petticoats without waiting for the driver to help her. Abigail followed more discreetly while Carl assisted his aunt and Ida. By this time the driver had started to unload the luggage and Carl was fitting a large key into a massive lock. They all waited, breathless with curiosity, and he turned to look at each of them, as if reluctant to turn it.

'Go on. I can't wait to see the place,' urged Emilia.

Polly was jumping up and down on the spot, unable to control her excitement. 'Is it furnished, do you know? Will there be cobwebs?'

'Assuredly, young lady, and you can help sweep them away,' Abigail told her with a laugh, and Polly wrinkled her small nose in distaste.

'Have you lost your nerve, boy?' Emilia challenged, seeing he still hesitated.

If there had been any such danger the eyes now darkened, and the shoulders lifted. The next moment the door swung open with a satisfying creak.

'Wait. Before you go in we must have a picture. Smile please.'

And as they all turned to pose for her, only Abigail saw the movement at an upper window. No more than the faintest of silver shadows, seen for a second, and then it was gone. But there was no mistaking its shape. It was the figure of a woman in a pearl-grey gown.

CHAPTER FOUR

THREE days of dusting, scrubbing, polishing and sweeping was not Abigail's idea of adventure. Nor did it leave any time at all for speculation over what she had seen, or rather thought she had seen. She found no difficulty in dismissing the image of the woman from her mind and putting it all down to too much sun and excessive fatigue. It was probably Carl Montegne's fault for planting the idea of ghosts into her mind in the first place. Absolute nonsense, and she was far too sensible to give credence to it. Besides, there were more important matters to occupy her. The whole of Italy lay beneath her window and here she was, on her hands and knees, attacking the floorboards with a wad of cloth impregnated with fuller's earth and fine sand, an effective remedy but time-consuming. And mind-numbingly boring.

Abigail had begged to be allowed to continue dusting the books in the grand library, using a goose feather she had found, but Emilia had stoutly refused, giving the task instead to the girl. Though disappointed, Abigail appreciated the justice of this decision, for Ida did actually get on with the task in hand, instead of trying to read the dusty volumes themselves. Abigail had been attempting to learn Italian and was anxious to try out her skills as well as to investigate the mysteries of the library.

Now she sighed and shifted her mat to the next portion of untreated floor. How long it would take to

clean the entire castle she dared not think. Perhaps
there was no money for extra staff, and that was why
every one of them had to work from dawn to dusk.
Carl cleaned window and lamps, Emilia scoured dishes,
and Ida beat and swept carpets till it was a wonder they
were not in shreds. Even Polly had set to work with a
will, declaring they were just like explorers in a foreign
land. And she must be working hard, for Abigail never
saw her sister from day's beginning to end. As for
Abigail, she ached in every muscle and was certain she
would have black bruises on both knees for her entire
life when this job was finally done.

But she would not waver from the task, which must
be done if they were to live in any degree of comfort.
Most of the *castello* was still unexplored as they
intended to live in only a small part of it, but Abigail
was itching to see what lay behind all the doors and
down the endless corridors.

And then there were the gardens, much of them
hidden under brushwood and weeds, but the outlines
were there in the overgrown remains of once neatly
clipped hedges, a riot of surviving plants wild with
colour spiralling around broken statues and fallen urns.
Who knew what she might find hidden in their tangled
depths if she could but be allowed the time to look?
Then there were the artificial lake, the groves of orange
and lemon trees, and beyond the west wing the remains
of a chapel with angels and gargoyles at each corner of
the high domed roof. It was altogether the most
exciting place Abigail had seen in her life and she could
scarcely believe her good fortune in being here.

Montegne had offered to take her round with him to
compile an inventory as soon as their living conditions
had been dragged out of the last century and become

moderately clean and habitable. She looked forward to this with eager anticipation, not least for the opportunity of a time alone with him.

Abigail had found herself often thinking of Carl Montegne while she laboured, her mind conjuring up pictures of his face, the way he moved, his crooked smile. And most of all the merry gleam in his nut-brown eyes, which sometimes seemed to follow her about the room. It made her feel most peculiar. As if he knew some pleasant secret about life, about herself, even, that she did not. Sitting back on her heels, she gave a little shudder now at the recollection, almost as if a thrill of anticipation rippled through her.

'You are tired, Abigail. It is time to stop.'

She whirled at the sound of his voice. Had she conjured him from her thoughts by some magic spell? It had happened before. So often when she'd been idly playing with these pictures in her head, or trying out witty conversations with him as they strolled hand in hand by a silver river, herself far more beautiful and fascinating in her imagination than in reality, he would suddenly appear before her, a knowing smile upon his face, as if he could read the fantasies in her head. It should have made her feel distinctly uncomfortable, but instead it excited her and she would meet his probing gaze with a tilt of her chin, and a half-smile on silken lips.

But such fancies were dangerous and she knew they must be stopped before she began to believe in them. They were merely the product of a female mind which should long since have attuned itself to spinsterhood. But how difficult that was proving to be now that Carl Montegne was around, reminding her by his constant virile presence of unexplored delights she might never taste, reminding her she was a woman.

'I am perfectly well,' she briskly replied. It would not do for him to think she was shirking, or to see her as a dreamer and idler. Abigail grabbed her neglected cloth and reapplied herself with excessive vigour. She heard his deep-throated chuckle.

'You don't need to convince me that you have worked hard; I can see it with my own eyes. But I may still regret that I allowed you to come.'

'It is good to know you have confidence in me,' said Abigail drily, shielding from his gaze the hot spurt of anger that seared her chest. Did he have to make it quite so plain that he did not want her around? She turned to him, lips tightly pursed, a frown marring her pale brow, but to her chagrin he only laughed. He was the most vexing man imaginable, one moment expressing concern for her tiredness and the next taking pleasure in insulting her. 'I have come at Mrs Goodenough's bidding, not yours,' she starkly reminded him, and allowed herself a prim smile.

'Quite so. And when Aunt Goody is settled, as I soon intend her to be, she may have no further use for a companion, and then you may return home with your recalcitrant sister.'

'Oh.' Abigail digested this unexpected and unpleasant piece of information fully, and, realising there was nothing she could do to prevent her being sent home, said again, 'Oh.'

'For the moment I am happy for you to stay, and grateful for your labours.' He quirked one merry eyebrow, knowing she hated to be thought of as a mere housemaid.

Almost choking on her pride, Abigail pulled stiff lips

into the semblance of a smile, for the last thing she
wanted was to be sent home. But when she looked up
at him to return his steady gaze it was a sideways
glance, through long lashes, as if some force within her
played the coquette and she could no more prevent it
than she could stop the sun shining or the breeze from
blowing over the mountain tops. 'I thank you kindly,
sir,' she said, trying to disguise her mistake by a teasing
tone, and saw how she had only made the matter
worse. He studied her with a sudden intentness that
was almost unnerving, a frown of puzzlement momentarily flickering between those awesome eyes.

'Come,' he said shortly. 'I said you might accompany
me around the *castello*. Why not now? You've done
enough housework for one day. Bring pencil and
paper. I'm eager to know what I have here.'

So was Abigail, for no reason that she could fathom
beyond normal curiosity. But she agreed about the
housekeeping and dropped her cloth with alacrity.

'Will you wait while I wash my hands and comb my
hair?' She hated to look a dowd in front of him, but he
dismissed her request with an impatient flick of a hand.
'No time for titivating. Goody will be calling us for
dinner soon. If we hurry we can at least investigate the
east wing.' And, without waiting to see if she followed,
he strode off down the corridor on his long-legged
stride. Abigail frantically flew about the room, found a
pencil stuck in a flower vase, and, grabbing her own
small notebook, skittered after him.

Back in the passage he quite disappeared and, picking up her skirts, she ran after him, decorum forgotten.

At the end she was forced to stop, for the passage
split into three. Spinning about, she looked down each
one for a sign of him or an open door through which

he might have passed. With still no sight of Carl she set off in the direction she believed to be east, swishing her skirts with annoyance. How irritating he was. Why wouldn't he wait? Too full of his own importance by far.

Abigail ignored the doors to the right and left of her and headed straight for the one at the end. It was of heavy, solid oak with a huge round brass handle, and she had some difficulty opening it. It probably hadn't been opened for years, maybe a decade or more. Abigail wondered who had last walked these corridors, and how long ago. She knew nothing of the *castello's* recent history, but the nobility of its architecture often led her to speculate and weave her fantasies around its turrets and towers, walkways and secret arbours. Somewhere in the dim recesses of this magic place had lived Elisabetta with her children, angry and weeping at her beloved husband's taking a princess for wife in addition to herself. But at first she had been happy, perhaps dancing and singing along this very passage all those centuries ago.

Abigail gave a heave and the door swung open. Glorious light blazed through upon her and for a moment she was half blinded, seeing only a kaleidoscopic picture of walls crowded with a dizzying range of landscapes and portraits in brilliant jewel colours. She thought she heard a ripple of laughter and she whirled about to see who it might be. But the long gallery was empty; Carl was not there. Closing the door quickly again, as if she were a trespasser, she ran back down the corridor and slammed into the solid wall of a male chest.

'Abigail.' Hands came out to grasp her, his face tight

with anger. 'Where the hell have you been? I've been looking for you everywhere.'

She stared up into his face, a mere inch above her own. She could feel the warmth of his breath caress her lips, the heat of his body hard against hers. It was pleasant to look up at a man, for it was an unusual experience for her and made her feel small and precious. She felt herself sink into him as if she belonged in his arms, and for a heady moment she thought he was about to kiss her. But his hands on her arm were bruising, shaking her a little.

'You foolish child,' he said, shaking her some more.

'I've been looking for you too. Leave hold; you are hurting me.'

His grip slackened not a jot. 'You scared the hell out of me. Don't you know that some of these floors are not sound? You can't go charging about the place as if——'

'As if I owned it? It that what you were about to say?'

'No, it was not what I was about to say, but it's a valid point since you make it. I meant that running on a rotten floor could end with you dropping through it into the cellar below. How would you like that, Miss Carter?'

'I'm sure you would love to see me make a fool of myself in that way. But I knew what I was doing, and I wasn't the least afraid.' It came to her then that that was perfectly true. She had been to all intents and purposes alone in this part of the house, not knowing where anyone else was, or where she herself was heading, and she had not minded at all. 'This is a friendly house,' she stated, quite irrationally. 'I was merely admiring the paintings.'

He made a low growl deep in his throat which gave some indication of his impatience. 'You are as stupid as your sister, wandering off when. . .' Then it seemed to register what she had said. 'Paintings, what paintings?'

'In the long gallery. Haven't you seen them? Come on, I'll show you. It is a beautiful room.'

Abigail led the way back up the corridor to the oaken door and, grasping the brass knob, twisted and pushed. It seemed even harder to open this time, though it should have been easier the second time. Carl had to put his shoulder to it to force it open. The wood seemed swollen with damp and lack of use.

Once inside, the long gallery stretched out before them, and this time Abigail could take her time for a proper look. The walls were indeed crowded with paintings, though there were faded squares where some had been removed. Some of the paintings were hanging crooked as if they'd been interfered with or been put up hurriedly, while others were propped in piles on the floor. There was that smell found in all old houses, of dust and old furniture, of mould and mildew. Because the shutters were tight closed, letting in not a morsel of air or light.

Carl walked the length of the room, carefully studying the pictures as he strolled. He had opened all the rickety shutters and now the light did stream in, but the colours on the canvasses did not light up as Abigail had imagined. They were dull and dark, coated with centuries of dust.

'I expect this is where the ladies walked on wet or too hot days, and where they held their masked balls. Shall we hold ours here?'

He cast Abigail a challenging glance, but she did not respond so he continued on his way. 'I very much doubt there is anything of value left. Most of them appear to be of rather solemn people, ancestors, I suppose. Even the landscapes are dark and forbidding.'

'I expect they need cleaning.' Abigail came out of her trance to join him as he stared at a rather gloomy picture which appeared to be a jumble of lines and squares.

'Rooftops of Florence, do you think?' he asked with a smile, and twisted his head to look at it from a different angle. 'It's not very good, is it? The walls aren't straight. It's rather like your portrait of Notre-Dame. I wonder if we should bring in an expert to look at these paintings, though I have little hope of finding a fortune hanging on these walls. What do you think? Abigail?' He gently shook her shoulder and stuck his face down close to hers to peer teasingly into her eyes. 'Abigail, I'm talking to you. Don't go into a sulk, for goodness' sake, just because I told you off.'

She started as if she had been a long way away. 'Oh, I'm sorry; I was only wondering why. . .I mean, I thought this room was better lit and the pictures. . .' She clicked her tongue as if with annoyance. 'They're extremely dirty. I didn't realise they'd got that way. How very careless. It can do them no good at all.'

'I beg your pardon?'

'I'm sure it will take more than a goose feather to bring back the colours. We must take care not to damage them even though you do not know their value, if only because they have been here such a long time.'

He was frowning as he stared down at her and when he spoke again his voice had become cold and clipped.

'Disappointed you haven't struck gold, is that it? Thought you might light upon undiscovered treasure which you could vicariously enjoy through increased wages or more treats from dear Aunt Goody?'

For once she seemed unmoved by his taunting, and merely walked over to the window shutters. Could one have blown open in the wind? But no, the windows behind were all closed. The truth was uncomfortable to accept, but it seemed she must. She'd allowed her fantasies to become confused with reality. She'd seen the room in her imagination as it must once have appeared, not as it now was, dusty, gloomy and lifeless. What on earth was wrong with her? Abigail half turned, addressing Carl Montegne over her shoulder.

'I feel rather tired. Perhaps we could continue with this another day.' The sound of her booted heels echoed on the bare boards as she strode out of the long gallery and back down the long corridor. Carl Montegne caught her up before she had got very far, grasping her arm with a firmness that could not be denied.

'I'd like to continue if you wouldn't mind. I'm sure we are all tired and would like to rest, but there is still work to be done.'

Abigail shot him a look of cold fury. How could he be so insensitive? Could he not see she was upset? But *why*? she asked herself. Why should she be upset simply because a room of old pictures showed neglect? Mentally she shook herself and tried a smile.

'Very well.' He would find no more weakness in her. She straightened her aching back. 'Let us continue.'

It soon became apparent to them both that at one time the *castello* had been a building of great splendour. It was smaller than a palace yet it clearly had attempted to ape the glories of such properties, perhaps to prove the prestige of its owners.

The groined ceilings were high and carved with all manner of emblems and devices, and, though some walls were bare, having probably once been hung with tapestries, many showed the outlines of faded frescoes.

'Do you think anyone famous painted these?' Abigail wondered aloud as she smoothed a finger over the cracked plaster. 'Could they be restored?'

'I doubt it, to both your questions, but we could investigate the matter.' Carl opened a door and went ahead of her into a large panelled room. 'This must have been the banqueting hall. Heavens, that sideboard must be ten feet high and twenty feet across. I wonder if they built it *in situ*?' Carl walked over to open drawers in the monstrous piece of furniture.

'Empty. Pity. We could do with a tablecloth to fit this huge table. How many would it seat, do you think? Ten? Twenty?'

'I expect there are cloths somewhere.' Abigail looked around her, opened a few drawers which were all empty, and resulted only in setting clouds of dust billowing into the air and making them both cough. 'Probably in the linen cupboard, when we find it,' she said, going to open the window. And then something rolled forward in one of the drawers she had recently looked in and she opened it again to see what it was. She held it out to him. 'Look, a tiny figure carved from marble.'

Carl came over and took it from her. 'Not marble, alabaster. Not so cold as marble and a popular craft in these parts. The figurine I seek is made of alabaster, but that one is said to be Mercury.'

'What is this one?'

'The god Saturn, I think.' Carl made a wry face.
'According to legend Zeus became head of all the gods
by overthrowing his father, Saturn, whom he hated.
Perhaps the person who made this was a di Montegelo,
for they too had a habit of not getting along with their
fathers.' He shrugged massive shoulders and walked
away, setting the figure down on the huge sideboard.
There was a small silence.

'I'll clean this room next if you like,' she said. 'It is
so beautiful; look at the mouldings over these windows.
They're shepherds and shepherdesses, and they too
seem to have been made in white alabaster. How
lovely. What will you do with this place?' she asked,
and Carl's jaw tightened as if she had no right to put
such a question.

'Live in it, what else?'

She stared at him consideringly for a moment, but
the question niggling in her mind had to be asked.
'How can you afford to?' By the narrowing of his eyes
and the white line that formed above the rigid mouth
Abigail saw she'd over stepped the boundary of good
manners despite her efforts to the contrary. 'I'm sorry;
it really is none of my business of course.' He looked
so infuriated and yet oddly flattened by her question
that she felt guilty and instinctively put out a hand.
'Forget it. I had no right to ask.' Desperately she
looked about her for a diversion. 'What a very splendid
fireplace. And that brass clock is showing the solar
system, is it not? How lovely.'

'My father was born here.'

Abigail looked up at him in surprise. She saw by the
tautness of the skin about the eyes the strain he was
under, and by the set of his shoulders how he fought it.
When he said nothing more she quickly averted her

eyes from his face. 'I dare say they used to cut logs the length of small trees for this dog grate.' Anything to fill the awkward silence, she thought.

Carl was still standing by the vast sideboard, fingering Saturn as if to etch it into his memory. 'There would once have been pewter and silver-plate on this sideboard, majolica from Urbino, and, on the floor, skins and embroidered rugs from the East. A house with money and style, but, I think, very little love. My father, Filippo, ran away from his home while still a young man because he did not get on with his own father, as I in my turn did not get on with mine.'

'How very sad.'

He shrugged as if it were of no account, yet she knew that was not the case. 'My grandfather, Guiliano di Montegelo, was said to be very autocratic and had it in mind for my father to marry a rather dull elderly lady who had ample funds but few charms.' Carl gave the ghost of a smile. 'My father refused and ran away with my mother, Vittoria, a girl he had known all his life.'

'How very romantic.' Abigail was staring at the softened face, entranced. But this sensitivity was soon masked and the tone became cool and practical once more.

'Not in the least. They spent half a lifetime wandering like gypsies, determined not to return here, waiting for the old man to die, so wrapped up in their own needs there was no place in their life for anything or anyone else, not even a small boy.'

'That's why they sent you to England, to school?'

'Let's say that I was an encumbrance.' The bitter tone showed how deeply the hurt had scored. 'But the castle, now that the old man is long dead, and with no

other di Montegelo left but me, is now entirely mine.'
There was grim satisfaction in the voice and the dark
eyes glittered with purpose. 'And I intend, for the first
time in my life, to have a real home. I intend to stay
here, in Italy, and build a new life, a home. Whatever
it takes to restore this place to its former beauty will be
done. I have to do it, do you see?' He glared at her
then, and as he looked into her eyes the gaze softened
slightly and he smiled. 'I don't mean to sound so
vehement, but it is important to me. Can you
understand?'

Abigail nodded and came to stand before him, to
rest her hands impulsively upon his. 'Oh, I do. And
I'm sure that you will achieve your aim. You can do
anything in the world if you want to; my mother always
says so, and I believe that, don't you?'

Carl laughed out loud and, taking her by surprise,
wrapped his arms about Abigail, hugging her to him. 'I
wish I could; it is a pleasantly comforting maxim. What
a treasure you are. But there was little money with the
inheritance, and precious few signs of family artefacts
here.' He sighed, looking about him with a grim
resignation, but still not releasing her from his hold.
She felt her own breathing move in accord with his. 'I
am not without funds, but this project is going to take
all of them and more besides.'

Abigail had both of her hands flat against his broad
chest and she was smiling up at him. '*I* believe you can
do it.'

His soft breath whispered over her lips as he looked
down into her upturned face, and she read a flicker of
delight and surprise in his eyes, and something else she
didn't dare name. After a long moment he allowed his
lips to tilt into a smile.

'Every man, they say, needs a woman to believe in him.' He continued to study her, his hands holding her fast against the hard length of him, so that Abigail could not have moved had she wanted to. Which she did not. But never had she been so close to a man before and it made her go hot and cold all over just thinking about it. 'I thank you,' he said, and, reaching down, put his lips gently upon hers and kissed her. They were warm and slightly salty and as she melted against him she felt his hands curl into her back, gripping her tightly as if a spasm had shot through him. Then it was over and he was giving a half-laugh, striding away from her, calling over his shoulder that they would do the rest of the house another day, while Abigail rocked upon her feet, her head in a spin.

Dinner was a quiet affair, the only one among them with the energy to talk being Polly.

'I suggest we take a rest from housekeeping for a while,' said Emilia, wincing with agony as she reached for a peach. 'My old back is giving me gyp. I shall declare a small holiday during which we can explore our new home, get to know the neighbours, perhaps hold a small party. What do you say?'

'Oooh, yes, please,' cried Polly. 'What kind of party will it be?'

'Haven't thought. In the garden, I suppose, since the house is still such a mess.'

'Mr Montegne suggested we clean the long gallery and hold a dance there,' said Abigail in soft tones. The thought of being presented with the opportunity to be held in Carl Montegne's arms for the length of a dance, perhaps two, made her blush and she had to dip her head quickly in case anyone should notice.

'A capital idea,' Emilia agreed. 'Do you think we could find anything approaching an orchestra in this quiet place?'

Carl Montegne chuckled. 'I dare say one or two can still be found in Florence, if not in the village.'

'Oh, Florence,' echoed Abigail, her voice almost as misty as her eyes. 'May we go soon, please? I so long to see it.'

'So that I can take you to lots of art galleries, and you can take lots of pictures with your camera? An excellent idea.' He was smiling at her as if he and she held some private secret of their own. Polly, looking uncertainly from one to the other, spoke up very firmly.

'Well, I should prefer a party, Emilia. We could invite the Count.'

Everyone turned to look at her. 'Count?' asked Emilia. 'What count is this? We have met no count.'

Polly's cheeks fired with guilt. 'I have,' she admitted in a mumble. 'But it was perfectly all right; he is very proper and genuine,' she hastened to add as she saw the shock register in her sister's wide eyes and felt the coming of a thorough scolding.

'In what respect was it all right for a young gel of your tender years to meet with a perfect stranger without having first been introduced?' The scolding came very firmly from Emilia before Abigail had time to draw breath.

'Oh, phoo. Who cares about such things nowadays?'

'*I* do.'

Polly shrank visibly before the censorious tone. Emilia Goodenough could be fearsome when crossed. 'I-I'm sorry. I didn't think.'

'Well, you should. A little thought goes a long way, my girl. It is an art you would do well to practise. Now, where did you meet this count — and what does he look like?' The earbobs danced with eager anticipation as Emilia sat up straighter in her seat to listen to Polly's tale. She'd made her point very soundly and did not harbour ill feeling. Besides, she was agog to learn about this Italian notable who must surely be a near neighbour.

'Well, then, miss, come on; tell us all about this count.'

CHAPTER FIVE

'HE IS most handsome,' giggled Polly, not wishing to disappoint her captive audience. 'He has hair as black as ebony and laughing, dancing eyes, a small moustache that sits oh, so delightfully upon his full upper lip and though he is not so tall as you, Carl, I thought him exceedingly good-looking.' Polly sighed. 'His name is Count Alfonso Ruggieri Paolo. Doesn't that sound splendid? I met him in the woodlands while he was out exercising his horse.' But looking at the faces of the others, she saw that yet again her tongue had run away with her.

'And what were you doing in the woodlands, might one ask,' Abigail very reasonably wanted to know, 'when you were supposed to be cleaning the green parlour?'

For a whole five seconds Polly was at a loss for words and then they all came out in a tumble. 'Oh, I came over all queer and had to go outside to get a breath of fresh air. It was from having been in a dusty atmosphere for overlong, I think. It is not good for your health, you know.'

Unable to help herself, Abigail let out a gurgle of laughter. How typical of Polly. No wonder they hadn't seen her for hours on end. She hadn't been busy working at all. She probably hadn't even been in the house half the time, but was no doubt by now fully conversant with the entire neighbourhood as well as the neighbours. Abigail was about to ask further questions about her truancy when Carl interrupted.

'You said his name was Paolo?' He was sitting straight up in his high-backed chair, the skin of his face pale beneath his tan, eyes narrowed but alert as a tiger.

'That is so,' Polly agreed. 'He was most interested to hear that we had moved in. And he took great pains to teach me to pronounce his name correctly. Don't you think I did well?'

'Admirably, well done,' murmured Carl, but his mind was clearly not on his words.

Abigail felt a prickle of alarm. 'What is it, Carl?' The use of his name came out quite naturally and though she felt the colour run up under her skin at her own temerity no one else at the table remarked upon it.

'Paolo. That was the name of the family involved in the long vendetta with the di Montegelos, my own family.'

Everyone looked somewhat stunned by this. Even Emilia appeared lost for words for a moment.

It was she who was the first to rally. 'Oh, stuff. We can't stand by old vendettas. The new century has begun. This is nineteen hundred and seven and I think we should have our party, and invite this count. Polly may take round the invitation herself. I'm sure she'd like to.'

'Well said.' Abigail very nearly laughed out loud at the expression of delight on her young sister's face, but stopped herself just in time. The ferocity of Carl's stare cut through her light-heartedness and brought new warmth to her cheeks, but she met his furious gaze with defiance. 'Do you not think that would be a good idea?' she asked, rather lamely.

'No, dammit, I do not. This man's family hounded my own for year after year, right down the centuries. I think it might be a good idea if I was to meet him first before any females start planning pretty-pretty social conventions.'

Abigail bridled. 'You mean *mere* females, don't you? And it isn't simply for the sake of social convention. Emilia's right; if we are to live here it is foolish to continue with this old vendetta. We should make the effort to be friendly towards our neighbours, start as we mean to go on.'

'You believe the first move should come from us, do you?'

His face was quite stiff with disapproval.

'Oh, for goodness' sake,' she cried, slapping her hand on the table. 'Yes, of course I do. Whyever not? Vendettas have to be stopped some time. I swear I would not have come if I'd thought you meant to carry this one on.'

'Would you not? I wonder.'

His eyes challenged her with a dangerous glitter. 'Perhaps you have some particular reason why you wish to meet this glamorous count. Perhaps because Polly thinks him so good-looking.'

'I intend to. It is my house.'

'I am going to bed.'

'Splendid.'

As she pushed back her chair Emilia gave a throaty laugh. 'I do love to listen to you two sparring. It is really most entertaining. Of course it is your house, Carl, dear, as you so rightly say, but we all are entitled to our opinions. And I have to say that on this occasion you are outvoted. I want no more feuds if I am to stay here.'

'I didn't say we should continue with the feud,' argued Carl, rather put off his stroke by this concerted attack. 'I was merely declaring a desire to see the gentleman before we invite him into my house.'

'To *vet* him first, presumably because you don't trust Polly, a *mere* female, to know whether he is presentable or not.' Abigail thrust the words at him, her fists balled into angry little stubs on the tabletop. 'How very patronising of you.'

'I do think it a good idea to size the man up before we declare ourselves his bosom friends, yes.' Montegne's voice was cold with contempt. 'And I consider my views may be more mature than Polly's.'

Silence followed this eminently sensible remark and, while the two combatants continued to glare at each other across the table, Emilia tapped her fingers together, a considering look on her piquant face. Polly, who was only too aware how she had started all of this, hardly dared breathe, but forced herself to whisper.

'He did seem a very nice sort of count.' She wondered if she should mention that he had let her ride his horse, but decided against it. On the whole that small piece of information might unleash another barrage of trouble. She bit down hard upon her lower lip to help keep her errant tongue under proper control.

After a while Emilia spoke again. 'Surely a social function where there are lots of other people present will give you a splendid opportunity, Carl, to size up this Paolo person without his realising it.' She issued her pronouncement in a voice that defied further dispute. 'It could be, as I said in the beginning, the perfect way to make the acqaintance of our neighbours. And I really do think that we should not be prejudiced about a person in advance. Let us wait and see, shall we?'

And so it was decided. The party would take place in exactly one week from Friday. Invitations would be written and Abigail would drive round with them, taking Polly with her.

'I assume you do intend to purchase a carriage and hire a driver for us, Carl?' she asked.

'I might run to a cart and donkey,' said he, and strode from the table. At the door he paused to glare back at them. 'I knew it was a mistake to bring a peck of women with me, but, make no mistake, I will have my way. This Count Paolo will be thoroughly investigated and if I think he is any kind of a threat to us the house and grounds will be barred to him in future. In which case none of you—I repeat, none of you—will ever speak with him again.' He moved back into the room, the muscles of his thighs knotting with tension as he stood before them, legs astride.

'And not one word about our reason for being here. Not one of you. Goody, Polly, Abigail, you must say nothing about my quest for the figurine. Is that clear?'

'As crystal,' said Abigail calmly, quite unmoved by his threats. 'I'm sure we would never dream of doing such a thing, though why it should matter I cannot imagine. But let us give Count Paolo the benefit of the doubt till we at least meet him, shall we? You may well find him perfectly charming.'

White teeth glinted in the candlelight. 'Now why do I think that you most certainly will?'

Alfonso Ruggieri Paolo threw his racket on the ground and kicked it into the bushes with all the energy his volatile temper could provide. Its progress was assisted by a stream of Italian invective which no one, not even his mother — perhaps particularly his dear mother, were she there to hear it — would understand.

'No one could play with such an instrument,' he screamed at his would-be tutor.

'Then I shall procure you another,' said he with a well concealed sigh. Professor Edward Latham, late of Oxford, was willing to attempt to teach his young charge whatever his heart desired — tennis, fencing, hunting, even dancing and music — but had never been so foolish as to promise success. 'Patience and practice, my lord, are essential if you are to master the game.' It was the nearest to criticism he dared go and it could as easily win him a stinging rebuke or roaring laughter.

'Do not blame me for your own incompetence,' Alfonso complained, preening himself. 'I have breeding, a noble disposition, grace.' He smoothed both hands over a not very impressive chest. 'I ask you merely to improve upon the talents which I already possess in abundance.'

Edward Latham had heard this so many times that not a flicker of expression marred his face. At twenty-six the greatest talent the young Count possessed was conceit, and his undoubted good looks of course. Hardly a mother in all of Tuscany, and perhaps half of Italy, would not willingly marry off any one of her daughters to such a charmer. But in Edward's humble opinion, built up over three long, trying months, they would be misguided to do so. The only person the boy would ever truly love would be himself.

'The classics are more my subject than tennis, I'm afraid. When I return to England you must find yourself a different kind of tutor.'

The professor had left his beloved Oxford on a

mission to teach the Count something of Latin and Greek, art and literature, but the young man had shown scant interest, being more concerned with the development of his muscles and perfecting his social techniques than the mysteries of the ancients. Edward had thought it might be interesting to spend a summer in Italy teaching the kind of skills Alfonso's ancestors once devoted a lifetime to attaining. But it would take that and more before this young man achieved half their abilities. Now he was tired of the boy's priggish ill manners; he was tired of the blazing blue skies, the dust and the heat. He longed for the streets of Oxford, rain and a good cricket match.

Now he wiped the perspiration from his forehead and replaced his panama hat. 'I do my best, sire. I am but a humble teacher trying to earn an honest crust.' This kind of humility, however insincere, usually managed to bend Alfonso to a better humour. But not today.

'Who are these people? Have you found out where they come from, why they have come here? We are not wanting them to litter our valley. And why do they take over the Castello Falenza? What right do they have?' Alfonso began to storm back and forth across the tennis court.

The professor thought longingly of the dark, dusty corridors of his college in Oxford and vowed never to leave them again. He was too old for adventuring. 'Perhaps, sire, you would care for a cool drink. It is near to midday and the August sun grows hot.'

'I have no wish to go inside,' said Alfonso, determined to vent his ill temper even at cost to himself.

'Then I'll have something brought out to the terrace where we can drink it in the shade.' Edward walked deliberately away from his companion, guessing that, having lost his audience, he would follow. He was right. Alfonso hurried after Edward on his short, stabbing stride.

'It was meant to be mine, you know,' he called after his tutor's retreating back. 'No Britisher can win it from me. It is meant to be mine, I say. I have the right to it. *I* am Italian.'

Edward dropped thankfully into a wicker chair. He sighed yet again as he drank deep of the ice-cold ale brought out by one of the endless and anonymous stream of servants. 'I heard the new owner is of Italian extraction himself. That he is the last of the di Montegelo family and has come to reclaim his inheritance.'

The snort of disbelief gave lie to the young Count's claim for charm and grace. 'I do not believe it. I will never believe it. He is the impostor. No one ever expected the *castello* to be occupied again.'

Edward set down his glass. He would be leaving soon, so what did it matter what he said to this empty-headed young man? 'Why have you only just now decided that you want the castle when it has stood empty for years? Isn't it only because you see someone else taking it? Otherwise you would not ever think of it.'

Alfonso glowered sulkily at Edward Latham, surprised that his tutor dared criticise him so openly. He did not like criticism. It made him feel inadequate and uncomfortable. How could he, a count from an ancient noble family, be made to feel such a thing? It was unthinkable. 'I did not then know that anyone would come and take it from me,' he said, quite illogically. 'I knew it was there, should I wish to do anything with it. Now it is not. Instead it is filled with the people from

England with the miserable faces, funny food and no sympathy with my countryside.'

'Oh, I don't know that this is quite true,' returned Edward. He got to his feet with weary resignation. If this diatribe were not stopped soon it would limp on endlessly. 'Shall we repair for an early luncheon?' Then he heard the approach of a vehicle and, looking up, beamed with pleasure. 'Ah, if I am not mistaken, here they are in person, so you can judge for yourself.'

Abigail was climbing down from the donkey cart which was all Carl would trust her with on these uncertain roads, and Polly was following, her pretty golden hair glowing in the sun. The young Count caught at the breath in his throat.

'*Bella, bella.*'

Edward went forward to meet them. 'Miss Carter, I believe?' Word of any newcomers travelled fast in this hill country where little stirred the even pace of life. He knew a good deal more about the newcomers than they might expect.

Abigail saw a man in his late forties, lean, with greying dark hair and a short beard, but no moustache. Not the Count. Perhaps he was hidden in the black shadows of the terrace. She held out a hand and smiled. 'Good morning. I hope we are not intruding.'

'Of course not. In truth we are glad of any visitor, particularly in my case one from England.' He shook the proffered hand with enthusiasm and Abigail laughed.

'Do you miss England so much?'

'I go home soon. Shan't be sorry, I must admit. Italy is wonderful but exhausting. And I've scarce seen a half of Florence. There are so many wonders to see I think it must take a lifetime. I shall gladly come again, but in the meantime it's back to the dreaming spires and my equally dreamy undergraduates.' He beamed, looked around her at Polly. 'This must be your sister.'

'How can you tell? We are not at all alike,' disputed Polly, her eyes straying about her, drinking in every detail of the grand surroundings, seeking another face. But she gracefully offered a curtsy, spreading out her candy-striped skirts with demure elegance.

A gentle applause came from the depths of the terrace. 'Delightfully executed. It could only be my pretty Polly.'

'Oh, there you are, hiding.' And, hitching her skirts above her ankles in a most unladylike manner, Polly giggled with delight and skipped lightly up the steps to vanish into the gloom of the terrace. Slightly alarmed by this unbounded show of affection, Abigail hurried after her.

Count Alfonso Ruggieri Paolo stepped forward from the darkness and, taking Abigail's small white-gloved hand in his, lifted it to his lips. She was not as moved by this demonstrative gesture as he might have wished, but he could see how she studied him with care. She must surely think him handsome, he decided. For his part he was not uninterested in Abigail herself. She too was a handsome personage, though Polly was the prettier and the more feminine with the big, big blue eyes.

'Please, ladies, be seated. Will you take refreshment?'

Proper introductions were made and the Count had his servants bring slices of melon and fruit cordial for his guests to enjoy.

Abigail laid aside her straw hat and dabbed at her

damp brow with relief. 'I dare say we should have left our call until later in the day, but I was afraid it might grow too hot. I do hope you do not mind our calling unannounced.' She fanned herself gently with her lace handkerchief.

'We are always pleased to see the ladies,' smiled Alfonso. 'You light up the shadows of our day.'

A charmer indeed.

'You must tell us all your news,' he went on. 'And then you must join us in lunch.'

'Oh, I wouldn't presume——'

He waved an expansive hand. 'I will take no refusal. But first you must tell me how you can bear to live in that dusty old mansion. It is so very creepy and full of lizards and snakes.'

'*Snakes*?' Polly cried, horrified.

Alfonso laughed. 'I only jest. In any case they would not hurt you. They are—how you say?—shy. My English, it is good, yes?'

'Most commendable.'

'I learnt it at Oxford, where I spent my youth. My lettuce days, *sì*?'

'Salad. Salad days.' Abigail dipped her head and sipped at her cordial to hide a smile. She found the Count, though of about her own age, rather immature, as if he was too conscious of himself, too anxious to please. Rather like someone posing for her camera. He certainly did not have Carl Montegne's assured presence, nor his physique. Abigail was idly making further comparisons when she realised she was being addressed by Polly.

'Tell Alfonso why we have come, Abby; why do you not?'

Abigail gave a pained smile. 'I am forever trying to

instil in her virtues of patience and good manners. Is it not enough to enjoy meeting new people first?' She turned to the Count with a slight bow of her neatly coiffured head. 'You have a beautiful setting for your elegant home, Count. You must be very proud of it.' Now she let her gaze drift out over the Tuscan hillside, at the silvered green of the olive groves and the taller, darker cypress and ilex trees. The sun shimmered in a haze on purple hillsides, washed patches of red roofs and white wall, lit brilliant flowers to startling colour and warmed the stones for lazy lizards to enjoy. She watched one now slowly slip down the steps of the terrace. What a delightfully uncomplicated, unemotional life it must lead.

'And have you seen much of our beautiful country-side since you arrived?'

Abigail laughingly shook her head. 'I'm afraid we've all been too busy cleaning to go anywhere.'

'But we go to Florence on Thursday,' Polly interrupted. 'Carl has promised. We are to see all the museums and galleries.' She wrinkled her small nose in distaste and the Count put back his handsome head and laughed quite charmingly at her.

'But the museums they are Florence, my little elfin. You will enjoy your day.'

Abigail wished he would not call Polly by that name. The way she was blushing and fluttering her eyelashes at him was doing her no good at all.

'Certainly she will,' put in Abigail in quenching tones. 'This whole trip is to be a valuable part of Polly's education, and mine too. It will be most illuminating.'

But Polly had put on her mutinous expression. 'I'd much rather visit the shops. I declare I have no interest in museums of any kind.'

'Then perhaps I may be allowed to escort you to the shops while your family visit with the pictures and the artefacts?' He raised one aristocratic brow as Polly gave a little gasp of pleasure.

'No,' said Abigail, very quickly and very sternly. 'I'm afraid that is quite out of the question.' And as Polly would have protested Abigail fixed her with a piercing glare which silenced her at once. 'We are companions to Emilia Goodenough and must not neglect our duties.'

'Some other time, then, perhaps,' said Alfonso smoothly, and Polly sighed, slightly mollified.

'Perhaps,' said Abigail, not really meaning it but glad to change the subject. 'How long has your family lived here, Count?'

'For many hundreds of years. It is my *palazzo*. Perhaps one day you will permit me to show it to you in its entirety. The land you see all around, it is mine and always will be.' His tone almost challenged her to defy possession.

Abigail slanted a glance at him, noting the proud profile, the stubborn thrust of the pointed chin. Not a clever man perhaps, academically, else the professor would not show so clearly his boredom; but not stupid either. And fiercely proud, with an inborn sense of dignity and elegance.

'That, of course, is the reason we called upon you first, because you are the oldest, most important family in the neighbourhood,' said Abigail with delicate tact, and saw how he accepted this as an acknowledged truth. Silently she wondered if Carl Montegne might perhaps feel the need to dispute this since Castello Falenza was at least as magnificent as the Count's *palazzo*.

'My employer, Mrs Emilia Goodenough, is to hold a small party in order to make herself acquainted with her new neighbours. It is to take place next Friday evening at the Castello Falenza and she would very much like you to come.'

'It is to be a very special kind of party,' said Polly with eager enthusiasm. 'At first we were only to have a small garden party but then Mrs Goodenough hit on the idea of making it a costume party with masks and fireworks and everything, just as they used to do in ancient times.'

Abigail rolled her eyes to heaven. 'I beg her pardon, Professor; she means of course in the time of Renaissance Italy and not the ancient Greeks.'

Polly flushed prettily. 'Alfonso knows what I mean, do you not? It seems ancient to me.'

Alfonso laughed and patted her hand as if she were a small, sweet child. 'Everyone would seem so to you, my little one. Tell Mrs Emilia I should be delighted to attend. And in costume. I had meant to call upon her in any case when she was settled and no longer brushing and doing the cleaning, you know?' The soft words were politely spoken, but perhaps the dark eyes were less charitable, and for some reason Abigail found herself irritated by his faintly patronising manner and hurried to her employer's defence.

'Mr Montegne will be hiring some help over the next week or two, I am sure.' What on earth had possessed her to say such a thing? Abigail shifted slightly in her chair so that she could not see Polly's startled expression. 'There was so much work to be done we could not wait a single day. The *castello* has been unoccupied for so long. We have barely scratched the surface with our brooms and buckets, and the gardens are an absolute tangle. Emilia hopes you will overlook these matters, in the circumstances. She thinks if everyone makes an extra effort to dress with sparkle and colour the rather dull surroundings will not matter.' Abigail smiled as if Emilia's honour had somehow been saved.

And now the Count leaned forward, seeming to warm towards her. 'It is far too much work to ask of a lady. Why is it that this Mr. . .?'

'Montegne.'

'Why does this Montegne ask it of her? He must be an unkind man who does not like to spend the money, yes? And cruel to bring his aunt to a strange foreign country, to a decaying old mansion that will never be as it was, whatever he does to it. Unless he is a millionaire,' scoffed Alfonso. 'And I think he is not that.'

Abigail bit back a wave of annoyance with a winning smile and thought she read admiration and understanding in the eyes of the knowing professor. 'Carl Montegne is not at all unkind. He is excited at returning to his family home and anxious to restore it to some semblance of decency.' She wondered why she troubled to defend him when they did nought but quarrel, yet somehow she did not wish this self-opinionated nobleman to gain the wrong impression.

'But why has he come at all? He is an Englishman.'

'No, no,' cried Polly, as distressed as her sister that her hero should be criticised. 'He is, or at least his family *was* Italian. Montegne is merely the English version of di Montegelo. You must have heard of them.'

The Count's smile looked very slightly forced. 'Indeed, my pretty Polly. Who has not? I know of them very well and had heard that a descendant had taken over the *castello*. Perhaps Mr Montegne is ignorant of the fact that they were in the *bellavendetta* with my own family for years.'

Polly frowned. 'What is that, *bellaven*——?'

'It means in your English way a feud, I suppose. But much, much more. A feud that has waited many years, a lifetime or more, perhaps, to be fulfilled.'

Polly, eyes riveted upon the beautiful olive-skinned face turned down towards hers, was completely entranced. 'Oh,' she breathed. 'But there is no vendetta now. Renaissance Italy is long gone, is it not, with all those troublesome princes who were always going to war, and spent a fortune on magnificent palaces and churches to outdo each other? You see, Abigail, I do remember something of my history lessons.'

'You are very clever, little elfin,' said Alfonso, and, reaching out a fine elegant hand, stroked Polly's sweetly pointed face. Abigail was on her feet in an instant.

'Come, Polly, it is time we were on our way. I must decline lunch today, Count, since we are expected back. Another time perhaps?'

And now Alfonso was reaching for Abigail's hand and she relinquished it to him. 'Indeed, I shall make sure of it. I shall escort you to your carriage.'

'Oh, there is no need,' protested Abigail, thinking of the patient donkey waiting in the shafts of the small cart. 'But there is one thing you could do for us, Count.'

The dark eyes shone with pleasure. 'Name it.'

'Mrs Goodenough is anxious not to leave anyone

out. If you could make a list? Perhaps one of your servants could bring it tomorrow.'

'Of course. With pleasure. It shall be done. You will find us a small community, Miss Carter, but one of quality.' Once more he bent over her hand and brushed the palm of her white kid glove with a light kiss. As he lifted his head again the challenge in his darkly sensual eyes were provocative. For a moment Abigail was so stunned that she forgot to remove her hand.

'I shall conduct the Misses Carter to their trap, sire, and then join you for the luncheon,' put in the professor.

'Till next Friday, pretty Polly.'

'Oh, yes,' she breathed. 'I do so love a party. Perhaps when Carl has fully restored the castle we can have lots and lots.'

Alfonso shrugged expressive shoulders. 'He will need to raise much money first, little one, so do not bank it.'

Polly gurgled with laughter. 'Bank *on* it. Of course he will need money, but that will be all taken care of soon when he finds his family's —— '

'*Polly*.' Abigail grabbed her sister's arm with a grip meant to hurt and certainly to silence. 'We have taken up enough of the Count's time already. Come.' And with a bow and a smile the two sisters hurried away down the flower-decked path.

The professor brought the donkey from the straw shelter and helped the two ladies on board. As Abigail picked up the reins he placed his hand lightly upon hers.

'I hope we will meet again before I leave. May I call? I would very much like to speak with Mr Montegne. I feel I could be of use to him.'

'Oh.' Abigail was surprised and slightly flustered. What possible use could a middle-aged Oxford don be to Carl Montegne? Or could it be herself he wished to see? No, of course not. She smiled with a brisk affability. 'We too always welcome visitors, particularly from home. Come tomorrow if you can, for tea.'

He withdrew his hand, but there was still a hint of tension in his stance. 'I shall do so. Till tomorrow.' He raised his hat elegantly as Abigail clipped the reins and urged the donkey into life.

'We shall look forward to it,' she called over her shoulder as the animal set off at a surprisingly brisk gait. 'What do you think all that can mean, Polly?'

But Polly had noticed nothing at all peculiar in the professor's manner for she was far too preoccupied with her own thoughts and emotions.

CHAPTER SIX

SHE would have to speak to Polly, of course, not least about the Count as well as her wilful tongue. But it was too hot to broach an argument just now. Abigail decided she would leave it for the moment, at least until after lunch.

And as they drove back at a leisurely pace, carefully negotiating the pot-holes in the rutted road, Abigail's lips curled into a smile as she thought of Alfonso Ruggieri Paolo. A professional charmer, one might say, full of his own importance, with the startlingly attractive good looks of the Latin. But in her view he paled into insignificance beside another, more familiar face. And she couldn't help idly wondering why this should be.

What was it about Carl Montegne that both infuriated and fascinated her at one and the same time? He gave out his edicts as if he himself were a god. But not sad, overturned Saturn. Mars, perhaps, though Abigail suspected he would prefer to be Zeus, ruler of all gods as well as mere mortals.

She was sorry that Carl's unhappy childhood had affected him so badly. There must be much more to it than he had confided in her. Abigail, having known the solid comfort of love from both her parents, found it hard to imagine a life without it. But Carl Montegne did not welcome or want her sympathy. He had made that plain enough. He seemed to have built the protective walls strong, as strong as the walls of his *castello*.

Would he ever allow love to penetrate such a soundly constructed fortress? And did she wish to be the one to breach the walls? Fortunately, she told herself stoutly, she did not.

'How can you have been so careless?' Carl Montegne spoke with icy control and poor Abigail was at a loss to know how to answer.

Professor Latham had come, as invited, and a most pleasant afternoon tea had been enjoyed by all. His particular brand of old-world charm had certainly delighted Emilia. But before leaving he had spent a long hour closeted with Carl Montegne in the library, and almost as soon as he had gone Abigail had been sent for. She had not been at all pleased by the summons for she had agreed to assist Polly to alter an old dress and find some suitable trimmings for the costume party. But the peremptory tone had brooked no argument and so she had hurried obediently to Montegne's bidding, reminding herself she was no more than an employee and must keep her natural pride in check. Now that she faced him, his fury was all too evident.

'Did I not specifically instruct you to make no mention of our reason for being here?'

'Yes.' Abigail had gone quite cold, so stunned by his attack and the implications that she was rendered monosyllabic. Whatever had the professor said?

'Yet you hurry at once to this confounded Count and tell him, quite bluntly, I presume, that I am here seeking the figurine. Can you have any brains at all in that empty, selfish head of yours?'

Abigail was so relieved that the professor had not divulged it was Polly who was the informer that some of the tension went out of her and she almost smiled on her breath of relief. 'I cannot imagine what you have heard, but I assure you I did no such thing. None of us did,' she added for good measure, crossing her fingers behind her back at the half-truth.

Eyes glinted almost coal-black. 'Don't play games with me, Miss Carter. You must have said something. How else would Professor Latham know that I was seeking it? And if you cannot be trusted I see no reason for keeping you here. What was it you said? You had better tell me for I shall find out in my own way if you do not.' Somehow Montegne had got nearer and his face was mere inches from her own. Taut and angry, he looked as if he would very much like to strangle her.

Abigail found she was trembling. 'There was nothing,' she murmured.

'I beg your pardon?' The voice was fearsome. Never in her life had she seen anyone so furious.

She did not want to be sent home. Her body cried out against the prospect of leaving. She needed to stay, needed to be near him. Her throat had gone dry and her body shook as if with the ague. She couldn't possibly leave him. 'There was nothing. I said nothing.'

'If you are lying to me you'll rue the day, I promise you.'

Abigail put out a hand to grasp a corner of the desk, a sudden weakness attacking her limbs. She must convince him or he would bludgeon the truth out of her and then her dreams, her hopes, her life would collapse. 'No mention was made of the figurine, I swear it,' she said with some degree of accuracy, but then in her anxiety she went further. 'Nothing at all, in fact, was said to lead the professor to surmise you were here to seek your family's fortune, not by intent nor by accident.'

He frowned. 'Not by either of you?'

'No, not by either of us.'

But that is not true, her mind screamed. That is a *lie*. The professor was an astute, learned man, and Polly had undoubtedly been indiscreet. What would Carl Montegne do if he found her out? Abigail met his gaze without flinching, and, believing that attack was always the best method of defence, she went on, 'Why make such a mystery of it in any case? The Count would surely find out sooner or later.' It was the wrong thing to say.

'Because it is no one's business but my own and I don't want any tomfool Paolo finding the figurine before I do.'

'But he has no rights to it. It belongs to your family.'

'That has never stopped a Paolo in the past.'

'I see.' Her voice came out as if Montegne had indeed strangled her, for the full horror of what Polly had done was now coming clear to her. Count Paolo was not so stupid as to have missed what she'd inadvertently suggested. He'd already started wondering why they were here and it would take very little for him to discover the rest, particularly from Polly's prattling tongue. The professor had clearly experienced no difficulty. And what would happen then? The Count's acquisitiveness was all too apparent, feud or no feud. And if he succeeded in gaining Falenza for himself, Carl Montegne would, without doubt, blame Abigail.

And Abigail would lose the opportunity of living here with Carl while he restored his home. Abigail's head swam giddily and her defiance dissolved to bitter ash, and then of their own volition her fingers flew up to whipser over the silk lapels of his jacket. 'And what would you do. . .have done, if I'd said that by a slip of the tongue I'd inadvertently told the Count of your quest?'

If she'd expected her sudden weakness to win sympathy she was all too soon disenchanted. Grasping both her wrists with an iron grip, he glared down into her wretched eyes with sour disapproval. 'I think, Miss Carter, it would be wise if you gave some very serious thought to your position here.' Twisting away from her, he walked behind the desk. 'I'd as lief send you home in any case, but I know Goody would protest. I have decided, on this occasion, to give you the benefit of the doubt.'

He felt her sigh of relief and waited, presumably to allow her to offer her gratitude. Abigail could not make her tongue work. He looked entirely forbidding standing there casting judgement upon her, and, since she could offer no explanation, was it any wonder? If she owned up to the fact that it had been Polly, however accidentally, then her sister would be sent home and she with her. And their whole adventure would be over, along with her own secret hopes and dreams. For inwardly Abigail knew much, much more would be lost. She would never see Carl Montegne ever again and such a prospect brought unbearable pain to her heart.

'I-I'm s-sorry,' she managed, and hated herself for stuttering. 'It is simply that the professor as a classical scholar must have worked it out for himself.'

Carl Montegne stared at her and for a long moment said nothing, merely looking Abigail over with a more probing gaze than usual. She seemed unhappy. He knew he had a tendency to blast off first and think later. Had she lost weight since they'd arrived? She looked somehow thinner and gaunt of cheek. Perhaps he had distressed her more than he realised since she probably spoke the truth and it was simply the astuteness of the professor. He would soon find out whether any great harm had been done, and at least Latham's comments had been useful.

'We'll say no more about it for now. But I warn you, Miss Carter, that I shall be keeping an even closer watch on your behaviour in the future. If you mean to stay you must obey my wishes to the letter, and do all you can, in fact, to please me. If my good will has any value to you, that is.' The tone was uncompromising and Abigail met the bold challenge in his gaze with a pounding heart.

What was he saying? Was he implying that there were ways in which she could buy his good will? Heat flooded her body and she longed only to quit his presence and nurse her troubled thoughts in private.

'I would advise you to keep a guard on your tongue and your fingers out of my affairs,' he continued. 'Is that clear?'

Abigail could do no more than nod her head with misery. She felt crushed beneath his scorn, and somehow cheapened. 'May I be excused?' she asked in trembling tones, rather like some forlorn child scolded by an irate parent.

'Indeed.' Carl watched her turn and almost stumble to the door, suddenly frowningly uncertain that he had handled things correctly. This whipped cur of a woman was not the Abigail Carter he had met on his aunt's doorstep. Nor the one who had bluntly resisted all his efforts to buy her off and stop her coming. Had he knocked the spirit out of her, and why should that trouble him? He knew he had a tendency to harshness, brought on by the self-sufficiency of a difficult childhood. But the fact that she had thought so little of him to easily break her word hurt far more than seemed reasonable.

Perhaps there was some other reason for her mood. Could she have fallen for the Count? She had hardly met the man. Or would it be Goody that she would miss if she were sent packing? No doubt it was simply an attack of hurt pride. He resolved to watch her closely over the next week or so, then he could more properly judge, for he got the feeling that Miss Abigail Carter was keeping something from him. If so he meant to discover what it was. Perhaps then he could lift this weight that felt like a stone inside his chest.

But he couldn't bear to see her like this, to see anyone like this.

'Abigail.' For some reason he had followed her to the door and was now taking her hand. It was very cold and fragile.

'Yes.'

Overbright eyes turned up to his, valiantly holding back tears that were all too real. Carl felt a prickle of discomfort and a surge of such protectiveness that it very nearly unmanned him. He let go her hand abruptly, as if it had burned him, for in another moment he would have swept her into his arms and. . . and what? He took a pace away from her. There was no necessity for him to behave like a total cad. 'Maybe I over-reacted. There's no reason to suppose this Count fellow is at all interested in me or my quest. It was a mite unfair for me to blow your head off.'

Abigail swallowed hard on the lump that had grown in her throat, with a rush of relief. Carl Montegne was not a man who normally found the need to apologise, and she sympathised with his awkwardness. 'What did the professor say to you?' she softly enquired.

Carl gave a rueful smile. 'He seemed to know a great deal about my family, and had guessed or been told that my purpose for coming here was more than returning to an old family home. He suggested it was possible that the figurine might be found in a museum. He is of the opinion that he could well have come across it, or certainly something similar. But, a vague man, he cannot remember quite where or when.'

'That is most helpful information in a city with as many museums as Florence,' said Abigail with an attempt at a wry smile.

'I dare say. But I would still much rather the subject were not one for public debate. The professor has promised not to speak of this matter to the Count.' Still that coldness in his tone. 'But I'm not sure how much I can rely on his discretion. Loyalty is hard won, it seems.'

Abigail opened the door and halfway through it said in a small, choking voice, 'Perhaps it would be better if Polly and I did return to England. The professor is going next week, I believe, after the party. I am sure he would be happy to escort us.'

Dark eyes took her measure. 'Is that what you want?'

For a long, telling moment she met his gaze, not even caring what he read in it. 'No,' she said at last with painful truth. 'It is not. But since your trust in me is quite gone perhaps it would be for the best.' She could sense the tension in his body. Did he want her to leave? Would he miss her? Did she but know it, that was precisely what he asked himself.

After a moment he spoke again, the bitterness back

in his voice, and the train his thoughts had taken
became clear to her. 'I can see that it would be a great
pity for you to leave so soon after you've met the
Count, would it not?'

How very much he must hate her. In his eyes she
was a traitor, the very worst kind of gossip and fortune-
seeker who would sell information to the highest
bidder. She longed to tell him that this was not the
case, but knew he would not believe her. 'I doubt the
Count would notice we were gone. And I'm sure it is
of no consequence to me.'

He was holding open the door, staring at her through
narrowed eyes, the square jaw rigid with distate. 'We'll
see how things develop, shall we?'

It was what she expected. Drawing in a shaky breath,
Abigail thanked him and quietly left. Carl Montegne
stood for a long time watching her walk down the
passage before he closed the door.

Florence was every bit as wonderful as Abigail had
imagined it would be.

She wanted to look everywhere at once.

At the tall, ornate buildings, at the tantalising
glimpses of courtyards a riot of colourful flowers, at
granite gateways and marble columns. Abigail was
entranced. The sun shone, the flowers bloomed, and,
putting the recent unpleasant scene from her mind,
Abigail vowed to make the most of her day. Even Carl
Montegne was in a benign mood.

'There is no need for you and Polly to accompany
me around all the museums. I have already visited
some while you were busy cleaning. The professor has
suggested several more obscure and out-of-the-way

places which specialise in alabaster and ceramics which he thinks are the most likely.'

The thought of spending an entire day alone with Polly was more than Abigail felt she could endure. Besides, she wanted to stay close to Carl Montegne. 'Oh, but we don't mind in the least. I for one am looking forward to visiting the museums.'

Carl looked doubtful. 'And Polly?' he asked with the teasing lift of one brow.

Abigail lowered her voice. 'Polly will do as she is bid.'

'What are you saying, Abby? May we visit the craftworkers' street?' cried Polly, as if guessing she was under discussion. 'Emilia says they make the most wonderful leather belts. And I am looking for something most particular for my new blue costume.'

Abigail rolled her eyes to heaven and Carl burst out laughing. A small argument ensued, at the end of which it had been agreed that they would all visit the Duomo and Il Battistero together.

'It is important that we do not attempt to do too much in one day,' said Emilia. 'There is plenty of time, after all. We can come again. After lunch Polly may come with myself and Ida to examine the craft shops and artisans in the narrow streets, while you, Abigail, if you wish, may accompany Carl on his quest.' And when he looked doubtful she continued, 'I vow I have no wish to go on this museum trail you are set upon myself, and another pair of eyes looking for your precious figurine would be useful, would it not?'

Carl had to concede the truth of this.

'Then it is all settled.'

The green, white and pink marbled Duomo was certainly worth seeing.

'It was built as the very last word in cathedrals,' Carl told them, reading from the guidebook. 'It can hold twenty thousand people, would you believe, and took almost two hundred years to build.'

'Heavens, didn't the builders get dreadfully bored?' cried Polly, much to everyone's amusement.

They admired the magnificent cupola designed by the architect Brunelleschi.

'The Florentines held a competition to find the finest dome for their museum. Rich or poor, anyone could enter.' And with a quizzical smile at Abigail, 'Art was all important, as I think I have mentioned before. This is something that even your most artistic photography cannot do justice to.'

'Oh, my camera, I had quite forgotten,' said Abigail. 'The film is almost finished. I must find somewhere to have it developed. Emilia, will you take it with you when you go around the shops?'

'But of course. I would be delighted.'

'And ask them to put in a new film too, please.'

'May we go on now?' asked Carl with exaggerated patience, making it clear he considered her intervention wasteful of precious time. Abigail flushed.

'Of course. I'm sorry.'

'Would you like to climb to the top of the Campanile?' he asked.

'What is that?'

'The bell tower. It has over four hundred steps so perhaps not.'

It was a challenge Abigail could not resist. 'But of course. Lead the way.' Polly too was eager to go.

Smiling with malicious pleasure, certain she would never make it to the top, Carl told Abigail she could return whenever her breath ran out. 'But pray, Miss

Carter, do not over-tax yourself and collapse. Even I should have great difficulty in carrying you back down again.'

'I assure you I am perfectly capable of going up, and coming down, under my own steam.' And she did. Every last step right to the very top. And it was worth it, for the view was magnificent. Before them lay the whole mysterious majesty that was Florence. Polly puffed and blowed but did not offer one word of complaint either and daringly leaned from one of the windows to wave to Emilia and Ida below, quite frightening the life out of them.

Abigail saw with some satisfaction that Carl was thoroughly impressed with them both though he tried not to show it. He seemed altogether more relaxed, enjoying the day away from chores as much as they were.

Once or twice as they made their way around the sights Abigail felt him watching her, but tried not to show that she noticed his attention. He'd said that he would watch her, but she had not expected him to be quite so literal about it. He scarcely seemed to lift his eyes from her. And what eyes. She couldn't think what it was that interested him so. But then she could not see the rapt expression upon her own face as she studied the pictures and the statuary. She could not see the golden glow come to her sun-kissed skin or the shine that sparkled in her amber eyes. Carl watched these changes in her because he could not help himself. He found, to his own astonishment, that Abigail grew in beauty before his very eyes.

In the Baptistry they admired the Romanesque architecture, the mosaics and the beautiful bronze doors. Then they moved on for a welcome lunch in the

Piazza della Signoria where they could eat in the sun if they wished or sit beneath huge brightly coloured parasols. Pigeons came to feed from their hands and Abigail joyfully finished the remaining few snaps on her film.

'Aha, I thought we might find you here, my friends.' Like a shadow crossing the sun the day was suddenly blighted by the appearance of the Count with an apologetic professor in tow. Abigail's heart sank as she saw the smile fade from Carl's face and his eyes darken with ill-concealed anger.

Hastily she tried to smooth things over. 'How very well met, Count. Allow me to introduce to you my employer, Mrs Emilia Goodenough, and her nephew, Mr Carl Montegne. Not forgetting her maid, Ida.'

Full introductions made, hands kissed or grudgingly shaken, Emilia invited the Count to join them for lunch, which he did with alacrity. His timing, Abigail noted, had been impeccable. One might almost think that he had carefully planned his appearance to coincide with their lunch break. But that would imply that he had been watching them.

Polly was not so reticent with her welcome and managed to move her chair so that she sat beside Alfonso. Here she was able to enjoy private conversations and asides with him during lunch, to which the others were not privy.

The Count did manage, however, to inform his new friends at length of his skills and prowess in the physical arts and social graces, even offering some credit to Professor Latham.

But in the main their interest was far surpassed by Polly, who was the only one who really gave Alfonso the attention he felt he deserved. Though even she was too much engrossed with her own concerns for his entire satisfaction.

'Have you visited the museums yet, which will so bore my little friend Polly?' Alfonso suddenly asked Carl, interrupting Polly in a lengthy discourse of what she might or might not wear for the coming masked party.

'Some,' Carl told him shortly, with little regard to courtesy.

'The professor tells me he was able to offer you advice on the most interesting ones to visit.'

Carl shot a quelling look at the poor professor, who had been forced to produce some excuse for his visit to the *castello* by his overcurious employer. It would not do to offend the Count. Latham might wish to visit Italy again. 'I happened to mention that you were interested in seeing them,' he stuttered. 'Nothing more,' he daringly added.

The dark brows lowered in a way now familiar to Abigail, and she got hastily to her feet. 'Mr Montegne and I must beg you to excuse us, but we have business to attend to.' She looked questioningly across at Carl and saw his look of surprise. He was on his feet in a second, however, offering a deferential if curt bow to the uninvited guests.

'Till a week tomorrow, then, Count.'

'Indeed. I look forward to deepening our acquaintance,' said that gentleman with smooth gentility.

'Well done,' Carl told Abigail as she hurried to keep up with his long-legged stride. 'What an indefatigable bore the man is.' And, spluttering with laughter, Abigail had to agree.

* * *

It was a wearing afternoon to say the least. There was an alarming number of museums to be got through. They visited any number, large and small, the first afternoon, some of them in the most unlikely places. They searched the displays with scrupulous care and Carl questioned the owners and museum guides, but with little result. No one had the figurine in their care nor knew who did. He began to think that the professor must have been mistaken.

But the next day found him in Florence once again and Abigail with him. He had demurred at first but she had been insistent.

'You need someone by you if only to remind you to eat.' She grinned. 'Besides, it's fun, and I really would like to help.'

He gave her a considering look and then relented, not admitting to himself that he rather enjoyed her company.

The following week they again trekked down street after street till Abigail's muscles screamed with protest. She wished there was an easier way but dared say nothing for fear he might refuse to let her accompany him. They were becoming quite adept in scanning the relevant catalogues, asking the right questions, scouring the ceramics and statuette departments and quickly moving on to the next. But they both were so afraid of missing the figurine that it soon became apparent that having two of them to look was essential.

At last, however, even Carl was in despair and almost on the point of giving up. 'It is like looking for a needle in a haystack. Do you think the professor can have deliberately sent me on the wrong trail?'

'No, of course not,' said Abigail, rather slowly. Her eyes felt so heavy that she could hardly keep them open. 'The sun is so hot today,' she said. 'We are too tired to look properly, that is all. Professor Latham may be vague, but I'm sure he is a man of honour.'

Carl believed that too, for the professor had made a point of seeking him out after their last meeting to assure Carl that he had not broken his word by telling his employer of Carl's quest.

He glanced down now at where Abigail lay slumped in a chair, an untasted cup of coffee on the small café table before her. 'Abigail? Are you asleep?'

'No, of course not,' she murmured, not very convincingly.

He was filled with a rush of remorse. What was he doing to her, to himself? They had already searched the *castello* during their massive clean-out to no avail, which was why he'd grasped at the professor's suggestion so eagerly. As a scholar he would be likely to notice such things, yet his memory seemed flawed. Carl realised that he might never find the figurine and this exhaustion, the whole expense of coming to Italy, would have been for nothing. He gazed down again at Abigail, a smile coming to his lips as he saw her head start to nod.

Her straw sunhat had fallen off and he replaced it. Very gently he rested her arms upon the table and laid her head upon them. She did not move. She was instantly and deeply asleep. With tender fingers he brushed back the wing of hair that had escaped the confines of her chignon. Then he sat quietly beside her, never taking his eyes from her face.

CHAPTER SEVEN

'WHY did you not wake me?' Abigail rubbed the sleep from her eyes and stared at Carl, appalled that she should have been so negligent.

'You clearly needed your beauty sleep,' he said, the corners of his wide mouth tilted upwards into a grin.

'Oh, poppycock.' Abigail got very quickly to her feet. 'Come on, we're wasting time.' But he surprised her by taking hold of her hand and making her sit down again.

'Enough. We are visiting no more museums today.'

'What?'

'I've been sitting here thinking while you've been asleep. I've ordered you another coffee, by the way, since that one has gone quite cold.'

'Thinking? What kind of thinking?' Abigail cast him a suspicious glance. Thankful though she was for the coffee she did not like the look upon his face. It was very nearly defeat.

'I think perhaps it is time I faced up to reality. The chances of my finding this damned figurine were always slight to say the least. I certainly will not ask you to wear yourself out with it any further.'

'But I don't mind.' She was horrified. 'You can't give up now. We have hardly started yet. And certainly not because of me.'

The wide shoulders seemed to lift and straighten. 'I didn't say I was going to give up entirely. At least I've certainly no intention of giving up the *castello*. Who knows? I may still find it there.' He leaned forward, resting his arms on the table, brushing casually against hers, and it set palpitations shivering in her throat. 'It is so very important to me, Abigail. I want to stay very badly. There may be some other way I can raise further funds. I've one or two ideas in progress.'

'Couldn't we try for one more day?' But Carl very vehemently shook his head.

'I doubt there are any museums of note left that we haven't tried at least once. And I keep getting the feeling that we are going round in circles.'

Abigail was thoughtful. 'Couldn't you ask the professor to try to remember where he saw it?'

'I tried. It is useless. Besides, the figurine may have been sold on to another museum by now. Who knows?' He sounded despondent, but was attempting to be philosophical, and his strength of character was unmarked, she was glad to note. 'Perhaps one day I will find it. They say you do find things when you are least looking for them.' He met her gaze then and something passed between them as if he sent some other, more tangible message to her. She shivered with sweet ecstasy.

Carl stood up. 'Come. We will declare a holiday for the rest of the day, and be tourists. Then we will go home and prepare for this party. It is time we enjoyed ourselves for a change.'

'Heavens, the party. I had quite forgotten.' Abigail blenched. She had given no thought for days about what she was to wear. And now there were only a few days to go. She would miss this time in Florence with Carl, but at least she had the party to look forward to.

But she would not think of that now. It was much more exciting to be alone with Carl and find that he was no longer rushing three paces ahead but taking her arm and strolling with her down the Via del Campidoglio, which once boasted real Roman baths. He took her to the Via de' Calzaiuoli, the street of the shoemakers, where he ordered some new shoes for her despite her protests, asking the man if he could have them ready to collect later in the afternoon before they returned home.

'*Sì, sì*,' said the delighted man.

'*Grazie*.'

'*Prego*.'

'Oh, ask him where I can take my camera. Emilia forgot the other day.' The cobbler kindly directed them to a small narrow street running at right-angles to this one.

The photographic shop was almost at the end, close to yet another museum. 'Have we visited this one?' Abigail wanted to know.

Carl frowned. 'I don't think so.'

'Then tell me how to ask for a new film for my camera then you can go and look while I wait for my film.'

But Carl only laughed. 'You'll never remember it.'

Abigail put on a rebellious expression which looked so like Polly's that it made him laugh all the more. 'Of course I will,' she vehemently declared. 'Do you think me an idiot?'

'Very well. You asked for it. *Vorrei una pellicola per questa macchina fotografica*?'

Abigail stared at him transfixed and then it was her turn to burst out laughing. 'You're quite right. I'd never remember all of that. And I dare not ask what to say for, "When will it be ready?" And I probably wouldn't understand the answer anyway.' And then they were both laughing, she with her delightfully merry gurgle and he with lively guffaws of glee.

'How very happy you both sound.' As one they turned to face the speaker. Count Alfonso Paolo smiled graciously at each of them. 'This is yet another happy coincidence, my friends, is it not?'

The laughter faded as quickly as it had come and Abigail felt an unreasonable resentment that the Count should intrude upon their happy afternoon.

Carl, however, was looking past Alfonso, back in the direction from which he had come. 'Where is the professor?' he asked.

'Still in the museum. What a slowcoach he is. But I have had sufficient culture for one day.'

'I should have thought, living here all your life, that you had had your fill of museums long since?' enquired Carl with a tilt of one questioning brow.

'I confess that like little Polly I prefer the shopping. I never appreciated their appeal until the professor drew my attention to them.'

There followed a small silence, which Abigail for once felt at a loss to heal. It was Carl who broke it by taking her very firmly by the elbow and steering her through the shop door. 'We have done with museums ourselves for today and are dealing with Abigail's photographs. Good day to you, sir.' And with a brief nod, Carl abandoned the Count and whisked Abigail into the little shop.

'You were quite rude to him,' Abigail breathlessly protested, and received a keen-eyed glare as reward for her temerity.

'Does it matter? I don't trust the man. He is up to something. I know it.'

It did not take long for the man in the shop to take

Abigail's camera into his dark-room, take out the old film, and reload with new.

'Now you can start happily snapping again,' said Carl as they left, promising to return in ten days to collect the developed prints.

'Good. I shall get lots and lots at the party.'

'Are you looking forward to it?' he asked her as they made their way back to Carl's carriage. They had paid a young urchin to hold and feed the horses in order to give them a rest. But they progressed rather slowly since both Carl and Abigail were somewhat footsore and weary.

'Indeed I am.' Her dreams were haunted with how it would feel to be held in his arms. 'Are you? Have you decided what you will wear?' Abigail slanted a teasing glance at him, but saw that he was abstracted, his thoughts clearly elsewhere. And while she contemplated questioning him about it he half spoke his thoughts aloud.

'What is the Count doing wandering about museums? He never struck me as a man interested in culture.'

Abigail's heart went cold. Surely Alfonso could not also be looking for the figurine? She dared not think so. But she was forced to conclude that yet again in some way the Count had spoiled her day. He had certainly lost her Carl's attention.

'I dare say the professor is anxious to see as many museums as he can before he returns home,' she offered.

Carl Montegne turned shrewd eyes upon her. 'It wouldn't be that the Count is following you about, would it?'

Abigail gasped. 'Good heavens above. Whyever should he do that?'

'Perhaps because he has eyes in his head and cannot resist a handsome woman.'

Abigail looked at him in surprise. 'I do believe you are jealous,' she teased, and was pleased to see his jaw tighten in anger.

'Or because you told him what I was doing here?' Again that accusation that she might be a traitor. But Abigail was too far into her lie to retract it now. She justified it to herself by maintaining that the truth would only hurt Carl the more, when he had enough to think about. And Polly too, for no benefit to anyone. So she merely sniffed disdainfully and turned her face away.

'You refuse to believe a word I say so what is the use of my replying?'

'As you will,' he said, and they sat in stiff silence all the way home, Abigail with a lump of misery in her heart as heavy and solid as the granite churches they had so recently visited.

'Whatever can we wear?' mourned Polly. 'Putting frills upon this old dress simply isn't working, Abigail; I feel like a frump. We must ask Emilia for help at once.'

Abigail took the pins from her tightly clenched teeth but held fast to her slipping patience. '*No*, Polly. I have no intention of asking Emilia for any more money to buy clothes. She has done enough for us already. We must simply do the best we can.'

'But we will look quite dreadful. Nothing we have can vaguely be called Renaissance,' Polly quite reasonably pointed out and, sitting back on her heels to view her efforts, Abigail had to admit that this was true enough. 'We don't even know exactly what a Renaissance dress looked like, which is ridiculous in a place like this.'

Abigail looked startled for a moment. 'Goodness, Polly, sometimes you say exactly the right thing.'

'Do I?'

'Yes. Why didn't I think of it before? Here we are in this old fifteenth-century house filled with books and pictures. We should have studied them an age ago. Come on, Polly, to the library.'

Ripping off the offending frill, Polly pulled a wrap over the thin muslin dress she wore and let out one of her famous sighs which spoke volumes about her opinion without her actually voicing it. 'Oh, very well. I suppose it is a start in the right direction.'

The library was dark and cold and smelt of old leather and musty books. Shivering, Abigail went to open all the shutters and windows to let in the sun. 'Now,' she said and could not stifle a groan as she viewed the vast expanse of shelves, row upon row of dusty volumes, some of which had stood there for hundreds of years. 'Where to begin?'

Polly too looked somewhat overawed for a moment but then rallied. 'You start at that end and I'll start at this. Do you think we might find a book with pictures in it?' she asked, not very hopefully, and, catching her sister's eye, they both giggled.

'Is this a *very* silly idea, do you think?' Abigail queried, and Polly gave an expressive shrug.

'It is the only one we have. Come on.'

For over forty minutes the only sound in the room was that of studious breathing and the flick of paper as the two girls leafed through volume after volume. Most of the books were in Italian and quite unreadable, a consideration that Abigail had quite forgotten to take into account. And none of them, so far as she could see, had any pictures. 'This isn't going to work either,' she said at last.

Stepping back, she viewed the lines of shelves, and for no particular reason her eyes lighted upon a small desk, its polished marquetry surface gleaming in a ray of sunshine. She went over to it and opened one of the many drawers. Inside was a roll of papers tied together with a faded pink ribbon. Half curious, she pulled these out and unrolled them. They contained several drawings. Some were of the house and its furnishings. Another showed the gardens as they had been laid out in the sixteenth century.

'These papers should be in a museum,' she said. Then, delving further into the drawer, she found an even older scroll, grey and torn at the edges, but still in one piece. And as she carefully unrolled it she saw that it bore the faint outline of a gown.

'Polly, come and look at this.' She was rifling through the drawer again, pulling out more papers, spreading them out on the desk. 'See, designs of gowns, dresses, caps, collars. Isn't this amazing? Some of them are more recent, but others. . . Look, these are so old the paper is crumbling. We must be very careful. Oh, Polly, this is just what we have been looking for.'

'And there are notes attached.'

'Oh, but of course, they are in Italian.' Abigail sounded crestfallen. 'But at least we have the drawings. We must tell Carl about these; they may be quite valuable.' Could they bring in enough money to restore the *castello*? she wondered.

'Just look at the length of those sleeves, Abby. They are all trimmed with ermine and encrusted with pearls.

They must weigh a *ton*, and see how they trail on the floor. Why, I would trip over them in an instant. Can you imagine my being introduced to some handsome prince? I'd fall flat on my face right in front of him.' Polly demonstrated and Abigail began to giggle, partly because the thought of little Polly in such an extravagant gown was too funny for words, and partly in relief from her recent strain. Perhaps all their problems were over and the *castello* could be saved, after all, and her guilt would thus be assuaged.

'You would rip it to shreds in a day, for certain. And look, this design is covered with birds and butterflies, flowers — '

'And even dragons and parrots,' interrupted Polly with a squeal. 'I'd be like a walking zoological garden.' And the two sisters clung together, suddenly weak with laughter.

'I hardly think the ladies who wore those costumes at their grand balls and festivals would appreciate your finding them so amusing,' said a cool voice from behind them.

Both girls swung round, scarlet-faced with embarrassment.

'We weren't meaning to be unkind,' said Abigail, swallowing her laughter, but unable to quench the merry light in her amber eyes. 'It was the thought of *Polly* in these extravagant designs which amused us. They would quite overwhelm her for she is so slender — and such a rapscallion that she would simply fall over. . .' And, unable to prevent herself, she was off again, peals of laughter robbing her of equilibrium or dignity. Polly was almost squeaking with hysteria and mopping up tears from both their eyes all at the same time.

Despite himself Carl found his own lips begin to twitch and he walked over to join them. 'Let me see. Where did you find these pictures?'

Abigail, valiantly stiffening her cheeks to sobriety, showed him and pointed out that a museum might pay a considerable sum for them.

He looked thoughtful. 'You may be right. Then again, the Florentine museums may be full of this sort of thing already. They probably belonged to the ladies who once lived in this house.' He glanced at Abigail. 'Why were you looking at them? Did Aunt Goody give you permission to rifle through my desk?'

A cold chill flickered along Abigail's spine. Why did he always have to accuse her, as if she'd been found out in some misdemeanour, like a small child? Or a traitor. And just as they'd started to enjoy themselves. 'N-no, I'm afraid we didn't ask. We were actually looking for a book which might describe the kind of dress we should be trying to produce for the party, but we forgot to take into account the fact they would all be in Italian.'

Carl Montegne looked down into Abigail's softly troubled eyes. There was gold fire in their depths, the thick lashes open entrancingly wide. He hadn't before noticed just how striking they were. And all at once he relaxed and smiled, not taking his eyes from her face. 'The masked party, of course. I'd forgotten. Perhaps I can help. Let's take them over to the window where we can see better.'

Carl spread out the papers on the wide polished table before the window, weighted them with a flower vase, and began to read. '"The robe will be of costly satin, velvet or brocade and sweep the ground with a tightness of bodice and loose-hanging sleeves as every good lady should wear. The girdle can be studded with gems according to taste and the buttons as many as are allowed".'

'What does that mean, "allowed"?' asked Polly.

Abigail attempted to supply the answer. 'I believe the Renaissance fashions became so outrageous the sober city fathers tried to curb the more outlandish styles by setting limits on design. Of course a lady always found ways round it if she was clever enough,' chuckled Abigail. 'Perhaps by pretending they were really not buttons at all but simply harmless ornamentation if they did not all have matching buttonholes.'

'I should not care to count a lady's buttons nowadays.' And Carl, his eyes moving instinctively over Abigail's full-breasted bodice, was forced to quickly avert them to her laughing face, and found himself strangely moved by her girlishness. He'd forgotten how young she was. Quite captivating. But then she had also made a good companion these last days in Florence. Unfussy, uncomplaining, full of sensible suggestions and lively, intelligent discussion. Could he trust her after all? He would very much like to.

'Go on, read some more,' urged Polly.

Carl dragged his gaze from Abigail and returned to the page. 'There seems little more of interest except details of how to dress the hair. "Thick and long with a high forehead smooth and serene".' Glancing back at Abigail, whose own hair was unbraided today and hung loosely down her back almost to her waist, he added, 'You would make a perfect fifteenth-century princess.' Carl smoothed one hand down Abigail's chestnut tresses and his eyes smiled at her as if he had noted her shivered response at his touch. The hair was thick, yet fine and silky, and swung about as if with a life of its own.

Lifting the hand, he traced a finger over the outline of one slender eyebrow. 'It says here that the brow must be "dark and silky". As yours are.' His voice softened. '"And with a good space between the eyes which themselves should be large and white". Yours, Miss Carter, are exceeding bright.'

His hand had moved somehow along the line of her chin to tilt it upwards, and Abigail's breath was like a tightly coiled spring in her breast. Carl glanced briefly at the paper then returned his study to Abigail's blushing face. '"The skin of delicate hue with a chin round and marked by a dimple".'

'Abby has no dimple,' quipped Polly, but subsided at once as neither noticed her interruption.

He was holding Abigail's hand now, laying it in one of his own while the other stroked it with sensuous care. 'A milk-white hand I should think was essential for any princess worthy of the name, and as for the mouth. . .' His eyes fastened upon Abigail's moistened lips. '"Small and rosebud with a sweet taste", it says here. Does your mouth answer these criteria, Abigail?' The thrum of his voice seemed to vibrate along every nerve-ending and Abigail could only gaze helplessly into his eyes, mesmerised by his words, by his voice. And then, impossibly, 'Let us see,' he whispered, and his mouth was upon her own, moving over hers with a leisurely, sensual movement that shot fire through to the burning soles of her feet, awakening a dormant desire in her that she had not known existed.

It was not a hurried kiss. His mouth lingered on hers as if reluctant to abandon its sweetness, and Abigail had ample time for her traitorous lips to open in response. And like an oyster shell giving up its pearl she gave the sweetness of her own mouth to Carl Montegne without a care or a thought. She remembered that other, more fragile kiss that had fleetingly startled her that day in the banqueting hall. But this was altogether different. With this one, all rational sense flew from her head. She could think of nothing but the pressure of his mouth on hers, the heat of his body hard against hers. She gave not a thought to her sister Polly standing by watching, nor of the consequences of such wantonness. She was aware only of the glorious new sensation that swept through her, banishing all other considerations before it.

When it was done, Carl looked down on her from dark, unreadable eyes, then laid one gentling thumb upon her lips. 'Sweet indeed.' His voice was hoarse and deep and he seemed not to wish to break the spell that held them, softly rubbing the heel of his thumb till her lower lip trembled and opened again of its own volition and he seemed to recall their particular situation. He dropped his hand and glanced at the roll of papers lying abandoned on the table. There was the drone of insects outside the open windows and he seemed to shake his head as if bringing his senses to heel.

Abigail was still standing motionless, the shock of her discovery robbing her of speech and adequate thought.

'Ah, yes, costumes. That is the thing. We cannot have our beautiful ladies of the Castello Falenza outstripped by our guests.' He straightened up and attempted to beam genially at them both. It didn't quite come off, but smiles flickered in response. 'I think we should investigate the attics, don't you? If these dresses were made here, they may still live here, or their descendants might.'

'Ooh, what a glorious thought,' Polly cried, and, not wishing to be outdone, flung her arms around Carl's neck and kissed him loud and long full upon his lips.

'*Polly*.' Abigail was shocked.

Polly pulled away, laughing and blushing but defiant. 'Heavens, whyever not? *You* did.' And Carl, who was beginning to wish he had never ventured into the library at all that morning, hurriedly suggested that they should go at once.

'Oh, yes, please,' agreed Polly. 'There is so little time. And I do so wish to capture everyone's undying admiration.'

Carl put back his head and roared with laughter. 'You are a captivating minx, young lady, do you know that?'

'It has been said before,' chuckled Polly, falsely demure.

'Very well.' He crooked an arm for each of them. 'To the attics, then, in search of some magnificent costumes which will delight and astonish our new neighbours. For you, Polly, I think pink or blue or some other soft shade, and for Abigail——' his eyes lingered on hers for one last time '—crimson or scarlet, don't you think? To set off your hair.'

The colour ran high under Abigail's skin. 'You make me sound like a scarlet woman.'

'Do I?' He hesitated fractionally before answering, a small frown starting to gather between straight brows. 'Now why should you think so?'

There were no Renaissance costumes in the attics but they did find a chest in the corner of one of the towers that was full of early Victorian clothes. Many were almost fifty years old, but Abigail was hopeful that these could be easily adapted.

'Here is a pale gold brocade for you, Polly. It will look enchanting with your hair colouring.'

'Golden hair was very popular with princesses,' agreed Carl, entering into the spirit of things. 'I doubt you'll need to recourse to spreading it out in the sun to bleach it, as they did.'

Polly giggled. 'I'd be quite willing to do so, but I think Abigail might lecture me about my skin.'

'I didn't think you paid so much attention to your sister's scolding.'

'Not nearly enough,' put in Abigail.

'Ah, and here, if I am not mistaken, is a dress for Abigail.' Carl pulled out a gown of scarlet silk shot with gold thread, its wide skirt and full sleeves stunningly beautiful.

'Oh.' Once again he had surprised her and left her empty of words.

'If you unpick the skirt up the front seam, Abby, you could open it up, trim the edge with braid, and wear this black velvet as an undergown,' suggested Polly with excitement. 'Oh, Abby, you will look quite lovely in it, I know you would. And you could wear a tiny black velvet cap to match.'

But Abigail was scarcely listening to Polly's plans; she was staring into Carl Montegne's suddenly serious face, her heart performing wild dances in her breast.

'And your hair should be left loose, Abigail,' said he, his voice scarcely above a whisper, 'just as it is today.' He reached out a hand to touch it as he had before, but then dropped it by his side instead. 'Will you do that for me?'

'If you wish.'

'I do.'

She might have said, I will do anything in the world for you, Carl Montegne, for I have discovered something wondrous about my feelings for you. But she merely smiled and offered a graceful curtsy in the Renaissance style. 'Then it shall be done, sire. Your wish is my command.'

CHAPTER EIGHT

THE house had come alive with noise and colour. If it wasn't quite the medieval pageant that Emilia had imagined it lacked nothing in colour, liveliness and laughter. Abigail decided it was good to see the house full of people and felt a foolish certainty that it enjoyed it quite as much as they did.

Count Paolo, perhaps determined to make a good impression, had sent half a dozen of his servants round to help with the preparation, together with a cartload of flowers. Emilia had been delighted and interpreted this as a friendly gesture. Carl Montegne, however, had taken a very different view of the matter and very nearly exploded, sending the lot of them packing at once.

'The Count is only being neighbourly,' Emilia protested. 'How are we to manage?'

'I'm perfectly capable of hiring my own labour and will do so this very afternoon,' he growled.

Emilia sighed heavily. 'As stubborn as ever. Very well, as you wish.' But she insisted on keeping the flowers.

The next morning a group of villagers had come straggling up the hillside. They were wreathed in their customary black attire and huge wide smiles.

'Goodness,' murmured Emilia to Abigail, 'some of them look perfectly decrepit.'

'So glad to come back to the *castello*,' said one

ancient, hugging Emilia and Abigail as if they were long-lost friends.

'And I will start with the garden,' said one grizzled old man who looked far from capable of wielding a knife and fork let alone a spade. 'And I bring my son, *sì*?'

'Thank goodness for that,' whispered Emilia, smiling and nodding with apparent pleasure. But it seemed that some of these villagers had worked as servants at Castello Falenza before and were delighted to do so again, bringing with them their sons, daughters, nieces and nephews.

'Can Carl afford all these people?' Abigail was moved to ask as a positive horde seemed to develop.

Emilia's earbobs danced as she laughed. 'Heavens, I don't know. But it is lovely to have help, isn't it? We'll be as clean as a whistle by the time they've done. We must thank the Count for galvanising Carl into positive action.' And by the end of the day the villagers had proved their value, many of them refusing any payment, saying they had come out of curiosity and friendship.

On the day of the party itself a half-dozen or so returned to prepare and serve the food and, as ever, the sun shone and the air was sweet with orange blossom. A perfect day.

Abigail and Polly helped to lay the tables on the terrace, watching entranced as a large earthenware bowl was set in the centre of each, filled with water and glasses of wine set in them to float and cool. Every table was decorated with vine and fig leaves, carnations and yellow roses, and looked, in the two girls' opinion, quite beautiful.

And there was food in plenty. The villagers prepared

traditional Italian dishes which would delight any palate. To begin there was *prosciutto crudo con fichi*, which was raw ham with fresh figs, and *crostini fettunta*, a kind of garlic bread, and of course the favourite minestrone soup. There was also turkey, capons, fish wrapped in olive leaves and *fritto misto*, a delicious fry of vegetables.

Dishes of fruit were set out, crusty rolls by the score, huge hams and long fat sausages which Abigail learned were called salami.

'Almost good enough to eat,' quipped Polly.

And to follow there was *torta* and a mouth-watering, honey-sweet fresh fruit sponge. But Abigail enjoyed her favourite sweet of juicy slices of water-melon, laughing as Carl tried to dispose of his pips politely.

He was dressed in cream jacket and trousers with a dark brown shirt and cravat which emphasised the deepness of his tan; Abigail decided she had never seen him look so attractive, nor so relaxed and content. Despite his opting not to wear costume he was quite the handsomest man present. Even the appearance of the Count, suave and mysterious in his mask and costume as Neptune, the god of the oceans, did not disturb him. Carl raised his eyebrows briefly, shook hands, and then ignored him, much to Abigail's amusement.

'I hardly think that attire appropriate for a man of his age,' was his only dry comment, whispered softly in Abigail's ear, which caused her to splutter with laughter at precisely the wrong moment.

An endless stream of neighbours was introduced to Abigail and she was sure she would not remember a half of them. Sometimes her stomach clenched as she watched Carl bend over an outstretched hand and touch it lightly with his lips, or smile down into some beauty's enchanting eyes. She would half turn away, trying not to look. She had brought her camera with her, loaded with its new film, and distracted herself by taking snapshots of the brilliant costumes.

'Isn't it all wonderful?' cried Polly excitedly, and Abigail paused in her photography to give her sister a warm hug.

'I'm glad you're enjoying it.'

'There are such glorious costumes here I feel quite dowdy,' pouted Polly, making Abigail laugh.

'What a vain little person you are. Did you think you would be the only beauty present?'

'Of course not. But I intend to have at least two dances with Carl so I would prefer him not to spend too much time cruising about getting to know them all, wouldn't you?' Polly slanted a teasing glance at her sister, who blushed bright red under her scrutiny and took immediate refuge behind her camera.

Abigail quickly focused on a figure standing in the doorway of the library. The sun shone brightly, lighting the woman with a brilliant silvery radiance that made Abigail catch at the breath in her throat.

'Who is that woman coming out of the house? I can't quite see her face from this angle.'

Polly looked to where Abigail was discreetly pointing. 'What woman? I see no one.'

'There, are you blind? She is dressed in a pale grey gown.' Abigail's blood ran suddenly cold, as if she had been douched in a shower of ice.

'Oh, phoo,' said Polly. 'It is you who are blind, Abby. You have spent too much time staring into your camera. Not a soul is wearing a grey gown. Everyone is in jewel-blues, greens and gold. Quite magnificent.'

Abigail became very still as she stared again at the empty doorway where a moment ago the figure had stood with her hand to her eyes as if in protection against the sun. 'You are right. My mistake. How silly.'

Polly giggled. 'You have drunk too much wine.'

'I think I must have.'

In the long gallery, dusted, scrubbed and polished to perfection especially for the occasion, a small orchestra sawed happily away, producing passable music among the growth of vines and mulberry leaves that the Italian ladies had devised.

Emilia and Carl danced the first waltz together to open the proceedings and Abigail waited with bated breath for her turn. She saw him look about the room. Seeking her? Abigail wondered, and her breast tingled with expectation. He moved amid a group of splendidly dressed ladies, all smiling and flirting prettily with him, and Abigail felt a twinge of jealousy. Surely he would ask her first before anyone else? Where was he now? She couldn't find him.

'Would you like to dance?' At last.

'Oh, yes,' she cried, swirling round to him eagerly, a ready smile upon her lips.

But it was not Carl Montegne who stood before her, smiling knowingly. It was the Count.

Abigail felt her cheeks light up with embarrassment. 'I thought. . .' She rallied. 'I'm sorry, Count, I confess I was expecting someone else. You quite took me by surprise. Your voice sounded——'

'English? I am good speaker, yes?'

She smiled at him — what else could she do? — though she longed to turn and scan the crowd that milled about her. Would Carl come if she waited? Her longing to have him hold her in his arms was almost a physical pain. 'Yes. Excellent. You are to be congratulated.'

The shapely lips pouted. 'I ask only the boon of a dance. But how did you know that it was me, in my splendid costume?'

'There can be only one Count,' said Abigail demurely. 'Quite unmistakable.'

He was holding out a hand for her and Abigail could think of no way to avoid it. Count Paolo led her out on to the dance-floor and as they began to dance Carl Montegne emerged from a group of people in the very spot she had been standing. Abigail caught his eye and gave a little expressive smile which she hoped would tell him that she had been unable to resist this offer. The Count whirled her away so that her scarlet skirts spun. He was an excellent dancer and in moments she was laughing merrily, joining in the fun of the evening.

And Carl frowningly watched her. She seemed full of laughter and thoroughly enjoying herself with that dratted Count. And what in damnation did they find to talk about with such vigour?

'Oh, we have had such fun getting everything ready,' Abigail was saying. 'I'm sorry we had to send your servants back, but Mr Montegne is a very independent-minded person. He likes to do things his own way, you understand?' She made a little moue, not wishing the two to become worse enemies.

The Count gracefully inclined his head. 'You have made this room very splendid. The artistic display of flowers and leaves must surely be your own creation.'

'With help from the village ladies, but yes, I do enjoy doing flowers,' Abigail acknowledged. 'The room was a sad mess. Many of the pictures have had to be taken down. We intend to have someone clean and restore them.'

'*We*?'

Abigail flushed. 'I mean Mr Montegne.'

'Ay, yes, Mr Montegne. He is rather brusque, *sì*?'

'He can be sometimes.'

They were engaged in a country dance so now they parted and skipped down the line of dancers to meet again at the top. 'How did he come to have this *castello*?' the Count asked as he took Abigail's hand again.

'It was left to him by his grandfather, I believe.' Carl Montegne was also dancing, with a very pretty dark-haired girl who couldn't be a day over sixteen. A shaft of unexpected pain struck Abigail's breastbone. How very silly of her to be jealous. Of course he must dance with his guests — as she was doing.

When the dance finished the Count led her back to her chair.

'A notable performance,' said Carl, with a slight drawl in his voice.

Alfonso smilingly agreed, puffing out his chest slightly. 'I am a good dancer, do you not think?'

Carl gave a crooked little smile. 'I was thinking of Miss Carter in point of fact. How very delightful she looks, do *you* not think?'

Abigail found herself flushing furiously beneath the scrutiny of the two men, but was spared from answering as Carl continued speaking.

'Miss Carter has become very like a friend these last months, though some would consider her as no more than a humble employee, being my aunt's companion.' He smiled, but there was little humour in it and Abigail felt a pang of irritation. Was there any need for him to mention that fact on this particular evening? 'We should not wish any harm to come to her.'

'Nor should I,' beamed the Count, and, lifting Abigail's hand, planted a kiss upon the back of it. His lips were moist and hot and Abigail delicately withdrew her hand as soon as was courteous. 'She is the delight, is she not? One day she has promised to come to my *palazzo* so that I can show her all my treasures. My pictures, my horses, my beautiful furniture, my land——'

'She has very little spare time,' cut in Carl, high-handedly. 'As you know we are working hard to restore my property.'

Abigail was indignant. How dared Carl Montegne decide whether she had time to visit the *palazzo*? She might be an employee, but not a slave, for goodness' sake. She helped with the cleaning as a gesture of good will, not because she had to. Stiff-lipped and straight-backed, Abigail turned to the Count.

'Mr Montegne exaggerates. I should be delighted to view your *palazzo*. It looks very beautiful from what I have seen.'

'Ah, that is good, yes. Perhaps next Sunday? You could stay for lunch and watch me play tennis. I have become very good.'

'I play tennis too,' said Abigail, stubbornly ignoring Carl's furious gaze. 'Prehaps we could have a game.'

The Count clapped his hands with delight. 'What women you English produce. Wonderful. Wonderful.'

'I shall bring Miss Carter and my aunt over for a visit when the time seems appropriate,' interrupted Carl with stolid determination. Abigail continued to ignore him.

'Next Sunday, then.' She heard his sharp intake of breath.

'I shall look forward to it.' The Count's eyes seemed to devour her as he kissed her hand again and as smoothly turned to Carl Montegne. 'Abigail was telling me that you inherited the *castello* from your grandfather. How was that? He has been dead these many years? I thought the estate was to stay empty.'

Carl stared into the smaller man's eyes, dark with curiosity, yet in them was also an awareness of his own importance. As Count Alfonso Ruggieri Paolo, a member of the dwindling Italian nobility and owner of vast tracts of land, and employer, even now in these modern times, of large numbers of people, he was unused to being set down or bettered by anything or anyone. Likewise Carl Montegne.

'It naturally passed to my parents first,' Carl told him in a matter-of-fact voice. 'Despite any differences between my father and grandfather, family ties are strong here in Italy, as you know only too well, so no other alternative would have been considered. My parents chose not to reside here.'

'Oh, and why was that?'

Carl's lips tightened at the persistent questioning, but he continued as if he had not been interrupted. 'On their deaths I was no more than a boy. Now I have the means to live here in reasonable comfort and can take up my inheritance, as is only right and proper.'

The Count's eyes glittered. 'You have papers?'

'Papers?'

'To prove your ownership.'

For a second Abigail felt sure that Carl meant to hit him, but with considerable effort he restrained himself.

'Of course I have documents. Would you like to see them?' The tone was not inviting.

'No, no, I will take your word. At this stage. However, I think you will find life in the Tuscan hills very dull after the excitement of London. I know, from the years I spent in Oxford. You English like the business — yes? — and the coming and the going of many people.'

'I see many people here now,' said Carl. 'I do not think we will lack companionship.'

The Count shrugged. 'A place this size takes a great deal of work, and money. It is like the beautiful woman, good bone-structure but expensive to deck out in the finery, *sì*? But you will soon return to your homeland. Like your father you will not wish to live here long.'

Abigail could almost hear Carl's teeth grinding. 'I doubt it. And you forget, this is my homeland. I was born here.'

The Count smiled his captivating Latin smile, which seemed to enrage Carl Montegne all the more. 'Oh, but I know how it is. You English like to travel, but not to stay; is that not so?'

'Not this Englishman.'

'When you decide to return home, to England, you must tell me. Perhaps I will relieve you of this ancient pile.'

'That is most generous of you,' said Carl, freezingly. But the Count merely replaced his mask, flicked back his brilliant green cloak, and began to move away.

'I have a fancy to take it on myself. I could use it as a guest house. So, if you do not find this family fortune you seek, then come and see me. You may then be glad of my offer.'

He walked away on swaggering little steps and Abigail felt as if she had been frozen to the spot. At that moment she longed to be a million miles away, in her father's ironmongery shop, in deepest Devon, counting linen endlessly for Emilia, or swallowed up deep in the bowels of the earth. Not once had she considered the possibility of the Count's revealing her lie. Now she faced it as she felt the cold fury permeate from Carl Montegne's rigid body to her own. He was glaring down at her as if he were planning her imminent demise and Abigail felt a rush of hot blood cloud her vision, the swirl of music and colour fade to the edges of her consciousness.

After an eternity Carl Montegne spoke in frigid, clipped tones. 'The library, Miss Carter, as soon as this shindig is done.' Whereupon he walked away from her, taking with him Abigail's dreams of being held close in his arms in some romantic Venetian waltz.

The rest of the evening passed by in a daze. With half her attention she watched Carl dance with every attractive woman in the room. Often she caught him glaring at her, or staring with a kind of cold triumph in his eyes as if he had expected her to betray him and had been proved right. The evening had entirely lost its glow for Abigail. Getting through it without entirely losing control was all she could hope for.

Polly danced with the Count at least three times and Emilia seemed to have the energy of a woman half her age. Coming to Italy had certainly done wonders for her constitution. There was no mention now of making endless lists of the contents of the *castello*. She was far too busy and fulfilled to worry about such things. Even Ida was laughing as she busily served out cups of wine and cut hunks of fresh bread.

Abigail should have been happy here. It was a beautiful place with friendly, kind people, and Emilia was the best of employers. But there was no hope of that. She saw no way of staying now that her lie had been discovered. Carl would never trust her again.

Leaving everyone to whoop and exclaim over the brilliance of the fireworks, Abigail went to her room and lay down upon her bed, dry-eyed and sick with misery.

She knew now that it had been foolish to try to protect Polly. She should have been quite straight with Carl, open and honest. She could have spoken up in her sister's defence and if necessary called upon Emilia's support. Why had she stubbornly determined not to?

Because she'd been quite unable to think clearly. The prospect of being sent home to the little ironmonger's shop like a whipped dog with no hope of seeing Italy, or, more particularly, Carl Montegne, ever again had been more painful than she could ever have imagined. Life without him would be intolerable. Her thoughts had been centred upon that certain fact.

And the reason was only too obvious to Abigail. It had been for some time, were she to admit it, for she could not get him out of her mind. She loved him. No matter that he treated her only as some pet servant upon whom he bestowed the favour of his good will from time to time; she loved him. She'd heard tales of girls being led astray — was that the term? — by their employers, and she knew it would take very little, very little indeed, for this to happen to her.

She had no hopes of marrying him. He was wealthy, not only by Abigail's standards but in terms of an excellent income from his inheritance and from his banking interests and investments. And one day, if and when he found his figurine, he would be even wealthier. Abigail had no wish to fulfil his accusation that she was a fortune-seeker.

But he was a strong man, used to calling the tune and being obeyed. Owning to her deceit would not be easy. If he thought her insincere he would fling her out of the house in an instant; she knew it. Apologising for Polly's misdemeanour was now not enough. She had the lie to explain. But how to prove her sincerity, her regret at having lied to him, without giving away this new and precious secret? How to tell him that she wanted to stay, without giving the reason?

The next second she was leaping from the bed and in a rustle of skirts was running down the passage. She needed to know more about Carl Montegne. Before she made any decisions, she must understand what it was she faced.

She found Ida in the kitchen polishing a silver platter with a cloth.

'Hello, my lovely,' she said in her warm, soft drawl. 'Now don't you go spoiling that pretty gown; I need no help in here.'

'Let me do something; I want to.'

Ida shot her a keen glance. 'Well, if'n you insist. You can put these away but take care, now.' After watching Abigail nervously bob to and fro with plates and mugs for a while, she said, 'Best to get it off'n your chest, where it will only worrit you.'

Abigail set another plate on the dresser and turned to Ida with a sheepish smile. 'Is it so obvious?' The kitchen was empty, the village ladies happily enjoying a feast themselves on the back terrace, as a reward for their hard work.

'You don't fool me, that's for sure.'

Abigail sank down on to a stool. 'Will you tell me about him?'

Ida did not ask who she meant. She looked at her for a long moment, then, setting aside her polishing cloth, came to take the seat opposite Abigail.

'He had a most miserable time as a boy. Nobody wanted him, do you see? Not his father, nor his mother. And it makes a deep impression, do that, upon a child.'

'But what was the reason?' Put so bluntly, the facts appalled Abigail.

Ida folded her hands in her skinny lap and Abigail thought she might be about to do the same with her lips, but she relented. 'His father was not a good man.' The old lady sniffed her disapproval. 'He was what you might call a ladies' man, a womaniser. Mistress Vittoria, she did her best to close her eyes to his dalliance, but when one of his flighty wenches produced him a son it wasn't any more possible, d'you see?'

'A son?'

Ida lowered her chin in a slow nod of acknowledgement. 'That be the size of it. Young Carl is his father's son all right, but not his mother's. And she, poor woman, refused to set eyes on the child.'

Abigail was horrified. No wonder Carl hated to talk about his parents. 'But what happened to Carl's real mother?'

'She died, and no one mourned her,' said Ida with country bluntness. 'Mr Filippo wanted to keep the child and there was a most fearful row, or so I heard. But Vittoria won and the little lost soul was left with a poor peasant family while they two went off somewhere. Once he was weaned his grandfather started to pay him some attention. Mebbe he thought the child was his only chance of a grandchild, which sadly proved to be true, and young Carl was a taking little babe, always smiling.'

'And when he was old enough he was packed off to England, to school. Carl told me that much.'

'By that time Vittoria had come to enjoy her wandering and her socialising, so refused to return to the *castello* even though the child had gone.'

'How dreadfully sad.'

Ida watched her for a moment.

'It's a terrible hard thing for a boy to accept, that not a soul in the world greatly cared about him, not even his own parents.'

Abigail was thoughtful. 'Why did not his grandfather let him stay?'

Ida shrugged. 'Dare say he thought the education would be good for the boy and I 'spect he wanted his own son to come home, which no one could blame him for, could they? But it has made Master Carl hard. If'n it weren't for his aunt Emilia he'd be even worse, I'm telling you.'

'I can believe it.' Abigail went to kneel at the old lady's feet. 'But what am I to do, Ida? He dislikes and distrusts me and wants to send me home. And I really dread. . . I don't want. . .' She could not go on; her eyes and her throat were blocked with tears.

Ida patted her hand with an awkward gesture before setting Abigail back upon her stool and returning to her drying and polishing. 'If'n you want something badly enough you have to find a way to get it. Sometimes you'm better making sacrifices. Love don't thrive where there's pride.'

'Who said anything of love?' said Abigail stoutly,

and Ida sent her a speaking glance before chuckling
with soft laughter.

'Not a soul, my lovely, not a soul.'

When the last guests had finally gone, many bestow-
ing invitations upon Emilia and her young companions
to call, Abigail went to her room to change and tidy
her hair before facing Carl Montegne.

She took off the small black cap painstakingly sewn
with tiny beads masquerading as jewels. She untied the
tapes of the voluminous skirts, dropped them to the
ground, and removed the tight basque bodice with its
low square neck and trailing sleeves.

Her mind was quite made up. She would own up to
her guilt and ask his forgiveness in a straightforward
honest manner. Surely then he could not refuse her?

She dressed in her plainest, most modest gown of
blue moire, though it clung to her shapely figure like a
glove. Her fingers trembled as she fastened the tiny
pearl buttons right up to the fast-beating pulse at her
throat, recalling that heart-throbbing moment when his
eyes had followed the line of those buttons over the
swell of her breast at first in jest and then more intently.
He was not disinterested, she would swear to it.

It seemed, in the circumstances, that she had only
two choices. Either she returned home with Polly and
the professor and never thought about Carl Montegne
again, or she used all her untried feminine wiles to
convince him she was no traitor to his quest and to let
her stay.

She rather thought this night might well change her
entire life. As she softly closed her bedroom door and
set off along the passage, she did not realise how true
a word she spoke, though it would not be at all in the
way she expected.

CHAPTER NINE

CARL MONTEGNE sat drumming his fingers upon the walnut desktop. He was not looking forward to the interview ahead one bit. He'd been surprised at his own reaction to the Count's revelation. It hurt bitterly that Abigail had lied to him. Did she think him such an ogre, then? Was he so unapproachable? He acknowledged his tendency to sound off first and think later, a fault he was only too aware of, but that was not reason enough. Abigail Carter must be a coward. She would rather offer a blatant lie than own up and take her punishment. That disappointed him too, for he had thought her above such poor-spirited behaviour.

She would have to leave, of course. He could never trust her again. He had no intention of putting the entire project in jeopardy for the sake of sentiment or burgeoning friendship, if you could call it that. But he wished he could feel better about the decision.

In the long hour he'd sat at his desk turning the matter over in his mind he had come to the conclusion that he did not wish her to leave at all. He very much wanted Abigail Carter to stay for he felt that life would be duller without her. And he could not think why that should be.

She was attractive, of course. A fine figure of a woman; handsome, one might say. She was lively and entertaining, full of vigour and common sense, or so he had believed, and with an adventurous spirit he admired. And he'd almost come to believe her to be totally unselfish. Now he wasn't so sure. All his conceptions of her had been thrown in the melting-pot again and it sickened him more than he could say.

There was a loud double rap upon the door. He strode over and opened it, mouth tight with anger, resolved not to be diverted from his purpose by a feminine smile, and found not Abigail but Ida.

'Can I have a word, master?'

Glancing along the empty passage, Carl reasserted his patience and said, 'But of course, Ida. Come in.'

But by the time Ida had unburdened her honest heart about how she had 'tittle-tattle-taled about him', in her own words, and Carl had assured her that no harm had been done, the small ormolu clock upon his desk struck one o'clock and he knew that Abigail was not coming.

'Go to bed, Ida, and think no more of it. If Miss Carter is so curious about my background, let her ask all she likes. I have no secrets to hide, nor do I care what she knows. I am not ashamed of my origins.' The grimness of his jaw said otherwise. 'I thought it was she just now when you knocked, Ida. I had asked her to call in before retiring to discuss a private matter.'

Ida remained discreetly impassive at this piece of information but added, 'She'm in bed, Master Carl. I saw her go myself a half-hour since.'

Carl stared at the little woman in furious disbelief. He was not used to having his word flouted. He had told Abigail to come to see him and not for a moment had he expected her to refuse. This proved her guilt beyond question. She had told the Count of his quest, and could not face him to own up to the fact that she had lied. He had been right to be disappointed in her.

She was a coward as well as a liar. He thrust open the door.

'Thank you, Ida. Go to bed. The fault lies with Miss Carter and not you.'

'Oh, but —'

'Goodnight, Ida. You are not in any way to blame.'

'Goodnight, master.' And, feeling slightly more troubled than she'd been when she'd come to unburden her guilt, Ida left.

Abigail had indeed gone to bed though that had been far from her intention when she had set out for the library more than an hour since.

Abigail had set out with her heart in her mouth. She knew that Emilia was in bed and that Ida was on her way to it as soon as the kitchen gleamed well enough for her to leave. Polly was already asleep, her arms flung out above her head like a child, soft round cheeks flushed with the excitement of her first adult party. The villagers had made their weary way home to their own beds, leaving the clearing and tidying for the morrow. All the candles had been snuffed, save the branch in her hand, every door safely locked and checked. There was nothing for Abigail to do but place her humble apologies before Carl Montegne and retire to bed herself to await his reaction.

Yet she hesitated, pausing in her steps to constantly glance back over her shoulder. The dark, shadowy passage was empty. Yet somewhere in its depths she could swear she heard the faintest echo of a whisper.

The clock downstairs in the hall struck twelve, finishing with its little carillon that they had all come to love. Easing the tension in her shoulders, she walked on. It must have been the old clock's machinery whirring that she had heard.

It was then that she heard the door slam. Abigail's heart stopped, raced on, hammering against her chest like a mad thing wanting release.

'Carl?'

No answer. She lifted the branch of candles and let the light spread its yellow pool further over the passageway. Quite empty. She turned again to walk on, but her steps at once faltered as the whispering this time was unmistakable. She was disgusted with herself to find her palms damp with perspiration. Not the thing at all for a lady. And what was there to be afraid of? Merely because the house was in darkness did not invest it with bogeymen.

And then it came to her. 'It will be Carl clearing away the chairs and the greenery in the long gallery,' she said out loud, and her voice buffeted the panelled walls of the passage, filling her with a new confidence. Of course. Ever impatient, he had probably decided not to wait for the villagers to do it. She turned and retraced her steps, turning at the bottom of the passage in the direction of the gallery. The whispering had stopped now. It must indeed have been the clock.

Abigail saw the light first, spilling out along the corridor from the wide-open double doors. Really, she thought, was there any necessity for him to use quite so many candles? Reckless extravagance. She marched straight into the room, but the scold died upon her lips. Every branch of candles in the long room was blazing, every chair was in its allotted place upon the wall, and every scrap of greenery had been removed with not a speck upon the polished floor to show that a dance had taken place at all. And it was quite, quite empty.

Where, then, was Carl? Abigail stepped into the room to walk slowly across the floor. When she reached the centre she stopped. And for no reason she could fathom she found herself quite unable to proceed further. She had no wish to move. A torpor possessed her limbs, as if she were no longer in control of her own actions. She seemed to watch herself set her candlestick upon the floor. Then she lifted up her skirt with one hand and began to dance. She did not dance with anybody, for she was quite alone.

Except in her imagination. For as clear as day she could see Carl Montegne. She could feel his arms about her, smell the tangy, outdoor scent of him, hear the whisper of his laugh.

Whispers. Voices. Colours dancing before her eyes as if there were a multitude of dancers in the long gallery. She could swear she heard music, not the sawing of violins they had had tonight, but pipes and something very like a harpsichord. It was all very puzzling, but delightful fun. She whirled and stepped, pointed her toes and dipped her skirts in a way she had never imagined herself doing, breathless with excitement and desire. Abigail was so happy that she didn't care if it was only a dream. Carl was dancing with her after all, and had done her the courtesy of dressing in costume.

Most handsome he looked too in doublet and hose of brilliant blue satin threaded with gold, a velvet cloak swirling about his broad shoulders and upon his dark head a soft hat with a blue feather. How handsome he was. She could hear him laughing, see his bewitching smile, the deep, dark eyes filled with promises. They were telling her that he cared for her too, that this magic between them was imprinted as clearly upon his soul as her own. Abigail felt so happy, so secure in his arms that she could almost believe that it was real. For this was where she was meant to be. Their two bodies moved instinctively through the intricate patterns of the dance, even their pulses beating as one.

Then it seemed that the dance was over for she had stopped and was staring at Carl dancing with another woman. She was small and dark, little more than a child, and she was laughing enchantingly up into his face.

A part of Abigail was inside herself watching and feeling all of this, while another part seemed to stand outside, knowing it was a dream. She looked to the opposite door which led through to the east wing of the house which they had not yet cleaned.

A woman stood in the doorway. Abigail recognised her at once. This was the woman she had seen twice before — once on the day they had first arrived and again at the party this evening. She took a step towards her, tried to speak to her, but as in the way of dreams no sound came out. And Carl was still standing with the beautiful young girl.

Abigail put her hands to her ears. The whispering was growing louder, louder, words echoing in her head, but she could scarce make them out except for odd ones. *Love. Hurt. Jealousy.* She was almost sure of it. And in her heart such pain. Pain. Pain. Pain. The room spun in a giddy whirl and Abigail fell to the floor, watching the woman walk away, leaving her bereft. She put out a hand, wanting to call her back, but she took no notice. Abigail would have liked to run after her, but she could not move. She closed her eyes tightly. Perhaps if she did this she would find herself waking up in her own bed and the dream would be over.

But even with her eyes closed she could see the woman walking away. She was dragging her feet, her shoulders hunched as if she was crying. Then she half turned and raised a hand to Abigail, cupping it as if holding something precious, then pressing it to her breast.

Then she was gone. Blackness closed in. When Abigail opened her eyes, she was not in her bed. She was still lying on the floor of the long gallery, but all the brilliance had gone, much as it had done once before. The wilting greenery was still waiting to be removed, the floor was unswept, and there were chairs scattered about everywhere. And the only light came from the double branch of candlesticks she had set upon the floor.

She shivered, feeling suddenly cold and clammy with shock. Very slowly she got to her feet. She could scarce remember a thing. What was she doing here? Abigail rubbed her eyes. Had she been sleep-walking? But she was still dressed. Had she fainted? Whatever had brought her here, the dream was over. And she felt strangely refreshed by it. Calm and certain inside.

She was not trembling or perspiring now. Nor was she in the least afraid. For now she knew what she must do. She could deal with Carl Montegne. But not tonight. It was too late and she was exhausted. A smile played about her lips for she felt so warm, so certain, so secure in her new-found decision that it was very like coming home. As if all her life had moved towards this moment. She meant to stay in Italy, with Carl. It was not through travel that she would find the adventure and fulfilment that she sought, but through love.

He had himself half suggested a way that she might stay, certainly implied it. She viewed this now with frank courage. Surely she was not wrong in her interpretation? He was a virile man, and had made no secret of his attraction to her, in physical terms. And could not be entirely ignorant of hers to him.

And he was, after all, his father's son.

Abigail sat in the garden, gently steeling herself to face him. All she need do was put her proposition forward. He was a strong, fair-minded man, and he did want her. She knew it. But how to frame the words? Snatching this moment of quietude to escape from the singing and laughter of the villagers clearing up after the dance, she tried to organise her thoughts, and did not hear the crunch of gravel as he approached.

'You did not come. I waited half the night, but you did not come.'

She jumped to her feet, pulses racing as the carefully planned words dissolved upon her lips. Once again he had taken the initiative from her and she felt her new-found resolutions fade to dry ash in her mouth. How was it that he either brought out her bullishness or sapped her courage completely? She should not let it happen.

'I was tired.'

The wide lips curled. 'From your dancing with the Count?'

'I danced only once with the Count.' She knew it was an inadequate excuse, but balked at the truth. He would think her entirely out of her mind. 'I suppose I may dance with whom I please?'

He was glaring at her with cold disdain. 'Once. Twice, perhaps. You will not do so again.'

'I beg your pardon?'

'I forbid you, and your foolish sister, to have anything more to do with the man.'

'You forbid?' Abigail gazed at him, wide-eyed with shock. 'How dare you —— ?'

He took a step nearer, grasping her chin mercilessly between finger and thumb. 'I dare, Miss Carter, because *I* pay your wages. I will repeat my instruction, very carefully, so that there can be no mistake. You will not see Count Paolo again. You will not visit him in his *palazzo*. You will not invite him here to my home. And the same goes for Polly. Social interchange between you is at an end. This is not a request but an order. Is that clear?'

She wriggled herself free, amber eyes flashing with fire and all her new resolutions to deal with him calmly quite evaporated. 'He has already invited us to a return of hospitality next Sunday, remember. It would be discourteous not to go, an insult to a neighbour which would not go unnoticed. Emilia would never be able to hold her head up again.'

Carl frowned, clearly not liking to be crossed. 'Very well, you may go next Sunday. But that is the last time. And I will take you myself.'

'Why, that is quite ludicrous. I am not a child that needs escorting about. Whether you pay my wages or no I do not see that you have any rights over whom I choose for my friends.'

He gave a short, harsh laugh. 'I doubt you have any rights at all. You have certainly not earned the right of trust. I never took you for a coward, Miss Carter. But then I did not take you for a liar either. And it seems I was wrong on both counts.'

'I can explain. . .' she began.

But he was already walking away. 'I am sure you can, most ably. However, I have more important matters to occupy my time just now than the foibles of foolish companions. I will speak to you later. For now, remember what I say.' And he left her stamping her foot with such fury upon the ground that she stepped upon a violet and was instantly desolate. What an abominable man he was. Why did she trouble herself with him? And then all the heat of her anger melted as her eyes followed his progress across the uncut lawns. She sank down on to the garden seat again, but her idyll had quite gone; her peace of mind was shattered, and every nerve-ending trembled.

She knew the subject was not closed. He had promised he would speak again to her and Abigail knew that that particular interview would not be an easy one. She must simply prepare herself, hold fast to her courage, and be ready. And on that occasion she must not let him win. But putting her proposal into effect was going to prove far more difficult than she had imagined.

Over the next few days Abigail waited anxiously for the call to the library. It did not come. Carl Montegne was far too occupied with his business affairs. Men came to the *castello*, offering advice about its possible development as a vineyard. They studied the soil, the lie of the land, and poked in every corner of every building, reassigning their purpose for the new project. Here could be sited the pressing-room, here the bottling plant, and the magnificent cellars of Castello Falenza were ordered to be swept out and thoroughly cleansed. A new future beckoned, a new beginning, one that did not depend upon the discovery of a long-lost figurine of dubious value.

Abigail watched the activity with interest, and a touch of sadness. It seemed all so practical and prosaic after their more romantic search of Florence for hidden treasure.

But mostly she missed the close camaraderie that had grown up between them during that time. She saw little of Carl these days, little of anyone, in fact. Emilia was happily visiting her new-found friends and had scarce use for a companion of any kind. Ida was thoroughly engrossed bringing her new love, the *castello*, to new and shining life. And Polly was sulking.

She had taken the news that she must not visit the Count again very badly indeed.

'What am I to do? He is the only person in the whole world who seems at all interested in me,' she mourned.

'Oh, Polly, what nonsense you do talk. That is not at all the case and you know it.'

'But we are in an impossible position here, Abby; do you not feel it? Not quite servants nor yet part of the family. You are sometimes invited to visit with Emilia, I know, but not always and not often. What are we? And what is to become of us?'

Abigail found it hard to answer these woes for she suffered similar misgivings herself. If she could find a proper place for herself in the hierarchy of society perhaps then she could better deal with her feelings for Carl Montegne. Perhaps then there might be some hope for them. But she knew it was not to be. There was only one possible course for their relationship, if it was to develop at all, and one day she must face him with that fact.

'Forget about the Count, Polly,' Abigail said, scarcely able to take proper note of Polly's very real distress, so wrapped up was she in her own. 'He is too

old for you, too rich, too powerful. Besides knowing
nothing about him, you must realise that he is only
amusing himself with you, the little servant girl.'

Polly was enraged. 'That is not true. He is the
kindest, sweetest of men, a perfect gentleman.'

Abigail gave Polly her sternest look. 'Then he will
understand that this attachment you have formed must
be stopped forthwith, or it will end in tears, mark my
words.'

'I hate you, I hate you,' cried Polly, bursting at once
into tears exactly on cue. 'You don't care at all about
my happiness.'

'Polly, that is not ——'

'Yes, it is true.' Polly was quite distraught, tears
rolling unchecked down fever-flushed cheeks. 'You
care only for yourself. You don't even *notice* what I
feel.' She was gulping out her emotions now without
thought or restraint. 'When you saw how I cared for
Carl, you *kissed* him, right there in front of me. Now
you see the Count taking an interest in me you forbid
me to see him. I know what is wrong with you, Abigail
Carter.' She was almost shouting now. 'You are *jealous*. Jealous, jealous, jealous. You have made my life
impossible here and I hate you.' And the poor child
whirled upon her heel, picked up her skirts, and flew
back to the house in floods of anguished tears.

A sigh of despair escaped Abigail's lips as she
watched her sister go. Did she not have enough problems of her own without Polly's? In truth it had been
Polly who had created her own difficulties in the first
place. What a trial she was. And what was to be done
about her? Abigail wearily shook her head, but her
eyes were soft as she sympathised with the anguish of
burgeoning womanhood. Growing up was never easy.

To fall in love at the same time made it doubly impossible. Poor Polly. She would go to her later, when she had calmed down, and talk with her gently.

And poor me, she thought. For Polly did have a point. Abigail knew only too well that there was some truth in the accusation of jealousy, and she hated herself for it. How very difficult it was to always have to be the brave and sensible adult. Would no one help carry her own burden? Then she remembered her dream of the night before and smiled. She was not entirely alone so long as she had that. But dreams were insubstantial whispering shadows, and more than anything she longed to feel Carl Montegne's arms about her in reality, and forever.

The next morning Polly was up bright and early. A glance in her sister's room showed Abigail to be still fast asleep, which was unusual but pleasing. Polly wasn't to know of Abigail's sleepless night spent pacing the floor in anguish over her dilemma, until her hot, dry eyes and exhausted limbs had driven her to lie down and finally succumb to sleep.

She had one of the village boys put the donkey between the shafts of the trap and in no time was bowling merrily along the rutted track in the direction of the *palazzo*, congratulating herself at her clever escape.

Unfortunately the Count too was still in his bed, it being not yet seven o'clock, but his manservant was willing to wake him for the sake of the pretty maid. Half an hour later Polly was enjoying breakfast with Alfonso out on the terrace, he dressed in his dressing-gown, and she in her smart new riding outfit. Polly rebelliously decided that this was the most daring thing she had ever done in her life.

The Count nibbled his bread roll and watched her with appreciation. Her sky-blue skirt and jacket perfectly matched her brilliant eyes and set off her lovely golden hair. He enjoyed too watching the way her pert young breasts pressed against the fine linen and the way her narrow waist sat tightly above the burgeoning swell of her hips. She was young yet and would mature nicely, but was already a pretty little sweetheart whom anyone would be glad to tumble. He considered the possibility of trying it today, since she had recklessly come without a chaperon, but thought better of it. A prize of such a quality would not be gained by clumsiness. Besides, he had a fancy to get to know her better. She was an entertaining little sprite and he rather liked her.

'And where is your dear sister?' he politely asked, offering Polly more fruit juice.

Polly pulled a face. 'Still sleeping. She has been most grumpy since the party. But then she is much older than I, you see,' she finished very seriously, and was surprised and delighted when the Count laughed. She wanted to please him.

'I can see that early rising does not take the edge off your energy.' He wondered if the sister knew that Polly had come, and decided probably not. 'What will Abigail do when she wakes and finds you gone?'

'Oh, phoo, who knows?' Polly shook her shoulders with distaste. 'Abby makes far too much fuss, when I am always perfectly all right.'

'I am flattered in your trust in me,' said Alfonso, and, lifting the girl's hand, kissed it with slow and

lingering care. 'But you should not always be so
trusting, little one.'

Polly shivered with excitement. Life had taken a turn
for the better since they had left the dreary villa by the
sea in Devon and been released from their endless
counting of linen. Now she could really enjoy life and
she meant to make the most of it, despite any strictures
her sister might impose. 'Abigail is a splendid sister,
but so very noble and caring. It would be just like her
to decide that Italy was not quite the thing for me and
pack me off home.'

The Count looked troubled. 'That is the last thing
we want. And what of you, little Polly? Do you like
my country?'

'Oh, yes. What I have seen of it,' Polly amended,
and Alfonso's eyes grew alert.

'But of course, you have scarcely arrived. Then I
shall make it my business to show you my beautiful
home and my land. If you will permit me.'

Polly sighed dreamily, suddenly feeling unusually
shy at the expression upon his face. 'Well,' she said
doubtfully, 'I cannot stay very long. But oh, I should
like that very much. If you have the time.'

'I can find the time, for you, little one.'

Polly unconsciously batted her eyelashes as she
looked up at him and her heart lifted with pleasure.
But then she remembered the ban. She was not supposed to be here at all. 'Perhaps I should ask Abigail
first,' she said, not really meaning it, but filled with the
need to show propriety, to prove that she was a good
girl.

'But most certainly. Perhaps she will come too, as
the chaperon?'

Polly's heart plunged in the opposite direction. Was

not a chaperon someone who sat between a couple on a bench? She did not want Abigail to do that. But oh, my, what was he saying? The thought that the Count might be courting her was too exciting for words. She very nearly squealed with delight, but then adopted a more mature expression just in time. It would not do for him to think her gauche. 'Oh, phooey, what need have we for a chaperon in these modern times, my lord? We could have such fun together, could we not?'

'I think we could,' he said, slowly smiling, half captivated by her laughing piquant face and so surprised by her trust in him that he felt duty bound to behave very much as the proper English gentleman might. At least for the moment. He was on his feet, bowing over her hand. 'I am a man of honour,' he said. 'You will be perfectly safe with me, little elfin.'

'I knew it at once,' said Polly, china-doll eyes laughing up at him. 'How could I not be with someone so clever and handsome?'

Alfonso took this as his just desert. 'You would like, perhaps, to go for a drive? Or a gallop on a fine white horse?'

Polly's eyes lit up. 'Oh, yes, please. Can we?'

'For you, my sweet, anything is possible. Do you ride?'

'Oh, yes,' said she, with her usual disregard for the truth. She had once or twice ridden a friend's horse while the friend very firmly held on to the reins. The horse, she remembered, had been little more than a pony and had not gone above a walk. 'If it is a small one,' she added in fairness, and smiled with natural coquettishness. 'I am such a tiny person, you see.'

The Count's eyes lingered upon her. 'I see that very well. So beautifully fragile, but growing into a lovely young woman, eh?' Polly sighed with ecstasy. It was so nice to be treated as a lady instead of a child all the time.

'Perhaps just a short ride,' she conceded, looking up at him through veiled lashes.

'Then a suitable mount shall be found for you at once, and I will show you my domain.' He called his man and made the arrangements. 'And while you refresh yourself for our ride, if you will excuse me, I shall go and dress.'

And, leading Polly across the terrace, he decided that life at the *palazzo* might very well grow much more interesting. What was more, this charming little elfin might be the very person to help him with his own quest. A most useful acquaintance he would do well to nurture.

CHAPTER TEN

THE following Sunday found the entire party setting out for the Count's *palazzo*. Abigail was thankful for the presence of Emilia on this occasion since Polly was still moody and it would help to ease the conversation.

Tea was to be served on the terrace but first Alfonso decreed it was time to show them around his property.

Its magnificence was legendary and they could not fail to marvel at the priceless tapestries which hung from the walls. Silk and brocade drapery, fastened with golden tassels, hung at doors and windows and formed baldaquin and counterpane upon each king-sized bed.

When they had toured and exclaimed over each and every room he led them to the upper loggia, which was an open-sided passage from where they could look out upon the inner courtyard through one of the many arches.

'It is built in a square with the inner court for our privacy and security. As you can see it is very fine with the noble colonnades and massive archways. But high above, upon the windows, you can appreciate the delicate tracery and beautiful mouldings in terracotta, can you not? My ancestors they were the greatest builders. It is good, *sì*?' Alfonso proudly pointed out. 'Many years ago the family made this into the fortress that could withstand many fierce battles. We allow no one to take our home from us. You understand?'

'Only too well,' said Carl quietly. 'I feel exactly the same.' The Count looked at him in surprise.

'But you are English, not Italian. How can you care so much?'

'Why should I not? Falenza is my home. Have I not had cause to remind you before that I was born there?'

The Count very nearly retorted, Yes, but to a serving wench, for it was common-enough knowledge. He stopped himself in time. There were boundaries to courtesy and this was not a man to push too far. 'Of course, my friend,' he acknowledged with a slight head bow. 'I forget.'

'Polly, hanging on every word, urged the Count to continue. 'Do go on, Alfonso; I want to hear all about your family.'

Smiling down at her, he took her hand in his. 'Come, elfin, I shall show you something truly remarkable. Mr Montegne knows all about the *bellavendetta* which exists between our two families. It was all a long time ago when my ancestor lost the lady he loved to a di Montegelo. It is best not to think on it too much. No one kills or seeks to kill another for love or jealousy now that we have grown civilised. We are all friends now, yes?'

'Oh, yes,' said Polly with shining eyes.

'I should think so,' said Emilia tartly. 'That has all been most interesting, Count, but I declare I am ready for that cup of tea you promised.'

'Of course.' He led them back down the stone stairs, but, before turning out on to the terrace again, he stopped. 'There is one thing which might interest you. The professor, who is now sadly returned to his beloved Oxford, found it for me. He insisted on a last tour of Florence before he left.' He glanced across at Abigail. 'As you know.'

Abigail nodded and felt herself grow still with suspicion. She dared not look at Carl, but instinct told her that his reaction matched her own.

'Come, see.' He led them along a passage and into a long, narrow antechamber. It was the first they had seen of this room and they were each of them astonished. Its walls were lined with glass-fronted cabinets, each one crammed with ceramics, glass, china and other artefacts, the impressive collection of an obsessive and acquisitive collector. 'I like the small things,' he said, with a half-smile, and went over to one cabinet at the end of the room.

Carl was the first to follow, and Abigail was not far from his side.

'Here, see my latest acquisition. A beautiful figurine. He is said to be the messenger of the gods—Mercury, he is called. Is he not a fine specimen?' Alfonso seemed to be unaware of the unnerving silence of the group behind him as he unlocked the glass door and lifted out the small alabaster model. 'Feel it,' he said. 'Is it not as fine as marble?' And the next instant it was in Abigail's hand. She stared at it in growing recognition and dismay.

'I-it is very beautiful,' she stuttered, and, unable to prevent herself, looked up into Carl's eyes in helpless anguish. And that gaze said so much. It told him how sorry she was for lying, for covering up for Polly. It expressed her hurt and aching hope that he would not blame her that a Paolo had got the figurine instead of him. It told Carl even more were he prepared to look deep enough.

But he was staring transfixed at the figure.

'Where did you get it?'

The Count shrugged. 'Some small private museum. I forget the name. They were not interested in it and were happy to sell it to me. I liked its shape. He is fine, yes?'

Abigail's mind surged with questions, and disbelief that the Count could be quite so ignorant about the true history of this piece.

'Let me see.' Emilia came forward for a closer look. But Abigail could not move for she was wedged between the two men and was far too occupied holding her breath, waiting for the storm to break over her head. She could actively feel Carl's patience slipping away and his volatile temper building.

Polly, too far in the background for her own liking, and not much caring for this particular attention that Abigail was getting, pushed forward too. 'What is it? I want to see.' Polly was small enough to intrude where the more bulky Emilia could not. 'Heavens, isn't that what you've been looking for, Carl?' Her fingers had closed upon the figurine and she'd snatched it from Abigail's hand before anything could be done to stop her, at the same time ousting her sister from the space next to her adored. 'Why, Alfonso has beaten you to it, Carl,' she said with a nervous giggle and held it up to her beloved with shining, worshipping eyes.

Just how it happened nobody quite knew. One moment the figurine was in Polly's outstretched hand and the Count was reaching for it. The next instant the fragile alabaster figure had somehow slipped from her grasp to lie in pieces on the floor. Polly's scream echoed in Abigail's head for days afterwards, but at the time she was far too engrossed watching Carl Montegne's expressionless face as he glared down upon the pieces for a mere half-second and then turned curtly upon his heel and strode from the room.

* * *

It was after dinner that evening when Abigail stood within the open door of the library and met Carl's coldly furious gaze with calm defiance. Closing the door behind her, she leaned back upon it, her cheeks stained with pink and her small oval chin held high. She had very nearly decided not to come at all, but then she was no green girl and could very easily fend for herself. Hadn't she made up her mind long since, on the night of the party, just what she was to do? Now was the moment to execute that decision before it was too late and their bags had been packed and she and Polly put on the next train.

Polly. What a trial the child had become, even to herself. Lying distraught in her bed, hysterical with remorse, she had needed a sleeping draught to settle her.

'So, you come at last.' Not a hint of compassion.

'It's true. I did lie,' Abigail said without preamble. 'I'm very sorry.'

Carl stood at his desk and glared at her. For no logical reason he found himself remembering her as she had looked at the dance. She had worn her hair loose and he owned to himself that he'd very much been looking forward to dancing with her, to enjoying the close proximity of that firm, slender young body. She had looked excited and exciting in her scarlet gown and he'd felt a keen disappointment that the party was over without them exchanging a civil word. Since then, relations had declined still further till they were now as broken as the poor figurine. He knew that it grieved him.

She was wearing a modest gown of amber satin that seemed to light up her eyes. Fastened right up to her small, determined round chin, it finished in a cascade of white lace at her throat. There was no cap on her hair this evening. The chestnut sheen of it could be admired in its full glory as it hung down her back. The longing to run his hand over its silky sheen was intense. He stared at her, willing her to look at him, but her beautiful eyes were veiled by dark lashes. He remembered well their brilliance and he wanted to see them smile as they had sometimes done. And he wanted to light them with desire.

He walked across to her.

'Why?'

Abigail swallowed. Indecision had long since gone but she was still tempted to plead hotly in Polly's defence or beg for sympathy. She did neither. Lifting her lashes at last, she gazed up at him with that frankness and clarity of vision that he remembered only too well. Now was the time for plain honesty.

'I was afraid,' she said. 'I didn't want to be sent home because of Polly's foolishness. I can see now that the result of that lie has brought disaster and I can only say that I am sorry. I wanted, desperately, to stay. It's as simple as that.'

The frown had not lessened and for a long, still moment the night ticked by and he said nothing. And then again, 'Why? Why did you want to stay?'

Abigail shifted with discomfort. She had known he would not make it easy for her, but this was a thousand times more difficult than she had imagined. He stood threateningly close and her skin prickled with awakening desire, filling her with shame. 'I-I've always wanted to travel,' she said with scrupulous honesty.

'That is not the whole of it. You could have sent Polly home with the professor and stayed yourself.'

Abigail's eyes widened. 'Oh, no, I couldn't do that. Polly couldn't possibly be left to fend for herself.'

'She has two parents who dote upon her, does she not?' asked Carl with acerbic cruelty.

Abigail flushed warmly. 'That is certainly true, but neither of them can. . .well. . .oh, how can I explain?' She sighed wearily, clasping and unclasping her hands. 'They are old. They had us rather late in life and, though they do their best to manage, and love us both dearly, they are really much more comfortable with each other.' Abigail smiled wanly. 'Some people are like that. The love is real enough but insubstantial. In short, Polly is a worry to them and they simply cannot cope with her.'

'You surprise me.'

'I know she can be difficult, somewhat vain, and stubborn to a fault, but she is kind and good-hearted and the best of sisters that anyone could wish for.' And now she did gaze at him, pleading with wide eyes which, had she known it, were quite beautiful and very appealing. 'Polly cannot be allowed to take all the blame. It was the Count. He took advantage of her youthful innocence, flattered her vanity. I hope you will find it in your heart to forgive her. She would be utterly distracted if she thought she was the cause of our being sent home.'

He gazed down at her with a surprising calm which she guessed could only indicate danger. 'It's a pity she didn't think of that earlier. I have since learned that Polly has made it a habit this last week to ride out with the Count every morning. Did you not give her my instructions?'

This was the first Abigail had heard of it, and her heart plummeted. If Polly had truly disobeyed Carl's instructions then all was lost. 'Yes, I did indeed. I had no idea. . .'

'It seems you have no more control over your sister than your aged parents.' And while Abigail frantically sought a defence to that just argument he continued, more bitingly, 'She allowed the Count to steal my family's figurine, and you expect me to simply smile and forgive?'

'I will speak with her, make her see what her silly prattling tongue has done. I assure you it will not happen again.'

'Assuming I agree to forgive her on this occasion,' he said coldly.

'Yes, of course.'

'And I really do not see why I should.' His anger plainly ran deep and Abigail did not wonder at it. 'If your parents have given up the ghost with her, why should I be saddled with the responsibility? I have risked my quest for the sake of your sister's sensibilities; is that not enough? Too much. She is a liability to man and beast.'

Abigail instinctively bridled. 'She meant no harm. She is simply. . .' Abigail searched for a word '. . .exuberant.'

Carl grunted, unconvinced.

And then, driven by her misery, Abigail burst out, 'Oh, why do *you* persist in this fantasy of finding a fortune hidden away somewhere, rather like some story in a penny novelette? How can one small alabaster figure be worth such a vast fortune? Why do you not accept the Count's offer to buy the *castello* and return home to England? I'm sure he would be generous in the circumstances and you could start a new life with funds aplenty.'

Carl let out a low growl. 'Do you imagine that I would sell my property to that vain peacock? You must think that I am soft in the head. And where has that understanding gone, that perspicacity I once so admired in you?' Wide lips curled with displeasure. 'You have easily managed to put from your head all that I told you of my reasons for being here. The Count deliberately set out to find that figurine, as we did, though for very different reasons. He wants only to rob me of what is rightfully mine, to prevent me from settling here. Unfortunately he was successful and we were not.'

'He had the professor's help,' said Abigail glumly. 'And I thought him such a nice man.'

'It is startling, is it not, how few people one can trust these days?' he said, in a drawling tone, and Abigail flushed crimson. 'Nevertheless, figurine or not, the Castello Falenza is mine. As the one and only remaining di Montegelo I intend it to stay that way. In fact, from now on, Miss Carter, you will address me as Carl di Montegelo. I have done with the counterfeit English name. It is time Count Alfonso Ruggieri Paolo realises who he is facing.'

Abigail gasped. 'You are not starting the vendetta over again?'

The brown eyes were dark and bitter. 'I shall do what must be done. The matter is by no means closed.'

'Oh, but ——'

He placed a finger upon her mouth. 'Enough. I will hear no more. Nor be lectured by you about matters that do not concern you.'

She shook herself free, but her skin was still imprinted with his touch. 'I was only going to say that I rather liked your old name. I shall continue to use it.'

'You will do no such thing. For once do as I say.'
She could scent the soap he had used upon his hands
before dinner. And in his turn he could scent honey-
suckle on her. And the keen memory of her soft lips
stayed stubbornly in the forefront of his mind. 'You
take too much upon yourself, Abigail. I'll make my
own decisions, as I think I've already told you. Is that
clear enough?'

'Perfectly.' Their eyes clashed. Carl was the first to
break it, for Abigail's attitude confused and confounded him. She apologised humbly enough, her eyes
spoke defiance, yet her body was giving him a different
message, and he wasn't entirely sure which to believe.
Her lips opened with a natural provocativeness and he
had a sudden urge to rip the lace from her throat and
bury his own lips in its place.

He walked over to the window where her nearness
was less troublesome. 'Your concern for your sister is
commendable, but I do not think you have told me the
whole of it. Tell me, was that your only reason for
wanting to stay, because you like to travel?'

Abigail rapidly considered every kind of prevarication; she even contemplated flirtation, but was sadly
unpractised at it. But today was the day for openness.
Hadn't she decided so? She shook her head. 'No.'

'So?' He was waiting for an answer. 'Are you going
to enlighten me further?'

For a moment Abigail squeezed shut her eyelids in
despair. Was there any other way? Did she want to
tread this path? Once she had set off upon it there
would be no turning back. She thought of the ironmongery shop with its collection of dark, dusty shelves, her
dear parents, and the rather dull life they led there.
But not for her.

She thought of employment as a companion with another elderly lady and knew none could compare with Emilia. She thought of 'going into service' in some capacity, as a housemaid or governess, perhaps, and shuddered. But none of that, however unwillingly she might view these prospects, was the real reason for her wanting to stay. She opened her eyes. 'I love it here. I love Emilia. I. . .' Her throat closed. She could not go on.

'Then you and your dratted sister should have thought of all that before.' He was glaring at her without a hint of compassion in those deep, dark eyes, and Abigail felt the depths of her misery sink still further.

She knew it was useless, but with sagging shoulders and quaking heart she went over to stand before him. He stood in a shaft of sunlight from the window, a patch of light enfolding him in its glory, touching the gloss of his hair, the sheen of his skin, as she so longed to do. Abigail put all the appeal she could muster into her voice.

'She is a child, besotted with Italy, and, though I sincerely hope not, perhaps also with the Count.'

'I can see why you would hope not.'

Abigail glanced up in surprise. Did he, then, understand her protectiveness towards Polly after all? But almost at once she saw that that was not the case, and her heart gave a little jump of joy. The expression in his gleaming eyes was not understanding or sympathy, but jealousy. It was unmistakable. He thought she cared for the Count herself and resented the attention Alfonso gave to Polly. Abigail found herself smiling. He must feel something for her after all. She could hear his ragged breathing, feel the heat from his body radiate against hers, and almost instinctively she arched her back as she looked up at him.

'I very much doubt that you do. Polly is, I'm afraid, most perverse, and if I tell her not to do something then she will most certainly consider it an open invitation to do so at the first opportunity. Which is of course the reason she has been riding with the Count in spite of your strict instructions that she must never visit. "Never" is an impossible word to use with a young girl.' Abigail smiled up into his eyes. 'It was perhaps unwise for if she fancies herself in love with him I shall have to tread most carefully to put a stop upon it or I could very well drive her straight into his arms.'

'A place you would much rather save for yourself.' Carl drew in a sharp breath, almost kicking himself for his stupidity. He had not meant to say any such thing. If he did not guard his tongue she might think it mattered to him which sister got the dratted follow, and of course it did not. To cover his blunder he hurried on, raising his voice with determined emphasis. 'Don't put the blame at my door for your sister's perverseness. I doubt she listens to a word anyone says. I told you both quite clearly to say nothing about my reason for being here. And she at once blurted it out to Paolo himself, no less. A mistake I find thoughtless in the extreme, and the result of which we have seen this day. Had Paolo not known about my intentions he would never had gone searching the Florentine museums and I would now have the figurine in my possession.

'What's more, your attempt to cover up for Polly by telling me a blatant untruth is nothing short of despicable, and when your lie was discovered you were even too cowardly to come and own up to it. Perhaps you imagined I would blame the professor, a man of

honour who has kept his word and long since returned
to England.'

'Oh, but I. . .' Abigail stopped, confused.

'You what?'

How could she tell him that she had been waylaid by
a dream? It was too ridiculous for words. She bit her
lip. 'I meant to come. I was tired. I'm sorry. Do you
wish me to grovel?' Her eyes challenged him, but she
felt herself losing ground. The longing to lie her head
upon that broad shoulder and beg his forgiveness at
any price was suddenly overwhelming.

'Just give me one good reason why I should forgive
either one of you and allow you to stay?'

Abigail dropped her gaze to stare at the floor, at the
toe of one black boot. The air seemed to thrum with
the vigour of her thoughts, the intangible magic that
drew them together. How could he not feel it? She was
powerless to resist. Lifting her chin, she looked him
full in the face. 'Because you want me in your bed.'

The silence went on for so long that she would have
thought he had not heard her but for the look of
startled astonishment upon his face, held there only
momentarily before he quickly concealed his feelings
by drawing over it the usual expressionless mask. Then
into his eyes came a very different expression, half
speculative and half amused. Abigail felt the hot blood
run under her skin and she looked quickly away. This
was going to be far more difficult in reality than any of
the rehearsals she had daydreamed.

'There is no need for you to deny it,' she murmured.

'I had not thought to do so.'

Her throat was ash-dry and she could not drag her
gaze beyond the lower points of his cravat. 'I rather
thought that the notion had already occurred to you,

in view of some of the. . .chance remarks you have
made.'

'Did you indeed?' He was enjoying this now, she
could tell. Abigail, however, was wishing very much
that she had never started it.

'Yes.'

His hands dropped upon her shoulders, twisting her
to look at him, but she resolutely kept her eyes fixed
upon his shirt front. There was no turning back now. 'I
know that there can be nothing — I mean there can be
no marriage between us.' The silence was heavy and
awesomely empty. She swallowed and struggled on,
shifting her gaze an inch or two upwards. 'I would not
expect that. But I do not think you are entirely
indifferent to me, nor I to you.' There, she had said it;
now she could face him. She did so and found his
expression no longer amused but totally unreadable.
And her stomach turned to water.

Carl was trying the idea out in his head and it was
not unpleasant. Surprising, perhaps, but agreeable. 'So
what are you suggesting?' The voice was barely above
a whisper, sending shivers up her spine.

That I love you, her heart cried, and will do anything
to remain by your side.

'That if you will only forgive Polly and let us both
remain as we so wish to do, then it can be under any
terms you wish.' She let that thought sink in.

'Any terms at all?' The corners of his mouth
twitched. 'That is a most generous offer.'

Her heart was racing so hard that she was sure he
must hear it, but she had seen his expression. 'I hope
you are not laughing at me.'

'I would not dream of doing so,' said he very
seriously. 'The prospect is too intriguing.' His hands

drifted down her arms, softly brushing her silky skin,
instinctively pulling her closer. He thought of her in his
bed, that thick veil of chestnut hair laid out upon his
pillow. His throat tightened alarmingly.

Abigail meanwhile felt she was not making the
progress she had envisaged. Her daydreams had never
got beyond this point. She'd expected Carl to take
charge in his usual authoritative way and sweep her up
into his arms. She snatched at a breath and blundered
on. 'I-I consider myself well past the age for matrimony. I have no dowry or fortune to offer, neither
exceptional skills nor moderate beauty, so no queue of
gentlemen is likely to line up with their offers.'

'That is a pity.'

'One should face the truth,' she said, watching his
lips, wondering when he would kiss her. Weren't men
always ready to make love to a woman? Mama had
said so often, and that love did not come into it. She
had instructed her daughter so well to guard her
emotions that Abigail knew not how to cope with them
any more. She could only be practical, open, honest
and painfully plain-speaking. Why, then, did he
hesitate?

Hadn't she already made that clear? Abigail swallowed carefully. Perhaps he was remembering their
frequent disagreements. 'We are, I hope, friends?'

He made no reply.

'Of course, friendship is one thing, being lovers quite
another matter, I know that. But I do not think you
would be—disappointed.' She met his gaze with a shy
smile. The prospect filled her with breathless excitement. And it had nothing at all to do with Polly.

He began to stroke her arms up and down with a

softly sensual movement. 'Have you any idea what that position might entail?'

He did think she was a green girl. Abigail was outraged. 'Of course I do. I am no schoolroom miss.'

Dark brows lifted. 'I never suggested you were.' He wondered how she would react if he sent her upstairs to his room now and put her to the test. He set the idea reluctantly aside. She was upset and would retract the offer in the morning. Then he would be riddled with guilt.

Abigail was gazing at him, willing him to accept. Now that she had dredged up the courage to speak it would be too awful for words if he was to refuse her. Not for a moment had she considered the possibility. She held her breath. He was regarding her with such intensity that even the air between them seemed to vibrate with tension. And his hands did not stop in their caressing. They were making her sway with weakness and longing.

'I have to say that your offer has somewhat taken me by surprise, coming from a young woman of respectability and good manners.'

Greatly daring, Abigail said, 'Manners make a lonely bedfellow, do they not?' But she saw at once that he was not amused by her quip and the frown deepened.

'You are serious, aren't you?'

'Of course.'

He straightened, staring down into her eyes, and Abigail thought, Here it comes; now he will kiss me and take me to his room. Her mind went blank at that point, for what happened behind closed bedroom doors was largely a blur, no more than a bare catalogue of facts. But she had an instinctive belief that, whatever these unknown details were, with Carl Montegne they would be entirely pleasurable.

Her breath quickened in her throat and she half closed her eyes, tilting her mouth up for him to kiss. Carl's mouth hovered above hers, his eyes devouring the lines of her face, the soft silkiness of her skin, the sweep of dark lashes laid upon her cheek. He was astonished by the surge of desire that soared through him. Dammit, he wanted her so badly in that moment he'd forgotten why she was here in his library at all. Now he recalled that he'd demanded she answer to the charge of betrayal. *She could not be trusted*. His hands dropped to his sides and he strode to the door, to hold it open for her.

'We'll leave it there for this evening. Allow me to consider your generous offer, Miss Carter. It is certainly a novel one.' He half bowed and smiled at her, but the smile did not reach his eyes.

Abigail stared at him bemused, her pulses still hot and throbbing from his touch. What had gone wrong? Did he not want her after all? He had gone quite cold and disapproving.

He was still speaking, as coldly and dispassionately as if this scene had not just taken place. 'For the moment you and Polly may stay at Falenza, but remember, no more visits to the Count, at least until I have made my decision.'

She had been rejected. Bile ran into her mouth and she felt a great urge to be sick. 'But——'

The wide lips twisted into a wry smile as if he saw her discomfort and for some reason was pleased by it. 'I shall give careful consideration to the—implications of your offer. I may still decide to send you both packing despite it; we shall see. Until then, Miss Carter, I wish you goodnight.'

And there was nothing else she could do but walk from the room.

CHAPTER ELEVEN

ABIGAIL spent yet another sleepless night, going over and over the little scene in her mind. Why had he rejected her? Her woman's instinct told her that he wanted her. Oh, not because he loved her; she knew that. But because of that certain *frisson* that sparked between them whenever he touched her, or even looked into her eyes. Yet he hated and distrusted her so much that it overrode any personal need. She was more disappointed than she had a right to be.

As the first rays of sunshine lit the dusty corners of her room she was glad to leave her bed. She dressed in a plain blue work dress and, after eating a lone breakfast of bread and thin wine in the kitchen, she went out in search of him, her mind occupied with yet more plans.

She found him, as expected, in the fields. He was helping a small group of men dig wide circular pits for the vines. He stared at her with dispassion, as if she was of no account.

Gathering up her flagging courage, she picked her way around the shallow pits to stand before him. 'If you will give me a spade I will help,' she said, and saw his eyes widen.

'Help?'

'Help dig holes or troughs for your vines. I must do something. I am being driven to distraction with inactivity. And if. . .if you are not interested in — in my other proposition, then this one will have to do instead.' Spotting a pile of implements upon the ground close by, she went to pick out the smallest spade she could find. It was still far too big for her, but she did not let that impede her resolution. All too aware of the village men watching her with mounting amusement, she marched over to a half-dug pit and thrust in the blade. The soil was harder than it looked, filled as it was with small stones, and the blade failed to penetrate. She tried again, pounding on the shoulders of the blade with her small feet. Success; the blade sank a good three inches into the soil.

'Abigail, what are you trying to do?' came a weary voice, ripe with amusement, from behind her.

One more time should do it, she thought, refusing to answer, and flung the spade at the soil for a third time, positively bouncing upon it with both feet. This time the blade sank for most of its length and she beamed with delight. But as she stepped off it in order to lift the spade with its load of soil, she had to put all her strength into it, and as she finally succeeded she lost her balance and fell over, legs in the air, soil flying, skirts in a flurry. '*Oh!*' she cried out, hastily trying to restore dignity, shamingly aware of the men's laughter.

Carl Montegne stood before her. With his legs astride, arms akimbo, grin splitting his handsome face from ear to ear, she would have very much liked to hit him. Only she was not in a position to. Reaching down both hands, he lifted her bodily and set her upon her feet.

'Go home, woman. When I have decided whether you are to go or to stay I will send for you. Till then, have patience.' And, giving her a little push, he set her off in the direction of the house. It did not even cross her mind to argue, so eager was she to escape the scene of her humiliation, and she fled from the hillside with the sound of laughter in her ears.

Ida, now well served by village help, dismissed Abigail just as briskly from the laundry-room, where she had finally succumbed to her in-built training and was in the process of listing every item in a household book especially bought for the purpose. In this instance, Abigail was not sorry to go and beat a hasty retreat.

Emilia had developed a passion for botany and horticulture and was busily planning gardens. And Polly, the very picture of contrition, was helping her. There seemed nothing for Abigail to do.

Feeling thoroughly depressed and sorry for herself, she decided to go for a walk. If she was to be leaving Italy soon, then she could at least enjoy the view and the sunshine while she was here. Tying on a wide straw bonnet and drawing in deep, relaxing breaths of warm air, she set out along the rutted track, nodding and smiling at passing villagers making their way to market with packs on their mules' backs.

Abigail felt totally rejected, unwanted by everyone. She felt bleak and alone and made herself look uncompromisingly into an even bleaker future, a future which featured a good deal of English rain and muffins, and very little of Italian sunshine or love. And without the least sign of Carl Montegne. The ache about her heart swelled and spread. How would she survive it?

Even her role as companion to Emilia had dwindled to nothing. For Ida could fulfil that role so much better now that Carl had taken on extra staff. Abigail had become almost entirely redundant and it was not a pleasant sensation.

As the days passed her isolation grew worse. The

plans for the garden and for the new vineyard went on apace, but no one asked for her assistance. She enjoyed her lonely walks. And she started carrying her camera with her so that she could take photographs of the villagers she met, of their homes, and of the beautiful Tuscan landscape. But somehow she felt them uninspired. The heart had gone out of her.

And daily she expected him to call her. Every time Carl glanced her way or passed her in one of the long passages, she half expected him to speak. But he did not. Always he hurried away with no more than a brief nod in her direction. If she had not known it to be ridiculous she would have thought he deliberately avoided her. But why should Carl Montegne do that? He was afraid of no one, and cared not a fig for her, so why should he waste energy on disapproval? He made it abundantly clear that her presence was not required, and so the intense excitement gradually faded from her breast and she very nearly began to pack her bags. It was only a matter of time, she knew, before he sent her back to England.

He still visited Florence frequently—perhaps to enquire about the possibility of travelling companions for her and Polly. When he was successful in this, her life, her dreams, would come to an end. She would be almost glad when it happened for the longer she stayed at Falenza the more she grew to love him.

Then one evening at supper the conversation turned yet again to the Count.

'I would dearly like to know what he is plotting,' growled Carl.

'Plotting?' asked Emilia, fork stopped midway to her mouth.

'He must be devising some scheme to find the other

figurine. If so, I would like very much to know what it is.'

Abigail listened in stunned bemusement. Of course. She'd forgotten there were two figurines. One for Elisabetta, the morganatic wife, and one for the Princess, Prince Giovanni's new bride.

'He is a gentleman,' protested Polly. 'He isn't plotting a thing.'

Carl looked at her, but made no reply. It was clear he thought her an innocent and not worth arguing with. He addressed himself again to Emilia, not even glancing at Abigail. He had ignored her presence totally for days.

'Can you manage on your own for a while, Goody? My visits to Florence have not yet been productive, but I live in hope. If one museum owned one figurine perhaps a second will own the other. I can only continue to look and to ask.'

He did not ask for Abigail's help and she lowered her chin, giving her full attention to her chicken, so that he would not see the hurt disappointment in her eyes.

But later in the solitary loneliness of her room she gave some thought to the matter. Perhaps Alfonso was planning something. If so, who better to find out what it was than herself? Carl still assumed she loved the Count. And if the Count had indeed taken a fancy to her, then she could at least use that to her advantage. The only answer was to make her mission successful and bring back the information Carl desired. Perhaps that way she could mend this great gulf which had opened between them and he would forgive her.

Abigail pulled out her prettiest dress ready to leave first thing the next morning. Alfonso was a man, wasn't

he? And she was a woman with at least some charm,
surely? And he was not resistant to a little discreet
flattery. She would not include Polly in the expedition,
however. Not on this occasion. She would go alone.

And that night she slept better, dreaming of a
handsome young prince who held her in his arms, and
he looked remarkably like Carl Montegne.

Polly meanwhile had grown tired of gardening. The
sun was hot, the insects buzzed irritatingly against her
hair, and although Emilia was a dear she was far too
finicky. Every time Polly measured out a bed Emilia
declared the lines were not straight or the soil was too
lumpy.

So the next morning Polly pleaded a headache, and
when everyone was at breakfast took the donkey cart
and drove the two short miles to the Count's *palazzo*.
She had done this so many times in the past that she
gave no thought to the precautions she took now. She
always kept to the quiet back road and hid the donkey
and trap beneath a straw shelter some distance from
the house. This way, should anyone be riding by, or
walking up the dusty road to the *castello*, they would
not see her. It was vital that she keep her visits a secret
for she knew she would be in the most dreadful trouble
if Abigail, or, worse, Carl himself, was to discover
them. So it was a considerable shock to Polly to see
Abigail already seated on the terrace sipping lemon tea
with Alfonso when she arrived.

They were chatting and laughing together as if they
were old friends. Polly quickly dropped down behind a
gorse bush and glared at them through wide, shocked
eyes.

How could Abby do it to her? To insist that visiting

the Count was out of bounds and then to come and breakfast with him herself when she thought no one was looking was shameful. So angry was Polly that she wanted to leap out and confront Abigail with her perfidy right away. Common sense, however, prevailed. She would have no way of explaining her own presence. Better to watch and listen and learn.

Abigail, however, was making disappointing progress. Alfonso had laughed when she asked him if he was still visiting Florentine museums. She tried again.

'You must have been devastated when Polly broke the figurine.'

The Count shrugged. 'I paid little for it. It is not important. And it may not have been Polly's fault.'

Polly warmed to his chivalrous defence of her.

'I dare say the second figurine was lost years ago,' Abigail said airily. 'And probably every bit as worthless as the first one.'

'We shall never know.'

'I suppose not.' There was a lengthening silence in which Abigail had ample time to gloomily realise she had no future as a secret spy. She considered asking him straight out in her frank way if he intended to look for it, but decided that discretion was the better part of valour, or so Ida often said. 'It is a pity, though. I think Carl would very much like to find it, even though it is not valuable, simply as a keepsake. It is good to find one's roots, is it not?'

'If you have lost them,' said Alfonso. 'It is not something of which I have any experience. Enough of this talk; it bores me. When will you come and ride with me?' he asked, shifting his chair closer to Abigail's.

'Oh, I don't think. . .' Abigail was caught off guard.

Should she accept in the hope of discovering more? Or
scurry back home while she was still safe? For she did
not trust those piercing eyes one little bit.

'Oh, but you must say yes,' said Alfonso, lifting her
hand to kiss it. 'Or I shall be devastated. What a lonely
life I lead here. No pretty ladies to talk to.'

Abigail couldn't help laughing, but she deemed it
wise not to remove her hand. 'I should think you could
have any number if you so wished. What mama would
not hasten to offer her daughter, given the slightest
encouragement?'

'Ah, but I am not speaking of the matrimony,' said
Alfonso, a worried expression coming into his eyes. 'I
speak of the friendship, which only you English can
understand.'

Abigail very much doubted it. 'I think you are a
wicked man,' she teased. 'I have heard of the Italian
love of romance,' said she, getting at last to her feet.
'And I think that I had better be getting back while I
still can.'

Alfonso burst out laughing, well pleased with this
compliment to his virility.

'You will come again?'

'Only if you promise to behave yourself,' Abigail
warned. 'Now I shall go. Good day to you.'

The Count was on his feet in a second. 'But how can
I promise such a thing when you are such a beautiful
woman? It is inhuman to ask it.'

He kissed her hand again. 'But how did you come?
By the donkey cart?

'No, I walked. It is a lovely morning and not quite
so hot now that autumn is coming.'

'How foolish to walk. It will be hot enough before

you get back to the *castello*. I will get my man to take you.'

But Abigail politely refused, saying she enjoyed the exercise, and left, not really any the wiser for her visit, but at least easier in her own mind that Alfonso had given no indication that he was planning any further attempts to rob Carl of his heritage. She chose not to think that neither had he given any assurances that he would not.

And Polly, hidden in the bushes, was scarlet-cheeked with mortification. How *could* Alfonso say that no ladies ever called upon him? How *dared* he kiss Abigail's hand in that familiar way and tell her that she was beautiful? She was not at all beautiful. Everyone knew that Abigail was quite plain; it was she, Polly, who was the pretty one. Hadn't it always been so?

Tears were starting in her eyes, but she meant to have it out with him. In an instant she had broken her cover and confronted a visibly startled Alfonso with an anguished wail of betrayal.

'How *could* you? You said that you *loved me*, not Abigail. That I was the beautiful one. Oh, how *could* you?' And, stamping her foot, Polly promptly burst into tears.

'Oh, my sweet child.'

'I am not a child.'

'Of course you are not. But I was put on the spot, as you say. It is you who are the important one to me, my little elfin. Have I not told you so many times?' he asked, holding out his arms wide. Polly gave a cry of despair and ran into them, sobbing uncontrollably.

Much later when Alfonso had dried her tears with kisses and fed her hot chocolate and sweetmeats her smiles appeared again and he breathed more easily. He trod a thorny path between the two sisters, but he thought this little one with the lovesick eyes was the one more likely to be of use. And he had very nearly undermined all his good work with her, simply because of his natural tendency to charm every woman who crossed his path. He must take better care.

'Now, my little elf, shall I tell you how you can best help us all?'

'Oh, yes, please,' she cried, giving a little hiccup of relief.

'Then you must help me to look for this silly model, the little figurine which is so important to Mr Montegne.'

Polly's face fell. This was not at all what she had been expecting. 'But why?' she wanted to know.

'Have another marzipan; they are so delicious.' He popped one into her rosy mouth, allowing his fingers to linger on her sweet lips, and heard her sigh. 'Because, little one, think how grateful he will be. If you are the one to find this treasure for him, then he will forgive you for the other — er — accident, will he not? And then we can be better friends, sì?'

'Oh, yes,' Polly breathed. 'I hadn't thought of that. But where can it be?'

He took both of her hands in his. 'Listen. It must be in the house somewhere. We have searched every museum in Florence. It was sheer good fortune that we found that other one. But none can have the second, I am sure of it.' He did not mention how many times he had trailed around the many museums, any more than he would own to the fact that he was as obsessed with the legend of the figurine and its supposed treasure as her employer. 'You must look in every corner, however unlikely. And remember to visit the attics and the wine cellars.'

Polly shuddered. 'I don't think I shall enjoy that.'

Alfonso leaned forward and rested his lips softly against her cheek. Enough to thrill but not frighten her. 'But you will try, yes?'

'Oh, yes,' breathed Polly. 'I will try.'

Abigail walked home briskly in her sturdy boots, stepping out on the road with a smile on her face. She was telling herself that the Count was innocent, that he had no intention of making any further attempts to interfere with Carl's quest. She was glad for him and would tell him so the moment she arrived back at the castle. It was a pity she had nothing concrete to offer by way of proof, but Abigail was certain she could convince Carl that all was well. Alfonso had trusted her, she was sure of it, and would have told her if he'd meant to continue with his search. She would tell Carl so and then the two of them could be friends again, and perhaps more. She broke into song as she rounded the bend and as she walked and skipped up the long drive she was unaware of watchful eyes following her progress.

Carl had seen her go and he watched her return. It did not take much imagination to work out where she had been. And it had obviously made her exceedingly happy. It hurt him more than he cared to admit to see that he had not been mistaken. Abigail was indeed a traitor, for what else would put such a smile upon her face, such a spring into her step, but love? And who else but the Count had she seen this day?

He strode away to spend his day sweating over the vines. Physical exhaustion at least left him little time to think. But the time was coming when he would have to make his decision.

It was Polly who brought his sandwiches at lunch-time. 'I've brought mine too. Can we eat them in the old chapel? It's cool in there.'

Carl followed her into the shadowy white-walled chapel and, sweeping the dust from a wooden bench with his handkerchief, they sat down together to enjoy their lunch. Carl found himself longing to ask after Abigail. It was usually she who brought the workers their lunch. Where was she? Visiting the Count again?

Unwittingly, Polly provided the answer. 'Abby sends her apologies, but she is not feeling too well. She has the migraine or a touch of the sun.' Polly shrugged and Carl gave her a sharp look.

'It is not like Abigail to suffer from headaches, is it?'

Polly looked irritated and uninterested. 'How should I know?' She hadn't forgiven her sister for stealing Alfonso's attention so she wasn't going to get in a pet over a little headache. 'I expect she is having a heat-stroke from too much walking out in the sun.'

'You may be right,' said Carl, his tone thoughtful. 'If she is not better by teatime we must call a doctor.'

'Might I ask you something?' Polly asked, setting her untouched sandwich back in the paper.

Carl's eyes twinkled. 'Of course. How very serious you sound.'

'It's about the figurine. I know what it looks like now. If I should find it would that — would that change anything? I mean — I know you're cross with me for breaking the other one, but. . .' Polly paused, cheeks bright crimson. 'It wasn't the Count. Oh, I know he found the figurine in the museum, but I'm sure he would have sold or even given it to you once he understood how much it meant to you.'

'Do you think so?'

Polly's eyes were wide. 'Oh, I'm sure of it. He is a most kind gentleman. And is most sorry for the trouble he has caused.' Here she paused again, curbing her tongue, warning herself to be careful. 'Not that I have seen much of him lately, you understand. But if I had, I'm sure he would be apologising.'

'Then you have more faith in human nature than I,' said Carl, his jaw tight. Then, regarding Polly with a thoughtful frown, he continued, 'You must not believe everything the Count says to you, Polly. Sometimes men do not always say what they mean.'

Polly gazed up at him, eyes wide and trusting, and he thought how naïve she was, how easy to trick. How old was she? Fifteen? Sixteen? 'Oh, but Alfonso does,' she said. 'He is most honourable.'

An innocent, no less. Carl cleared his throat. 'No, Polly. No man of Alfonso's selfish nature can be entirely honest.' Polly was frowning at him. She did not understand and he felt it his duty to finish the explanation now that he had started it. 'He may charm you simply because you are pretty, because he enjoys saying sweet things to you.'

Polly was flushing delightfully now and he smiled.

'It wouldn't be difficult to say pretty things to you, Polly. But that does not signify that the Count means them, or that he thinks of you in any particular way. Do you see? I expect he has a string of women whom he likes to charm and who in turn flatter him. His sort usually does. He has an ego that requires constant attention.'

Polly had paled slightly, remembering again the soft

words he had used to Abigail. 'Is that why he kissed Abigail's hand, because she flattered him?'

Carl became very still. 'When was this, Polly?'

Poor Polly. Once again her innate sense of childish selfishness had betrayed her, and her cheeks fired. 'Oh, I dare say it was nothing. Abby was just out on her walk and decided to call upon him for refreshment, I dare say. I was merely exercising the donkey, and ——'

'You were exercising the donkey?'

'W-well. . .' Polly stammered.

Carl looked fiercely at her. 'I shall know if you lie to me, Polly. Do not I always know?'

And the whole story came tumbling out. How Polly had gone to speak with the Count and found Abigail there already, giggling and simpering like a young girl. No, Polly hadn't heard what they were talking about, but the Count seemed very taken with her, and oh, why couldn't you trust men? What dreadful liars they were. Whereupon the tears were flowing again and Carl was hard put to to mop them up.

'Enough, Polly, before you wash me away. Yes, I agree to your earlier question. If you were to find the figurine that I seek, then I might very well look favourably upon you. Not that I blame you for anything now.'

Polly gazed up at him out of moist eyes and gratefully accepted the handkerchief he offered. 'But the other figurine. Your precious treasure. I broke it.'

But Carl only shook his head. 'No, indeed, Polly. You mustn't worry about it. Now dry your eyes and tell your sister I wish to have words with her in the conservatory, after dinner, if she pleases. At once.'

And, not daring to question further, Polly fled.

The day seemed endless, and the dinner interminable. Emilia chattered incessantly on and did not seem to notice the two girls' unusual silence, each one occupied with their own thoughts. Abigail decided to forgo coffee and made her way to the conservatory with heavy heart. It was empty, and she was forced to sit and wait for Carl to appear, very much the lowly servant waiting upon her employer's indulgence. The wait seemd endless, enough time for her to develop serious nerves fluttering in her stomach. What did he want her for? Was this the moment that he would tell her to leave his home?

Abigail sat very still, her hands clasped upon her lap. She would not argue, nor complain. The least she could do was keep a hold upon her dignity. She wanted desperately to stay here in Italy with him, but would not give him the satisfaction of letting him see her beg. She would agree to leave without any fuss.

The door opened and the next instant he was standing before her.

'Miss Carter.'

She inclined her head a little. 'Mr Montegne.' So formal. So painful.

'I understand from Polly that you have been out visiting today.'

He clasped his hands behind his back and gazed down at her. It was hard to see her as a traitor, yet that was what she was, without question. The moment he was occupied with his vines, or out visiting museums in Florence, she ran to that self-important imbecile, fawning before him, having him kiss her hand at the very least. Heaven alone knew how many times she had visited him when Polly was not there to see. She was evidently not, after all, a woman of scruples or fine morals. The thought filled him with an intense and bitter sadness, a heated anger that threatened to devour him.

Abigail was on her feet before him, her hands clasped, her eyes imploring. 'Yes, I did. I wanted to discover if he meant to pursue this race to find the figurine. But I'm sure that he does not. I'm certain that I won his trust.'

'I have no doubt of it.'

Abigail ploughed on. 'And he would have told me quite openly had he meant to continue looking. I swear to you that the Count is not at all interested in you, your family history, nor in finding the figurine. I do not think he believes it possible to find it at all. Nor do I believe he really wants the *castello*. He is all bluster and foolish pride, but not harmful; I am sure of it.'

'Would that I had your faith.'

'I assume you have been watching me, that you saw me return this morning. I'm sorry if you got the wrong idea.' Abigail straightened her back and looked him full in the face. 'I have already offered you my compliance. What more can I say?'

Carl met her frank gaze and saw the pleading in it, felt his desire for her harden. Why should he not test her? He could give her one more opportunity to prove her loyalty, if not her virtue.

'I have been giving careful consideration to your proposition.'

Abigail's heart was in her mouth. 'And?'

He gave a half-smile that did not reach the shadows of his eyes. 'I would be willing to take you up on your interesting offer. If you are still agreeable, pray attend me in my room within the hour.' And, turning on his heel, he strode away.

CHAPTER TWELVE

ABIGAIL lay back upon the pillows and thought she must have been mad to suggest she become his mistress. What had possessed her? Yet she could not deny that the fierce beating of her heart was not entirely brought on by fear. She wanted him. She loved him. Was she taking shameless advantage of the situation to try to win him? Was she a wanton? Her heart pounded. And then she was sitting up in bed, eyes wide, staring into the candlelit bedroom as the thought at last pierced her heart that perhaps he might think so. It was a prospect that until this moment she had naïvely not considered.

No. He wanted her too; she knew it. And they could never marry. The descendant of an Italian prince did not marry an ironmonger's daughter. For all they had entered a new century, such a thing would not be permitted. She did not ask who would not permit it, seeing it only as one of the faceless laws of society. One day Carl di Montegelo, as he now liked to be called, would marry his princess, and she, like Elisabetta, would be partially forgotten. But Elisabetta had at least enjoyed the love of her prince, even if in the end he had been unfaithful to her. When Carl came to her this night it would be for physical fulfilment, not love. He believed she had betrayed his trust and she did not know how to convince him otherwise except with the love she felt for him. But Abigail knew with bitter regret that she could not expect a lifetime's commitment from Carl Montegne.

Despite all her misgivings, a warm, excited glow was starting in the pit of her stomach, and she knew that shamefully, at this moment, she did not greatly care. But no, that was not strictly true. She wanted to stay with Carl for the rest of her life. How could she do that unless she was his wife? Could Carl ever fall in love with her? Could he abandon the strictures of society and take her for his wife in spite of them? For a blissful moment she allowed herself to contemplate this delicious prospect, smiling at the thought, snuggling back against the soft pillows, waiting for him to come. Perhaps he would. Giovanni had taken Elisabetta for his wife even though she had never been accepted by his family. And Carl had no family to consider.

She saw the years stretching ahead with herself and Carl living contentedly together here in the *castello*, making it beautiful, creating a vineyard whose name would be revered throughout Italy, raising children. Her cheeks grew warm at the thought.

But then again, perhaps not. Sometimes she thought that he hated her even as he desired her body. Perhaps tonight she would learn the answer to this puzzle. But even if she did not she would love him in any case. Abigail lay on, dreaming, watching the candlelight flicker upon the plasterwork ceiling.

She heard the scrape of a boot in the courtyard below and her heart stopped then raced on again. He was coming. Silence. A wind fluttered the curtains, threw back the shutters, and the candle guttered and died.

'Oh, bother.' She was out of bed in an instant, wrapping her lacy white peignoir close about her. She must light it again, but first to close the window. The wind was from the south and gusty. Her hands were on the shutters, pushing them closed, the wind streaming her hair back from her face, when she happened to glance down into the courtyard below, and looked into the face of a stranger.

She cried out, in surprise as much as fear. He seemed as startled as she and suddenly swivelled about and, taking to his heels, ran away from the house, across the cobbled yard, as if the devil himself were at his heels. Abigail watched him go in startled horror.

'I believe he thinks you a ghost.' The voice, softly caressing in her ear, made her start in fresh terror.

'Carl, how you frightened me.' She looked out across the yard, a small frown puckering her brow. 'I suppose he must have done. For the castle does seem to be haunted.'

'Does it?' The eyes searched hers. 'Wait here. Don't move, while I discover what our nervous friend was looking for.'

Carl strode out of the bedchamber and started for the stairs, but stopped almost at once, alerted by a sound. He had heard it before and now followed its direction, intrigued. It seemed to remain in front of him, but just beyond his vision.

When he found himself in the long gallery he stood stock-still, staring. There were voices in his head, in the room, speaking to him. He listened, wanting to answer yet saying nothing.

'Carl?' He swung round, eyes blazing.

'Abigail. What the hell are you doing here?'

She was taken aback and faltered in her step. 'I-I'm sorry. I thought you might need help. . .with the intruder. But you came here instead. Is there something the matter? Were you talking to someone?'

He came to her then, the anger smoothed from his face. 'No, of course not. And what use would you have been in your nightgown if I were seeing off a pack of villains? One glance at you and they might very well have decided to stay.' His gaze roved over the swell of her breasts above a tiny waist, clearly visible through the thin muslin of her gown, and Abigail felt her cheeks grow hot. 'Go back to your room, Abigail. I will join you there shortly as soon as I have seen off these louts you have invited.'

'I have not invited them,' she protested.

He took her very firmly by the elbow. 'I shall decide that for myself. Later.' There was a catch in his throat that set her pulses pounding and she made no resistance as he led her out of the gallery. But at the door curiosity, perhaps, or some sixth sense made her turn and look back. She saw the glimmer of a woman slipping away along the opposite passage, and heard the very faint sound of soft laughter.

'Does someone else live here?' The words had come of their own accord but Abigail was not sorry. She wanted to know.

But Carl did not pause in his stride as he hustled her back along the passage and Abigail was forced almost to run to keep up with him. 'What a very curious little companion you are. Why is it that you want an answer to everything? Because I assure you, you will not get it, not from me. I keep my own counsel, as you should keep yours. Life is healthier that way.' He thrust her into the bedroom and slammed shut the door.

Abigail stood watching through the darkened glass and in an instant saw Carl striding across the lawn in

pursuit of the strange intruder, disappearing into the
bushes. She kept her eyes concentrated on the spot.
When he returned he looked up at her window and she
saw his teeth glint white as he smiled. He would still
come to her, despite his ill temper, she knew it. All
thought of the other woman flew from her mind as she
smoothed down her gown, desperately trying to steady
her ragged breathing.

He was in the room, closing the door and leaning
back against it, his probing gaze insolently robbing her
of the last vestige of her modesty.

'I dare say he was no more than a prying villager,
fled for his life, thinking he has seen a ghost,' she said,
giving a nervous little laugh as he came towards her
again. 'I suppose I must have looked like one.'

'You look very beautiful.' His eyes were drinking in
every detail of her, her vibrant beauty lit by the silvered
moon, the soft pulsing at her white throat.

'I wonder why he came?' Abigail was scarcely thinking of what she was saying, but she saw Carl stiffen, as
if she had reminded him of something he'd much rather
not consider.

'I should think you know very well who sent him.'

Abigail gazed up into the dark pools that were his
eyes, too deeply etched in shadow to reveal his
thoughts. 'The Count? Of course. But what was he
doing here?'

'Snooping. Or trying to make an assignation with
some lady?' He unfastened the ribbon that held her
peignoir closed at the neck, pushing it back with his
fingers to bare her throat, the upper swell of her
breasts.

Abigail held on desperately to her thoughts. 'He
would hardly send his henchman in the middle of the

night for that. H-he must be here to look for the figurine after all. And I was sure he wasn't interested.'

Carl smoothed his hands across her shoulders and down her arms, pulling her back against his chest so that they both looked out across the courtyard to the night-dark hills beyond. The hard pressure of his body against hers made her weak with desire. Heavens, her knees were even shaking.

He rubbed his chin against her hair. 'You are too vulnerable by far, sweet Abigail. And too trusting.' The peignoir was on the floor by now and her flimsy nightgown would not be long after it if his fingers continued with their smoothing path over her shoulders. Her head was spinning so much that she could scarcely think. 'Was your visit with handsome Alfonso a pleasant one?'

Abigail's heart seemed to leap up and bang against her breast. Could he be jealous? She would like to have seen his face. Did it show jealousy, or simply disappointment, anger and curiosity? She tried to move but he kept her firmly pinned against him. A tremulous sigh escaped her lips. Was this what it was all about? This earth-shattering weakness? 'I did not go to make a social call. I went only to try to discover his plans since you had expressed a desire to know them. I told you.'

'How very considerate of you.'

'He gave no indication that he was still interested in the figurine. I really think you are worrying unduly.' She paused. 'A-at least, I thought so this morning, but now, having seen this man snooping, I-I'm not sure.'

She was most convincing. And Carl wanted to believe in her. After a moment he turned her in his arms and looked down into her face. He saw the familiar frankness, the wide, innocent eyes. Sensible, open-hearted Miss Abigail Carter. How could she be playing traitor to him, in particular with that self-opinionated idiot? But then why not? Her sister was besotted by the fellow, so why not her too? He could make her regret it if that were the case. But she was a woman, standing half naked in his arms, and he was a man, for God's sake.

Her eyes sparkled invitingly, the lips seemed to soften invitingly, and he could not tear his gaze from them. Was she a wanton? Would she truly sell herself body and soul to any man for the right price? Was this how she had looked at the Count this very morning? His mind closed upon the thought. It was too uncomfortable and it made him unusually, incredibly angry. His mouth lowered of its own accord to taste hers, slowly, softly exploring its contours. He teased her lips open, felt her tremble in his arms, her body grow limp and flaccid against his. He could do what he would with her. He could hurt her if he chose, make her regret she had ever thought to betray him, ever dared to hurt him.

His hands slid about her, smoothing the slender lines of her surprisingly tiny waist and the exciting swell of her hips as he pressed her into his awakened body. How could he think of harming this splendid woman? He wanted only to enjoy her. His lips were fondling her ears, her throat, and reason and common sense were fast slipping from him.

'Do you know what you do?' he asked into the fragrance of her hair.

'I know,' she whispered, against his lips.

'I hope to God that I do.' And with a deep groan of

desire he lifted her easily into his arms and carried her to the bed.

He did not trouble to re-light the candle. He took off her gown swiftly with gentle hands and studied the play of moonlight upon her naked body with dawning delight. She was more than handsome; she was beautiful, her skin as white and pure as that of the alabaster figurine. But he would not break this delectable body; he would crush it with his own, teach it the joys of lovemaking, of what the role of mistress involved.

Abigail sighed with deep satisfaction as he lowered himself beside her. And as his lips started on their journey of exploration her heartbeat quickened. She needed no teaching. Arousal came easily and she clung to him, crying his name, urging him on to greater heights of desire. She pushed her fingers up into those thick tousled curls, kissed the lobes of his delicious ears, the dark circles of his eyes, the passionate, insistent mouth.

Her body curled naturally against his as if it was meant to be there and as he slipped his hands beneath her, lifting her to him, she arched her back with a cry half of pleasure and half agony as he penetrated deep into that secret core of her. They moved as one, their bodily rhythms as fluid and beautiful as fern fronds waving in the sea.

She found she knew just how to please him and there was no unnatural modesty between them. He was the most gentle and generous of lovers, timing his need to hers till together they came to that perfect moment of ecstasy and lay spent together, stranded from an ocean of longing, beached upon sated fulfilment. Their limbs entwined, Abigail's head upon his chest, they slept.

It was Carl who woke first, and he lay for a long time

without moving, studying the pale oval of her face beside him. The tenderness he felt for her in that precious moment astonished him for it was almost painful. He saw her eyelids flutter open.

'I felt you watching me,' she said, and saw something very like a smile in his eyes. For a long moment they seemed content simply to look, as new lovers did. And then Abigail smiled with all the dawning power of womanhood. 'Do you believe in me now?'

The smile faded a fraction and she bit her lip with concern, but he only laughed, very softly. 'Perhaps.'

She pouted. 'Still doubts? How very cruel you are, Carl di Montegelo. I swear on my love that I am not at all interested in your figurine for myself or for the Count. I care not a jot for it, except in that I would like you to find it for your own sake. It is clearly important to you.'

He hardly seemed to be listening. 'You swear on what?'

Abigail snuggled closer into the warmth of his body as, heady with love and intoxicated by her new-found knowledge of its effects, discretion and even common sense had deserted her. She gave a little giggle. 'Do you imagine I would be here in your bed otherwise?'

'I think you don't know what you are saying,' Carl said, very quietly.

She kissed his chin, which jutted just above her head. 'I think I do. Would you rather I sleep with you simply for bodily gratification? I am not made that way. I was exceedingly well brought up. I dare not think what my mother would say if she knew. But you may rest easy; I don't ask you to love me.' She eased herself up on to one elbow so that she could look into his eyes. 'I cannot believe it is such a sin to love. If it is, then you must forgive me, for I think I loved you from that very first moment when you spoiled Polly's photograph.'

He looked into her eyes and saw that she spoke the truth. Certainly the truth so far as she believed it. But then if she was a virgin, as she no doubt had been, would she not love any man who had been the first to pleasure her? Carl had had many women and had responded to each in different ways. Each of them, like him, had been bent on pleasure. But this woman, he had to confess, had been different.

He had wanted to hate her, even to hurt and humiliate her. He had been ashamed when he had told her to go to his bedroom, knowing that intention in himself. But the moment he had held her in his arms by the window and looked into her moonlit eyes the desire to wound had fled. In its place had been burning desire. And something more. Something he preferred not to contemplate too closely.

'You have a most dangerous effect upon a man, Abigail Carter. You can make a man forget his principles.' Such as not to grow fond of any woman he bedded. Love, he'd always known, was not for him. As Emilia had so often said, it could lift you to the heights or plummet you to the depths. He had no wish for such acrobatics. Love, in his world, did not last. It abandoned you at a crucial moment for selfish pursuits, like parents leaving a lone child in a foreign country.

He withdrew his arm from her and sat up. She gave a litle moan of distress and wrapped her arms about his waist, stroking the dark hair upon his chest, leaning her cheek against his back.

'Don't be angry because I told you. I shall put no chains upon you if that is what you fear. I stand by my word on that, Carl. But I will not ask you to keep your word unless you truly wish to. If you want me to leave, to go back to England, I will do so without protest. I will not beg for your favours but I offer mine freely.'

He lifted the hands that had been caressing his chest and thoughtfully kissed each fingertip. He did not love her. She was not his type at all. This fire that was kindling yet again deep in his belly had nothing to do with love. He could quite easily have his fill of her this night and tomorrow send her back to England with that giddy sister of hers. And never think of her again.

But he knew he could not let her go. He knew this bed would be as empty as a desert if he slept in it alone. Relinquishing the inner battle for the moment, he pushed her back on to the pillows and smilingly kissed her eager mouth.

'You are a wanton. A minx in very truth. But an exciting one, without doubt.' And his mouth caught at the rosebud of her nipple, rolling it between his lips, making her cry out in her need. He took her the second time with less restraint and a passion that shattered any lingering remnants of her maidenhood. And she gloried in it, in him. They were one, as they had always been meant to be.

She was sure it must show. Abigail sat at breakfast with Polly and Emilia and was certain they must know of what had occurred last night in Carl's bed. How could it not be writ clear upon her face? Outwardly, in her burgundy, buttoned-up-to-the-neck gown, she appeared as demure and maidenly as ever. But inside she was in turmoil. Could they see that?

When Carl came in she dared not even glance in his

direction, but kept her gaze firmly upon the pieces of melon on her plate.

'And what do you plan for today?' asked Emilia of her nephew.

'I intend visiting Florence.'

Emilia sighed. 'Not more museums. I have been invited to attend Catherine Draywood's soirée. Ida and Polly will attend me if you can find someone to drive that dratted donkey cart. What about you, Abigail? Would you wish to come?'

Abigail cast a speaking glance of appeal in Carl's direction so that he found himself saying, 'Abigail is coming with me to Florence. Unless you have need for her.'

Emilia swiftly masked the rush of pleasure she felt at that little piece of news. She'd been rather hoping the two would come out of this ice war they'd been keeping up for some reason. Clearly something had occurred, judging by the spot of high colour upon each of Abigail's fine cheekbones, but she was not one to pry. 'Not at all. I shall have Polly.'

But Polly cleared her throat with a nervous little cough and begged leave to be excused also. She asked rather as if she expected great wrath to fall upon her head, but Emilia only laughed.

'I don't blame you. Who wants to spend the day with a gaggle of old women when they are pretty and blooming with the joys of youth? But you must tell me what you plan to do with your day, Polly, so that I can leave you with an easy conscience. I cannot have you idle.'

They all waited with various degrees of polite interest for Polly to answer. And Polly was thinking fast. She certainly could not say that she wished to explore the

castello from top to bottom and therefore needed a day
alone in which to do it. If everyone was going out, even
the all-seeing Ida, she couldn't hope for a better
opportunity. But she'd already claimed to be unwell
once before; if she tried that one again they would
hoist her off to a doctor. There was nothing else for it
but a fabrication. Abigail had made one once, by not
owning to the fact that Polly had told the Count about
Carl seeking his family fortune, so it couldn't be such a
dreadful thing to do. She would simply have to risk it,
for she could not let Alfonso down.

'The two Clarke sisters said they may pay me a call.
They are staying with their grandmother until the end
of the month.' There, that was only a half-lie, for there
had been vague talk of a visit, though no definite date
had been fixed.

'Oh, well, then, in that case, Ida and I will leave you
to it.' And Emilia got up from the table, smiling
benignly upon them all. 'How happy we all are here
now, are we not? Really, Carl, even if you never find
the figurine it won't trouble our happiness one iota.'
And, sweeping up her skirts, she bustled from the
room.

'But then she does not pay all the bills,' chuckled
Carl. 'Though she may like to think she does.'

The two girls joined him in gentle laughter for they
all loved Emilia and her bossy ways.

'Are you ready?' Carl asked Abigail, setting down
his coffee-cup. And, still keeping her blushing face
turned from his, she nodded. Why did she feel more
shy in the light of day than she had without a stitch on
in his bed?

'Now, Polly, please do behave,' she said tersely, only
to gain a scowling acquiescence.

Carl laughed. 'Leave the girl alone. What possible harm can she come to in this place?' He half hesitated, frowning. 'You could come to Florence with us if you wished?' he offered, though it was said with little enthusiasm — a fact which Polly did not fail to spot. She lifted her chin proudly.

'No, no. I am heartily tired of museums and art galleries and the endless numbers of churches you do like to explore. You are more than welcome to them. I shall enjoy a perfectly selfish day, all alone.'

'But I thought you said the Clarke sisters were coming?' said Abigail with sisterly sharpness.

'Oh, well, they said they *might* call. If they do not, I shall peacefully read, or weed Emilia's garden.' This delightful, if unusual picture of her lively sister troubled Abigail slightly, but Carl was in a hurry so there was no time to pursue the matter. 'I shall be perfectly all right, and I'm sure you do not need me drooling along beside you,' Polly insisted, and Abigail kissed her, knowing the truth of this and that she must therefore be content.

And as Carl had said, what possible harm could come to her sister here in the *castello*, with its fortress walls and battery of servants?

Florence was hot and crowded as ever. But somehow it didn't seem to matter. Carl seemed to have set any doubts about Abigail's loyalty aside as together they enjoyed the city's sights as tourists, as lovers.

'No museums today,' he said, pulling her into the crook of his arm. 'Today I wish to enjoy having you all to myself.' And Abigail's heart sang.

They took a boatride on the Arno, haggled over the price of a pair of apricots at the market-place, and then enjoyed an open-air concert in the Boboli Gardens.

Abigail had changed into a soft pale print gown, her hair neatly stowed away beneath her straw boater. With flushed cheeks and a sparkle to her eyes she was unaware quite how captivating she looked. Carl Montegne, however, was not. As she clapped and laughed with pleasure at the performance of the small orchestra and the superb singer who ought surely to be in the grand opera house, Carl scarcely took his eyes from her face. He kept forgetting how young she was — barely twenty-five for all her sensible, mature manner. But today the sobriety had gone. In its place was a delightful girlishness that warmed him. Would that he had had the opportunity for such reckless, uninhibited joy at her age. Instead he had worked long hours poring over figures, making his way in the merchant banking business. And he had been successful. But he had always meant to find his family's fortune and restore Falenza, to make it into the home he had always longed for. And he still intended to succeed with that too.

Did he wish to share that home with Abigail as his mistress? The prospect was tantalising. She was a beautiful, sensual woman who had given generously of her love last night in his bed. But there, perhaps, he had touched upon the core of his doubt. Had he been mistaken about her motives? And if her reason for that startling proposition had been because she loved him, how then did he cope with such a responsibility? The prospect alarmed him.

The concert ended and Abigail threw her arms about Carl's neck. 'Oh, that was lovely. Thank you for bringing me.'

He withdrew her arms. 'Abigail, it is not proper for

you to behave so in public,' he told her, but she only laughed, and pulled a face at him, uncaring.

'Oh, don't be such a grumpy. You'll become old before your time if you do not take care.' And he found himself laughing with her, hugging her to him.

'Very well, I shall take you for the largest, most delicious ice-cream I can find. The Italians are famous for it.'

'And then may we collect my photographs? They should be ready by now.'

He popped a kiss upon her forehead and again experienced that *frisson* of delight when he touched her. What was happening to him? Had he lost his reason?

The ice-cream fully lived up to his promise and afterwards they strolled together down the narrow streets, talking of nothing in particular, as lovers did. Then Abigail threw pennies to a group of beggar children while Carl collected and paid for her photographs.

'Here are your precious pictures,' he said, handing them to her. 'Don't take all day looking at them. I know I said no museums, but you must see the Uffizi. The very best of Italian art is there and I insist on showing you some real pictures. You must see the *Adoration of the Magi*.'

'Oh, I am far too tired. My feet are burning.'

'Then I shall transport you in the grand romantic style.'

Laughing, she let him take her hand, and, calling an open carriage, he held her close with his arms about her as they drove to this most famous museum.

As the carriage bowled along with Carl pointing out famous sights along the way, Abigail flicked through

the prints in her lap. She was pleased with them. Here
was Polly picking flowers in the garden. Here was
Maria, one of the village ladies, with very few teeth
and the widest grin imaginable. Here a picture of the
castello, and another of the Count puffing out his chest
in that way he had. Then she came to the very first
photograph they had taken on the steps of the *castello*
and she smiled at the sight of the happy group, relieved
to have arrived at their destination at last. And in the
left-hand corner of the photograph, looking out from
an upper window, was the woman in the pearl-grey
gown.

Abigail was so startled her hand suddenly shook.

'What is it? Haven't they come out?' Carl asked,
noticing her sudden quiet.

She handed some to him, including the one with the
woman. He glanced quickly through them, came to the
one on the steps, and looked at it. After a moment he
laughed.

'Polly looks so pleased with herself standing on that
step you'd think she had organised the entire journey
herself.'

'Do you notice anything particular about that picture?' Abigail asked, and held her breath as she waited
for his answer. Carl was studying it with apparent
attention.

'Yes. You are not on it.'

'Don't be foolish. Nothing else?'

He shook his head.

Abigail could not believe it. Could he really see
nothing? Or was he pretending?

Her one coherent thought was that she remembered
taking another photograph when the woman had
appeared on the night of the masked party when she

had suddenly come to stand in the library door. But Polly had seen no one in a grey gown so perhaps that photograph would be blank. She dared not look.

Without a word she handed the pack of photographs to Carl. 'Tell me what you think.'

CHAPTER THIRTEEN

HE LOOKED at every one, making the kind of polite remarks or exclamations of pleasure that people made when looking at snapshots. She watched him carefully from the corner of her eye, but nothing in his expression gave away the fact that he had seen anything untoward. When he had done, he gave them back to her with a smile.

'Very good. You are really quite talented. Here we are. The Uffizi.'

She felt quite unable to look at them and pushed them into the depths of her pocket.

Why had Carl not mentioned the woman? A sick feeling spread through Abigail's stomach, for all this time she had thought the figure a product of her imagination. Yet here she was in a photograph seeming as real as herself. *And Carl had denied her existence. Why?* Who was she? Had he known she would be there? The answer came at once. Of course he had known. Hadn't she found him talking with the woman in the long gallery only last night? Hadn't she seen the flick of her grey skirt and asked quite bluntly if anyone else lived in the *castello*? And what had Carl answered?

Nothing. As now, he had avoided answering.

Carl showed her the Uffizi with pride and humility in his voice, but the pleasure in the visit was quite gone for Abigail. She half stumbled along beside him, seeing nothing, caring less.

'What is the matter with you?' Carl asked, concern in his voice. 'You look quite pale.'

'I feel suddenly unwell. May we go home? Pehaps it is the heat and the crowds.'

'But of course.' Carl called for a hack to take them back to their own carriage and Abigail huddled at once into the corner of it, her romantic day in Florence turned to a sour taste in her mouth.

Could a camera photograph a ghost? Surely not. Then why had Carl not seen the figure? Because he did not wish to admit the woman existed? Perhaps he thought that if he pretended not to see her Abigail would believe the photograph a product of her imagination, or a ghost that haunted the *castello*. He had said something about ghosts on that very first day at Emilia's house in Devon. Had he been looking for a possible explanation in case any one of them should spot his secret guest?

But why was she a secret? The carriage bounced on the rutted road, flinging Abigail across the seat and against Carl's shoulder. Even this rough contact sent fires raging through her. She pulled herself away from him, ignoring the half-glance of surprise he cast in her direction. But he said nothing, only flicked the reins and urged the horses to a faster pace.

In the safety of her bedroom Abigail pulled the pictures out again and studied them with greater care. The doors leading out on to the terrace were not blank. There she was, half turned from the camera as she moved back into the shadowy room. A tall, slender figure in a pearl-grey gown. A mysterious woman who lived somewhere in this building and did not wish to be seen.

She could think of no other explanation but that the

woman had lived here all along, perhaps in the east wing. And if Carl had seen her in the photograph, then he must have some reason for not mentioning her. Abigail could think of only one logical explanation. She was his mistress and he did not wish them to know of it; neither his aunt, the impressionable Polly, nor, more particularly perhaps in the circumstances, herself.

Abigail sat stunned upon her bed. She had taken off her outer garments and knew she had only a little time before dinner, time enough to wash and change into something fresh and pretty. She did neither of those things. How could she keep still when there were secrets to unfold? How dared Carl Montegne look with faintly disguised disapproval upon herself, and Polly, for their female weakness of seeking love, when all the time he kept a mistress hidden in the unused wing of his *castello*?

The heat of anger and, though she did not admit to this, jealousy seared through her body, and she knew she would not rest until she had found the woman and confronted her.

Abigail was willing to devote her life to Carl as his mistress and accept the fact they could never marry. For all her pride she was no more than a servant after all. She would even accept the fact that he did not love her, certainly not in the way she loved him.

But she could not accept infidelity. She *would* not. If she was to be his mistress, she must be the *only* one. Therefore the woman, whoever and wherever she was, must be found at once, without delay.

Abigail headed for the east wing. The place she had seen the woman had often been in the long gallery. She would look there and beyond. Abigail's bare feet slithered upon the bare boards, her skirts flying about her ankles as she half ran along the dark passages. There was no time to be lost.

But what she found was a room full of wrecked pictures and Polly in a fainting fit.

'I tried to stop them.' Polly was in bed, the wonders of sal volatile having cured the hysteria, and her head was now being bathed with cool water and a gentle hand.

'Them? The Count's men?' Carl asked, his voice biting hard, and Polly looked up at him from anguished eyes and nodded.

'Is that why you chose to stay at the *castello*, to let them in?' He turned his ferocious glare upon Abigail. 'And you were the lure, to keep me out of the way? You wanted me to stay in Florence for as long as possible, and the only way to be sure I did that was to accompany me. I can also see that it would provide you with a very special alibi which for someone as fond of the Sherlock Holmes stories as Polly claims you are is exactly what you would plan.'

Abigail was stupefied. 'How can you think such a thing?'

'Then how come you knew exactly where to find your sister? Why did you hurry straight to the long gallery when you should have been changing for dinner?'

He was waiting for her answer, but Abigail found she could not give one. Her throat constricted on the accusations that filled her own heart. But she could not confront him with this new knowledge of hers, not now, in front of Polly. Unfortunately her stubborn silence was self-accusatory. She saw his lips twist with sardonic satisfaction, as if she had told him all he needed to know.

'No, of course I didn't let them in,' Polly said, rallying. 'But I had promised to search myself. Perhaps Alfonso wasn't satisfied with my efforts. The men just burst in, shouting, running everywhere. I tried to stop them, but they pushed me out of the way.'

'Search? You mean for the figurine?'

'Yes,' Polly glumly agreed. 'But I only wanted it for you. I thought that if I found it you would forgive me for breaking that other one. Alfonso told me you would.'

Carl gave a low growl. 'You listen too much to that ambitious young man. He wanted you to find the figurine for himself, not out of any generous gesture for you, or for me.'

Tears were welling up once again in Polly's eyes and Abigail put a comforting arm around her.

'Now is not the time for cross-questioning. Can you not see how upset she is? Leave her be.'

'I only wanted to help,' Polly mourned. 'Oh, I do wish I'd never touched that other one. I never meant it to fall.'

'Stop going on about breaking the other one,' said Carl, his voice tight with impatience. 'You did not break the dratted thing; I did.'

Both girls gasped, Abigail staring at him as if he had lost his reason. '*You* broke it? My God, *why*?'

'It was necessary. Stay here. I will have food sent up to you. Tomorrow I will see this dratted Count for myself. It is time the whole matter was settled.' And on this unsatisfactory note, he strode from the room.

Abigail sat in stunned silence for some long time, holding the sobbing girl in her arms.

'I shall never s-speak to Alfonso again,' sobbed poor

disillusioned Polly. 'He said that I was the most important thing that had ever h-happened to him.'

Abigail looked at her sister with great sadness in her
eyes. 'I fear men often say things they do not strictly
mean.' She recalled how Carl had called her beautiful,
and fascinating. He had said that he wanted her. But
he had never said that he loved her. Abigail looked
more fearfully at Polly.

'I hope he did not. . . I mean, I trust you recalled
what Mama——'

Polly gave her a scathing look. 'I am not quite a
goose, Abby. Oh, but I did *so* love him and he has
done this most dreadful thing to Carl. I *know* I would
have found the figurine, given the chance. I know it. I
was always good at finding things for Mama. Oh, it is
all my fault.'

Abigail soothed her young sister as best she could,
but her mind was not properly on Polly's woes, which
would pass soon enough for she was young and pretty,
and it had been no more than calf love, the first trials
of life. She was more concerned with her own troubles,
for she had not listened so well to Mama's excellent
advice.

'One day,' she told Polly, 'you will meet a prince of
your own who will love you to distraction, and you will
live happily ever after, just like in the fairy-tale.'

'And will he ride a white charger?' giggled Polly.

'But of course. You wait; he will come sure enough.'

But there would be no prince for sensible Abigail.
The relationship she had so briefly enjoyed with Carl
Montegne, so precariously built, had crumbled to dust
and she felt quite unable to retrieve it. He cared
nothing for her, any more than he did for poor Polly.
His one thought was for his precious *castello* and the

figurine, a figurine he had claimed to want desperately
and had then deliberately broken. And for all she knew
he might have a host of mistresses scattered about. Oh,
dear, would she ever understand him? Could he, in
fact, be quite sane?

Her heart clenched with cold fear as Abigail began
to wonder if this might not be the case. It would
explain a great deal about his behaviour, both over the
woman whose presence he denied, and the precious
figurine he'd so desperately sought and casually
destroyed. Could he be mad? And if he was, she would
still love him.

The moment Polly was asleep Abigail went straight to
Carl. She meant to tell him what she thought of his
behaviour in no uncertain terms. She would confront
him with her discovery, accuse him outright of keeping
a mistress hidden, and demand an explanation. Whatever it was that had possessed him to break the very
thing he had so assiduously sought and most valued,
she meant to discover it. She was done with secrets; it
was time for the truth.

He was not in the gallery, nor in the dining-room,
which was deserted, as was the rest of the house, it
seemed.

Polly had told Abigail that Emilia and Ida had
decided to stay overnight at the Draywoods' and would
not be back until late the next day.

Abigail longed suddenly for the warmth of their
company as a prickle of unease touched her nape. She
had bravely tapped on Carl's bedroom door only to
find the room silent, empty.

'Where is he?' she cried to the echoing kitchen.

She had no desire to search the east wing just now

and the only other possibility was the chapel. It was growing late, almost ten o'clock, and the night was black dark, the moon having been blotted out by clouds. So she picked her way with care, several times finding branches clawing her face or clutching at her skirts. But she bit down hard upon her lips so that she did not cry out. A light flickered in the chapel window and she quickened her pace.

She found him bent over the remains of a broken statue. He turned when he heard her, but did not get up, merely stared at her, a dreadful emptiness in his eyes. 'Are you well satisfied?'

Abigail hurried to him. One glance told the tale. The chapel had been ransacked and by a cruel hand. Every artefact, every piece of statue or shred of beautiful cloth or mouldings, had been broken or ripped from the walls. Abigail put out a hand to touch his shoulder in a gesture of shock and sympathy. 'I'm sorry.' She gazed at the broken madonna. 'Was she very valuable?'

Carl Montegne made an unspeakable sound deep in his throat. 'Is that all you can think of? The value of something? Do you never consider its beauty?'

Abigail was instantly hurt. She had spoken without thinking, an automatic reaction to a disaster, but of course she cared about beauty. She tried to explain, but Carl refused to listen. He strode away from her, the pieces of the madonna cradled in his arms.

'Those villains came here and took my property apart, and for something that does not even belong to them.'

'Perhaps they exceeded their orders,' Abigail suggested. 'I cannot imagine the Count, for all he is a silly young man, instructing his men to perform such sacrilege.' She stared at the destruction about her.

'They would not do it without his say-so.'

Abigail did not argue. Even in the dim light from the tapers Carl had lit, the devastation was plain to see.

He sank on to the altar steps, head in his hands, and her heart ached for him. She longed to go and take him in her arms. But he was a strong, proud man, a man whose distrust in her was once again rekindled, and he would not welcome her sympathy for he did not believe in it.

Abigail approached cautiously, picking her way among the broken shards of pottery and glass, her practical, sensible side already noting what could be mended and what would have to be thrown away. Her thoughts were in total disarray for she was badly shaken. 'Why should they break everything? It's wanton destruction. I never thought——'

'That he'd go this far? He is a Paolo. The vendetta, it seems, still lives.'

Abigail shook her head in dismay. 'No, no, that cannot be. A vendetta must not be allowed to go on for so long. What good does it do?'

'Paolo is after the same thing I am, but from greed, not a desire to rebuild his roots.'

Abigail came to kneel before Carl. 'Perhaps not. Perhaps he simply wished to frighten you away so that you will sell the place.'

'To him?' Carl grunted his disgust. 'So that he could then search the place unfettered? It is my property and I intend to keep it.'

Abigail put both hands upon his knees, desperate to soothe his anger, to have him trust her again. 'You must not allow him to. Hold fast.'

Dark brows raised in mockery. 'A short while ago

you scorned me for wanting to hold on to this place. "A draughty pile", you called it.'

Abigail had the grace to flush. 'I spoke in haste, in anger. I was upset. Really and truly I want you to keep the *castello* and find your Prince Giovanni's legacy, if it exists. But Carl, there is another matter which concerns me. I hesitate to mention it to you now, but I cannot help myself, no matter how much it pains you, or me, to do so.'

He glared at her, a threatening scowl marring his brow. 'Ask what you will. If you must. I don't promise to answer, but speak plain; I dislike prevarication.'

Was this the moment? She wished instantly that she had chosen another. Abigail swallowed carefully and drew in a deep, quavering breath. 'The woman in the pearl-grey gown. . .'

He looked at her in silence, waiting for her to continue.

'Who is she?' Abigail asked.

His face was quite expressionless. After a long moment he said, 'I don't know what you are talking about. Is this some kind of trick?'

'She was there on the photographs. You must have seen her. I know you said you saw nothing particular or odd about them, but you must have done. She was *there*. I saw her.' Her tongue had been loosened now and she hurried on. 'She was the only stranger on that picture of the party, dressed in a shimmering gown of palest grey. And she was framed in an upper window on that very first day we arrived. I *saw* her. Please tell me who she is. I must know. Is she your mistress? I can only think that she is; else why would you keep her secret?' Abigail was babbling, voice choked with her distress. 'Because if she is, I must know, do you see? For I don't think I could bear it.'

It was as if time itself stood still. Abigail ached for him to answer. She wanted him to take her in his arms, stroke her hair, and tell her there was no other woman in his life, not now, not ever, no one but herself for as long as he lived.

But Carl Montegne's brain was far too agile and too filled with hate and distrust for such romantical notions at this juncture. He kept his unwavering gaze fixed upon Abigail's face.

'Is that what you think?'

'I do.' Her voice was no more than a whisper.

Carl got very slowly to his feet. 'I don't understand one half of what you are saying, but I assure you that, much as I enjoyed your services, you do not own me. I took you to my bed against my better judgement.' His self-loathing turned his voice bitter. 'And without doubt you will make a charming, most fascinating mistress, Abigail, but if I should wish to take another at any time, I will do so. I see no reason to ask your permission or inform you of the fact.'

Abigail, still kneeling upon the floor, crouched at his feet, looked up the long, hard length of him to the fury in his face, and could find no strength to answer. A terrible weakness flooded her limbs, paralysed her mind, and dried the tears upon her burning cheeks. She knew she had lost him, but was powerless to act. Her mind sank into nothingness. What could she say or do to prevent him walking away from her, perhaps for good?

While Abigail had been trying and failing to save the love of the man she loved most in all the world, Polly slept fitfully on. She woke often during the course of the night and went over and over in her mind how everything she did seemed to go wrong. She'd always been eager to help, to share the work — within reasonable boundaries, of course, for she was but young and liked to enjoy life. She'd been happy to visit some of the museums looking for the figurine if not to spend all day at it as Abigail had done. Her heart plummeted; of course that was it exactly.

Abigail did everything so selflessly. She would happily spend all day trailing about to help Carl find the thing, without a thought for her own comfort. She had cared for Polly, so long bearing the brunt of her youthful misdemeanours that Polly had come to take it all for granted. But she knew in her heart she should not.

Dawn was breaking, that rare pink light lifting the burden of night from her eyes. She lay on her back and stared at the square of window, her mind locked in unaccustomed self-exploration.

And Carl. He was not for her, any more than the Count was. Abby was right there too. One day she would meet someone to love, but she was only just sixteen and in no real hurry.

Polly sighed and stretched out in the bed, drawing a face in her sleepy mind of how she would like him to look, this prince who would come on his white charger. She smiled into the darkness, but it faded almost at once into a frown. Fairy-tales were fun, but nothing like life. She had trusted Alfonso and he had used her. He did not love her at all, despite all those pretty kisses which she must never mention to Abigail. Her sister would have a blue fit.

Men were a snare and not to be trusted at all, she

decided, with all her sixteen-year-old wisdom. She would certainly give Alfonso a piece of her mind the very next time she saw him.

And as if conjured from her mind, there he was, framed in the window of her room as if the dawn itself had brought him. Polly cried out her alarm, but found a sweaty palm crushing the sound from her lips.

'No, no, my pretty elf. You must come with me. I wish to know where and what you have searched. Before the day fully comes I want to be holding that figurine in my hands. And you are going to help me. Be still or you may get more seriously hurt and I should be sorry for that, after all we have been to each other.'

The childlike eyes glittered threateningly in the rosy light and Polly squealed in her throat like a trapped rabbit, blue eyes wide, vigorously wriggling and thrashing at him with her young limbs. But, laughing, Alfonso picked her up easily in his arms and carried her from the room, Polly's last desperate thoughts being that surely Abigail would hear the commotion in her room next door and come to help.

But her sister's door remained firmly shut as Alfonso proceeded down the stairs with his wriggling burden clamped firmly to his side. Abigail's room, and her bed, were in fact empty.

In her moment of desperation Abigail had found the right words.

'I love you.'

Disbelief had registered in his eyes.

'I do,' she repeated. 'What more can I say?' She had got to her feet and stood bravely before him, tilting her chin to look him straight in the eye. He returned her gaze with astonishment in his.

'How can you still love me after what I have just said to you?'

Abigail smiled. 'You cannot switch love on and off like one of the new electric lights. I love you, and will always do so, no matter how many other mistresses you take.' She dropped her chin to shield the pain in her eyes, for such an event would be unbearable.

'And you would not mind if I had another mistress? You would still love me?'

Abigail clasped her hands before her in case they should wish to touch him. 'I did not say I would not mind. Of course I would.' She lifted her eyes to his and he saw they were moist with real tears. 'But I would not stop loving you. Is that very wicked?'

He gazed in wonder into her face, saw the tremble of her lower lip, the raw honesty in her face. How could he distrust this woman who bared her soul so openly to him? She did so knowing he might crush her, knowing he had little faith in the lasting properties of love. Yet she offered hers to him as an undying gift. Like this she was utterly irresistible.

She was in his arms. Unable to help himself, he was lifting her fast against his chest and covering her face and neck with kisses. His hands were in her hair, at her breasts, wanting to hold and learn each part of her anew. He could feel the pressure of those beautiful breasts hardening against him as he kissed the white column of her arched throat. The urge to possess her overwhelmed him by its suddenness and by its fierce intensity. He would like to shut off his mind, to refuse to allow it to question further. He wanted her, he needed her, and surely that was enough.

But he was bitterly disappointed in her, however hard he tried to disguise the fact, even from himself.

She had beguiled him to take her into his bed, no doubt with the express purpose of giving the Count's men time to look around. And like the fool that he was, he'd been so besotted by her that he hadn't followed that snooping fool they'd spotted from the window any further than the bushes that night. His mind had been filled with bedding her, just as it was now.

Then she had begged him with those delectable eyes of hers to allow her to accompany him to Florence. And while she had kept him busily occupied, fawning at her feet almost, the *castello* had been ransacked. Carl was disgusted with himself. Had he turned into a fool? She made an idiot out of him and now seemed to think she could place exclusive rights upon him also. His urgent fingers had opened most of the pearl buttons right down to her handsome breasts. It was long past time he made his position plain. His lips moved down to the crown of her breast, which rose hard and thrusting into the palm of his hand. He would make it very plain.

Later, in his bed, he made love to her with all the passion that surged and boiled within him. He did not ask if it was love. He took what she offered and gloried in it, treating her with care and respect even in his passion. He undressed her slowly, savouring the sweet discovery of her body, caressing and exploring each secret part of her with an urgent tenderness that sent Abigail's senses spinning.

He could not keep himself from her, no matter how hard he might try. They were good together, here, in his bed, but it was more, much more than that. It was as if it was meant to be. And for all Abigail's inexperience she seemed to know instinctively how to please

him, how he might pleasure her. As his kisses grew
more demanding she did not demur, and the warmth
of the soft Italian night folded them into its loving
embrace so that they were oblivious to all but their
own growing needs, and love.

They slept but little that night. Occasionally they
would doze, sated with loving, but then one of them
would wake and rouse the other and the touching and
kissing would start again. By unspoken agreement that
night was meant for loving and they wasted none of it.

By the first light of dawn they were relaxed and
laughing, talking sweet nonsense as lovers did. He was
examining the shape of her nose with critical lips,
devouring with his eyes, and a softly smoothing hand,
the curving magnificence of breast and shoulder and
throat.

'I do not want this day to come,' he murmured
against the pulse below her ear. 'Let us push back the
dawn and begin this night again. I would explore it,
and you, more thoroughly.'

Abigail laughed softly in her throat. 'There will be
another night, and another.' The loving quality of her
eyes never ceased to astonish him.

'Why do you love me?' he asked, not for the first
time that night, and Abigail gazed at him very
seriously.

'Because you are handsome and rich and live in an
Italian castle.'

He was startled for a moment; then he saw her
laughing.

'That is what you accused me of,' she reminded him,
and he grimaced.

'What a callow-hearted fellow I must be.'

'Do you, then, trust me? Do you believe that I am

not some kind of secret agent working in league with the Count?'

For a long moment he was silent, so silent that Abigail's heart faltered. If he said the wrong thing now she would die. But the lips twisted into a wry grin. 'I dare say I might, in time. I am unaccustomed to trusting in love.'

Abigail nuzzled her mouth against his. 'Then I shall teach you. How could you think that I would even look upon the strutting Count when I can have you?'

Despite himself Carl found himself chuckling. 'Is that why you came to Italy with me, because you were bowled over by my charm?'

'It must have been.'

'But you did not know that I would use you as a skivvy, to scrub my floors.'

Abigail playfully slapped at his hand as it stroked back her hair. 'No, I did not, nor that you would take me into your bed and ruin my reputation.'

'I believe that was your idea.' His mouth was on hers, kissing her deeply, feeling her respond with pleasure, unable to get enough of her. Then he was studying her face, ready to judge if her expression faltered. 'Do you think I am mad not to sell Falenza to the Count? To want to stay here?'

Abigail recalled how not so long ago she had thought him quite insane. He did not seem mad to her now, in the warmth of his bed, with his arms fast about her. The very idea was a foolishness. He was strong and masterful, fully in control of his life, and of her. But still a worry needled her mind. He had deliberately broken the one figurine they had found. He had denied seeing the woman in grey on her photographs. And this was not love he offered her, only pleasure. It masqueraded well as love, but she knew it would be a mistake to make too much of it and confuse the two.

'You are frowning.'

She quickly smoothed out her brow and nestled closer into his side. 'Am I? Perhaps I am fearful you will still leave me, afraid you may return to your secret mistress hidden in the east wing.' She spoke as if in jest, but she hoped her daring would bring an answer that a more probing enquiry would not. She was never to discover for at that moment the door of the bedroom banged open and a panic-stricken, tousle-haired Polly almost fell into the room.

'Carl, Carl, you must. . .' She stopped, eyes and jaw falling wide, face freezing as she stared at her sister so lovingly snuggled beside Carl Montegne in his huge four-poster bed.

He was out of bed in an instant, pulling on soft riding breeches, while her mind was thus in shock and her gaze fixed upon Abigail. 'What is it, Polly?' He gently touched her shoulder and she turned to him, released from her paralysis.

'I've found it. I-I know where it is. B-but you must hurry, for the Count knows that I have seen it and not told him where. I just ran and ran. But he'll find it any minute, I swear he will. You have to hurry.'

CHAPTER FOURTEEN

'HELP me dress, Polly, and don't say a word,' Abigail said, and with commendable self-control Polly did as she was bid, nevertheless managing to convey silent disapproval.

Various possible excuses and explanations flew through Abigail's mind as the two sisters fumbled hastily with buttons and tapes, but none seemed quite appropriate. In the circumstances silence seemed the best defence, but Polly's eyes were hot and accusing.

Abigail drew a trembling breath. 'We can talk about this later, if you must. Life is not always as clear-cut as we would like it to be, Polly. And I wouldn't like you to get the idea that this is the normal way a lady should behave.' She stopped, quite unable to continue.

Polly gave Abigail a tremulous smile. 'I have known for some time that you loved Carl. Not as I loved him, in an adoring, childlike way, but real love, as a woman. I do understand that. But——'

Abigail hastily set her fingertips upon Polly's lips, closing her eyes against her first pangs of guilt. 'My responsibility to you is great, but I have my own life to lead. It is difficult to. . . Later. We will talk of it later. For now there are more important matters to deal with.'

They met up with Carl again at the entrance to the small chapel, where fingers of light spilled out on to the cobbles.

'He is in there,' whispered Polly.

'Anyone with him?'

Polly shook her head. 'No, quite alone. He made me help him to look. He seems angry that his men failed and only made a mess of everything.'

'I'll make a mess of him,' growled Carl and started to move forward.

'Wait,' urged Polly, clutching at his shirt. 'Let me show you where the figurine stands. It's been in plain view all along and we never saw it.' The three of them crept on soft feet through the half-open door of the chapel and, keeping behind the marble pillars, edged their way around the side of the west wall.

Polly pulled them to a halt. 'There, can you see it?' She pointed upwards above the chancel steps to where the crossbeam spanned the roof of the small church. At each corner were the familiar angelic devices and in the centre a wooden cross. The space between these had been filled with a collection of simple silver urns and ceramic figures, their colours faded and chipped. But as they looked more closely they saw that one of them was different. Its white marble-like shape was unmistakable despite its covering of dust. Even had they not seen the first Mercury figurine they would have recognised it instantly, had they thought to look in the right place.

'Damn me,' Carl murmured in wonder. 'And it has been right there before our eyes all the time.'

'It must have stood there for centuries,' Abigail reminded him. 'But I suppose people simply do not look up. How clever of you to spot it, Polly.'

Polly preened herself in the knowledge she had at last reinstated her honour. 'How are we to get at it? That is the question.'

And then they saw him, Count Alfonso Ruggieri

Paolo, dignity set aside as he placed a simple wooden ladder against the wall of the church.

'He has discovered it,' gasped Polly. 'I thought I had disguised my surprise and delight at seeing it, but I must have failed. Oh, Carl, what are we to do?'

But Carl was already leaving his hiding-place. He leapt easily over the back of the ornate seating and, reaching the centre aisle, stood stock-still, legs astride, arms crossed against that impressive chest.

'Good morning, Count. Can I be of assistance?'

Alfonso almost fell off the bottom rungs of the ladder in his eagerness to turn and face his adversary. 'Montegne.'

'Carl di Montegelo, if you please. If this vendetta has to be resurrected let us at least keep the names right. You realise, of course, that you are trespassing?'

'Your family owe this figurine to me,' the Count said, peevishness strong in his voice.

'Now how do you arrive at that notion?'

'Your family had nothing, nothing, until they stole the bride of Ercole.'

Carl sighed heavily. 'You are speaking of something which took place over four hundred years ago. How can you know?'

Alfonso took a step towards him. 'I know. It is written in my family's diaries. They speak of how Giovanni lured Elisabetta away from Ercole, her intended husband. And it was all for her money, not her beauty. My family has made it their quest to win back not only lost honour but the fortune that should have been theirs.'

'Whatever truth there may be in your statement, Elisabetta did not marry your ancestor Ercole, she married mine, Giovanni. You have no claim, therefore, to her fortune. If it exists.'

Alfonso was far from done with his argument. He slammed his fist angrily upon the altar rail, making Carl glower with disapproval, his hands moving instinctively into fists. 'Of course it exists. She had more gold than could be spent in any one lifetime but she was no princess. She had a morganatic marriage with the Prince, not a true marriage, and she was already betrothed to Ercole, who was robbed of what was rightfully his without compensation. I have come to collect that compensation now.'

Carl put back his head and laughed. It had no mirth in it. 'Try it. Try, and see what you get in its place. There are no princes here now but the tenacity of the di Montegelos is still present, in me.'

The silence following this undisputed threat was awesome. Carl pressed home his advantage. 'Your family has had four hundred years to find this fortune. How come you have so consistently failed?'

Alfonso looked unhappy, but grudgingly admitted, 'We did not know where to look. We have already searched this *castello* many times and found no sign of gold or treasure of any kind. But then you came with some story of a figurine. I think perhaps that must hold the key to it all.' He slid a pistol from the pocket of his coat and, pointing it directly at Carl, began to edge back to the ladder. 'Clever little Polly has found it for me.'

He must have seen Polly hiding in the shadows for he laughed at her, eyes twinkling. 'What a sweet child you are, little elf, but too simple. You gave it away when you gasped with that childish excitement of yours. And now I too see the figurine high on that dusty beam above our heads. And I intend to be the one to collect it.'

'You are too late, Count. I have it already,' shouted Abigail. And, stepping down from the ladder, she held the figurine high in her hands. 'See, Carl, it is yours.'

And then everything happened at once. Alfonso dived towards her. Abigail, panicking, thrust the ladder at him so that it toppled right over, knocking the Count back on to the floor. Carl was upon him in seconds, but then came the most awful crack as the pistol went off and Abigail stared in horror as Carl slumped. The next instant Alfonso was on his feet, approaching Abigail on slow, measured steps.

'It was his own fault; he should not have jumped upon me. Give me the figurine, Abigail. I can shoot you too, you know.' Even as he spoke Abigail's stunned eyes watched him start to reload the pistol. In the background were Polly's screams, but from Carl nothing, not a sound. He lay unmoving upon the floor, a pool of blood spreading from his head. Abigail's instinct was to run to him, but if she did that she would lose the figurine, and everything Carl had planned for would be lost. She could at least save that for him. Swirling about, she gathered up her skirts and ran from the chapel. Leaving him there was like ripping the heart from her breast, but she knew it must be done.

Abigail ran and ran, not knowing where she ran but desperate to escape the pounding footsteps coming after her. Behind the altar was a small door. It was locked. Turning desperately, she started in another direction. A flight of stairs led upwards and she had no alternative but to take it. The Count was almost upon her. Grasping the iron rail, she flew up the winding stair on winged feet.

It led out upon the parapet. Abigail stumbled over the top step and she fell sobbing on to the cold stone walkway. The pain in her lungs was almost more than she could bear. She scrambled to her feet, not caring about the blood that ran down her knuckles from the grazes she had incurred. She looked wildly about her. Where to run now? Along the parapet, around the perimeter of the roof. But would there be a way down? There had to be. Clutching tightly her precious burden, she began again to run.

From here all of the di Montegelo lands lay spread out below. She could see the shallow pits dug ready for the vines. There were no men there at this hour for the day's work had not yet begun. She could see the *castello* close by, its windows still shuttered. It was a relief that Emilia and Ida were safely away, but the villagers who worked in the kitchens would not be here for an hour or more.

Who was there to help her? Polly? Abigail hoped her sister would be looking to Carl. She dared not think he was dead. Her life would be over if that were so. But the memory of that spreading pool of bright red blood blocked her vision so badly that once again she stumbled and had to grasp hold of the head of a gargoyle. She screamed in her terror for she could easily have tipped right over the edge and fallen forty feet to the courtyard below.

'Why do you not stop running, and hand it over to me? Where is there for you to run? You know there is no escape. I have won. I always win.'

Abigail half glanced behind her to see the grinning face of the Count, his hands outstretched mere inches from her. Then they were closing upon her arms, pulling her towards him, and she was powerless to protest. The next instant he was pushing her backwards, pinning her against the parapet wall. Still she clung obstinately to the figurine.

Alfonso said something very rapidly and angrily in Italian that thankfully Abigail did not understand, but she could feel the pressure of the low stone wall at her back. Any moment he would push her over the edge. And if she gave him the figurine? *He might still push her over.*

She could see it in the greedy set smile upon his beautiful face. He had always been given everything he wanted throughout his life. And if Abigail, like Carl, had something he needed he would take it without thought. He had shot Carl, however carelessly. He could throw Abigail off the roof of the chapel without a thought. She kicked and fought and tried even to bite at his hand. Her own hands were shot with pain at being so tightly clenched about the figure, but her fingers were now being prised open and there was nothing she could do. Once he had the figurine he would truly have won, and could snuff her out as easily as a candle flame.

'I wouldn't do that,' came a most welcome voice from behind him, and Abigail cried out with relief. In that instant her fingers relaxed and with a shout of triumph Alfonso wrenched the figurine from her. But Carl was quick too, and in a flash had caught the Count about the neck with one arm, bringing him crashing to the ground till he was screaming for mercy and the figurine was slipping from his grasp, rolling away across the stone walkway. Abigail snatched it up and held it to her breast, scarcely remembering to breathe in her excitement at seeing Carl restored to health.

He looked up at her and his eyes smiled into hers. 'I

was worried about you,' he said mildly, meaning much, much more.

'I was rather concerned for you, but I should have known you were far too stubborn to give up so easily.'

'Exactly.' Then, addressing his still wriggling prisoner, 'Get up and walk very slowly downstairs,' ordered Carl, in a quiet voice of authority. 'No tricks. I want you off my land.'

But back in the relative safety of the courtyard the two men still faced each other with sour expressions of distrust, Alfonso making no move to leave.

There was a long scratch along the side of Carl's head where the bullet had grazed him, but since he was standing on his own two feet and held the pistol very firmly in his own grasp the danger seemed to be over. Abigail handed him the figurine. She had wiped off the worst of the dust, but it still looked a sorry sight. The shape and features of Mercury were pleasantly enough executed and perhaps the alabaster would glow and shine once it was cleaned. For now it seemed incredible to her that it could be worth a great sum of money. Carl stared at it for a long moment. He seemed transfixed by its humble, stark beauty, as did Alfonso.

Polly came running out of the chapel straight to Abigail and flung her arms about her.

'Oh, Abby, I was so scared for you. Are you all right?'

Without taking her eyes from the tableau before her, Abigail assured her sister that she was perfectly well.

'I doubt you can rebuild on the strength of that amateurish effort. It is no better than the cheap little piece I picked up at the museum.' The Count shrugged, and half turned away.

'So it was the professor who gave away my secret.'

The Count laughed. 'No, no, I guessed what you
were up to. And I could retrace the steps the professor
had taken me on in his efforts to educate me. As for
your Giovanni, he was known to be an amateur artist
of meagre skills. You can see some of his efforts in
your long gallery. Dark and gloomy with little idea of
perspective.'

Abigail looked from one to the other of them. 'Do
you mean that attempt to paint Florence? We noticed
it when we first arrived.'

Alfonso gave a mirthless laugh. 'He had many lessons to learn the art, but did not succeed. There is no
talent in your family, my friend, and no treasure at
Falenza. It is all a story, just an old legend.'

'I agree,' said Carl. 'Just a legend.' He weighted the
figure in his hand and the dark eyes took on a wicked
twinkle. He laughed. 'Then we must declare a truce.
At least we had fun, eh, resurrecting an old vendetta?'

For a moment everyone stared at him in open-
mouthed astonishment. Even Alfonso appeared nonplussed. Then he too gave a shout of laughter. 'You
are right, my friend. We fought like the knights of old,
sì? And since there is no victor we must agree to be
friends, to be happy neighbours in this beautiful
country. That is, if you can afford to stay without the
help of Elisabetta's gold.'

'I'll stay,' said Carl, and, after a long moment in
which both men took the measure of the other, Carl
stuck out his hand. 'I'd rather have you as a friend than
an enemy, however uneasily.'

Alfonso bowed to the two ladies. 'I apologise to each
of you for my callous behaviour; the greed for gold
gets the better of one's good manners, I'm afraid. It
will not happen again.' He smiled at Polly and stroked

one peach-soft cheek. 'I am not worthy of such a treasure as you, my elfin, but I hope you will come to forgive me and in time come to look upon me as a friend. You may use the little mare for your gallops whenever you wish.'

Polly said nothing, only watched him with wide, startled eyes. At that moment she thought she could never forget or forgive how he had made heartless use of her infatuation of him. But she was young, and time was a great healer.

To Abigail he again bowed. 'I would not truly have hurt you, Miss Carter.'

'I never thought you would for a moment,' said Abigail stoutly, not quite believing it. And, seeing Carl approach, she smiled and lifted her chin. 'Not with Carl right close by.'

'As I always intend to be, Count, so I recommend you make no mistake on that score in the future.' He laid a hand possessively on Abigail's shoulder. 'Touch anything, or anyone, that is mine again and I'll chop you into mincemeat and feed you to the bulls.' Carl issued this threat with a smile upon his face, but Alfonso was in no doubt that he meant what he said. The two men shook hands very solemnly.

'It is time to end the *bellavendetta*, *sì*?'

'My own sentiments exactly,' said Carl. 'But you may have some surprises to come, Count. Don't think Falenza is finished quite yet.'

'We will see,' he said, and then he mounted his horse and rode away, still laughing.

Abigail went at once into Carl's arms. He gathered her hungrily to him as if he would never let her go. His lips nuzzled against her neck. He pressed her tight against him, smoothed back her hair, caressing her, kissing her, taking in every detail of her face, looking deeply into her eyes as if he could not get enough of her. 'I thought I had lost you.'

'And I you,' she whispered.

In that moment Carl Montegne had faced many truths, not least his feelings for this tall, sensible Englishwoman who was companion to his aunt. He knew that if she had died at the Count's hand no amount of fortune, no castle in all of Italy, could have compensated him for her loss. They continued to gaze at each other, drinking in the sheer joy of being together, safe and well, and beginning to consider the heady prospect of the future. Could it possibly lie together? Or were there still obstacles to overcome?

Polly, standing by and looking anywhere but at the two lovers, gave a polite little cough and they both broke away, laughing, two sets of cheeks rosy with the embarrassment of new-found happiness.

'We must see to that head, at once,' Abigail murmured, trying to be sensible.

'It can wait a moment,' he said. And, weighting the figurine once more in his hands, Carl suddenly let it drop. Both girls cried out in alarm as it broke into pieces on the stone cobbles. But while Abigail fell to her knees, quite distraught, searching for words to express this seeming catastrophe, Carl reached down and picked something up.

'I've got it,' he cried. 'I was right.' He was laughing, grabbing Abigail and swirling her around in a mad, careless dance. 'The figurine did hold a key, a real one. So all we have to do is find which lock it fits and our future is secure.'

Abigail made him stop spinning her so that she could

catch her breath. 'How did you know it contained a key? Is that why you broke the other figure?'

'I didn't know it was a key; I just felt sure that one of the figurines held something that would lead us to whatever fortune has been left me.' His gaze encompassed the fortress walls of the *castello*, the tall, shuttered windows, the cobbled courtyard and verandas. 'It is here somehow; all we have to do is find it.'

He lifted the key and held it up high, his gaze going instantly to the high, shuttered windows of the east wing. Abigail did not miss this gesture, nor the expression of love and triumph in his face as he called up to them, 'I have it. See, I told you I would find it. You were wrong to doubt me.' His shout of triumph sent a covey of pigeons flying out in a panic from the rooftops. And Abigail's heart turned as cold as the stone parapets and cornices. She half expected a shutter to open and the figure of a woman in a pearl-grey gown to lean out and smile upon him. But only the pigeons clamoured. Yet who else could he be speaking to but his secret mistress hidden in the east wing of the *castello*?

She had proof at last that he acknowledged her existence.

Slightly subdued, despite the exciting turn in events, Abigail knew that Carl's bleeding wound had to be attended to. She would have it no other way. And when it was bathed and dressed and she had made them all coffee to recover from their ordeal they sat around the big, scrubbed pine table, the large iron key before them, and discussed the matter.

Carl was so excited by his discovery that he did not notice Abigail's loss of vigour. 'If you recall, the legend states the Giovanni gave a figurine to each of his two wives—Elisabetta, and his young princess bride. He told them that one would lead to something of great value, but it would only be found by she who loved him the least.'

'I remember,' said Abigail.

'Well, don't you see? The woman who loved him the least would break her figurine to find out what secret it contained. Only it turned out that they both loved him and so both figurines survived.'

'And to find the answer, or, as it turns out, the key, you had to break each one.'

Carl picked up the key and turned it in his fingers. 'But where will this fellow lead us? Which door will it open?'

'I have searched the *castello* from attics to cellars in these last few days,' said Polly. 'And every door opened. Some were admittedly stiff with age, but none was locked.'

'Besides which, someone may have come upon this fortune by accident,' warned Abigail with a sigh. 'Do not get your hopes too high, Carl.' She cared nothing for his fortune, only for him, and it was very apparent to her now that he belonged to another. No wonder he wanted to come here, to stay in this beautiful place, where he had already installed his mistress. But he could not keep her a secret forever. Some day he must surely reveal her existence. Abigail meant him to do so, very soon.

Carl's excitement at finding the key had begun to fade and now he stared at it, his face grim as his mind went over the possibilities. 'Nevertheless, here it is in my hand, a key, and every key must have a lock. I do not give much credence to Paolo's tale of gold. I'm sure if Elisabetta brought any to the marriage, which is doubtful when she refused to marry the man her family had chosen for her, it would long since have been spent. But this key must open a lock somewhere in this castle. And if it is locked there must be a reason for it. We must simply look more diligently to find it.'

Abigail's thoughts were racing and she wondered how much she should say. Should she pursue the issue now, or wait until he volunteered the information? At last she said, 'Polly, did you go into the east wing?'

'I went everywhere.'

Then if the woman in the pearl-grey gown was in that part of the building she must indeed be well hidden. Could the key open her door? But Carl would know where she lived, and visit her there, perhaps on those days he purported to be searching Florence. The thought sent a shaft of pain piercing Abigail's heart. He might have denied her existence on the photographs, but he had not denied he knew of her, or that she was his mistress. Abigail was not unaware that he had avoided answering that question altogether. However, her room could not be the secret door he sought or he would know of that too. The mystery deepened.

Carl got to his feet. 'We'll not find it sitting here. Let us search.' He held out one hand to Abigail and, without thinking, she half smiled at him and very nearly took it, but the pain was still keen in her heart and, turning from him, she walked away. She could feel his gaze following her, but did not allow herself to look at him, for she knew the hurt that would be in it. He had been waiting for rejection and now she had supplied it.

For most of the day they searched till they were all worn out and almost dropping from exhaustion.

Once more they gathered together in the dining-

room, this time to eat cold meats, salad and bread, but
their hearts were heavy. Polly's because she had
thought the quest was over, Carl's from desperation
and Abigail's from despair and loss.

'Well, I give up,' mourned Polly. 'I know this castle
better than my own hand by now, but I have found
nothing.'

The expression on Carl's face said he was not ready
to give up, not by a long way, and Abigail's heart
squeezed tight as she watched him. How could he be
so certain? And what if he was wrong? There must
surely be a limit to how much of his life he should give
to this dream. She felt her faith lie dead within her, all
hope of sharing a future with him quite gone. And no
longer could she believe in this dream he stubbornly
clung to. She was ashamed of herself, knowing she
should wish him happiness even if it were with someone
else. But she could not, which had nothing to do with
love and a good deal to do with a woman with a grey
gown, for the jealousy cut deep.

'Have we investigated every tower?'

'Yes.'

'Yes.' Abigail, heavy-eyed, laid her head upon her
wrapped arms on the table.

'What about the roof?' Carl persisted.

Polly nodded. 'There are several doors up on the
roof. I have opened every one. Nothing.'

'And the chapel?'

'We were all in there at dawn,' mumbled Abigail
into her sleeve. Her hands were still sore from her fall
on the roof of the chapel. Her limbs ached and her
heart was bruised and throbbing within her. She
wanted only to go to her bed and weep her hopeless

sorrow into her pillow. Tomorrow she would enquire about trains home.

'But have we been back to search it? Polly, have you searched the chapel?'

Polly looked slightly nonplussed. 'What is there to search? It is a very small building. You can see the whole of it at a glance.'

'No, you can't; the pillars are in the way.' Abigail sat up with a jerk. And despite herself, her eyes were suddenly alight. 'I remember now. I found a door, this morning. I'd forgotten in my terror. I tried it, it was locked, and that's when I was forced to go up the stairs to the parapet.'

They stared at each other in shock for a whole half-minute, then Carl tossed aside his chair and was striding on his long legs out of the kitchen and across the courtyard, the girls scurrying after him as fast as they could.

CHAPTER FIFTEEN

No sun got into the chapel so it was cool and rather dark as Carl, Abigail and Polly slipped inside. Each of them knelt for a brief moment, remembering they were in a holy place, before making their way to the back of the little chapel where Abigail had found the locked door.

It was a small solid wood door and very firmly fastened. Taking a deep breath, Carl slipped the key into the lock. It turned. None of them dared speak or even draw breath. He pushed at the door and it opened with a creak to reveal a small room, quite empty.

The disappointment was keen.

'Do you think this room once held treasure?' asked Polly in a breathless whisper.

Carl seemed unable to answer. It was plain to both girls that he had so longed to find something, anything which would help him to keep the *castello* with which he had fallen in love, that he was choked with bitter disappointment. There was nothing in the room — no treasure, no gold, nothing of any value at all. And if his funds ran out before any vines grew to produce an alternative income, what would happen to the *castello*, to his dreams? Hope died in his eyes and Abigail's love went out to him. She tentatively touched his arm with her fingers, wanting him to feel her love for him. Despite their differences, despite the fact he had declared he could enjoy another mistress whenever he chose, she could not disguise her feelings from him.

'We can at least look,' she whispered.

He looked at her with something between defiance and gratitude printed on the strong lines of his face. 'We'll look, then,' he said.

'I'll try the floorboards,' said Polly, dropping on to her hands and knees and starting to knock and probe the solid oak floor.

Carl found a cupboard. It was empty, but he searched it anyway, stirred perhaps by Abigail's encouragement.

'What is this?' Abigail had been prowling about the dark walls and her hands had found something sharp and shiny buried in the stonework. She pulled and tugged at it and suddenly there was a grating sound and the wall opened. Gasping, she stood back in alarm.

The three of them gazed into blackness. 'Of course,' murmured Carl, half to himself. 'This must lead to the family crypt. Families often put their loved ones on to stone slab shelves in an underground room, not in the ground along with all the other peasants. Possibly in the hope of reincarnation. Wait while I find some light.'

He found a torch that was fastened into a sconce on the wall and lit it, and, holding it before them, led the way through the door, the flames flickering and dancing on the stone walls.

The stairs were dry and well worn in the centre from the passage of hundreds of feet. The steps seemed to go straight down into the bowels of the earth and Abigail grasped hold of Carl, nervously clinging to his shoulder, the feel of its strength beneath her hand giving her the courage she needed to go on. Polly's hand was tightly held in hers as she stumbled along behind.

They reached the bottom and, lifting the torch high, Carl looked all about him. They saw the familiar shelves that held very solid-looking coffins filled with long-dead ancestors, and Abigail shuddered. It didn't seem quite right for them to be here, disturbing the eternal peace.

The walls were daubed with cracked and faded paintings of naked nymphs and youths, flowers and trees. The domed ceiling, no more than seven or eight feet above their heads, was equally well decorated and at each corner was set a gargoyle to leer and grin down upon them. There was a dry, dead feel to the place and Abigail longed to be out in the sweet-scented sunshine.

Nothing in the crypt appeard to be of any particular value at all.

Abigail slipped an arm through Carl's. 'Perhaps the treasure, whatever it was, was discovered long since.'

'Or is in one of the coffins.'

She was shocked. 'Oh, surely not.' The thought of opening the casks was more than she could bear. But whatever Carl wanted to do, she must bear it, for his sake. She had the rest of her life to live without him; wasn't that long enough? For today, and tonight, she would do exactly as he wished.

'Oh, goodness,' breathed Polly. 'There it is again.'

'What?'

'The figurine. Mercury, or whatever you call him. There he is again, high up on the wall.'

They all looked where Polly pointed, and sure enough, halfway up the stone wall of the crypt, artfully disguised by several other carvings, was the likeness of the figurine. In two strides Carl had reached it, his great hand closing over it.

What he did, no one quite knew, but a grinding of

old machinery behind them brought them all jumping round. A second door had opened, revealing an inner crypt, and as they slowly entered it they found it to be almost a replica of the first. Except that in the centre it held a huge sarcophagus bearing the effigy of a young man, the relief depicting scenes from classical mythology.

'Can this be the remains of Prince Giovanni?' Abigail breathed, but Carl shook his head.

'No, he never returned from the wars, but his wives may well have had this made for him, in place of a funeral, I dare say.'

'There are pictures here,' murmured Abigail, very quietly, as if afraid to disturb the sacred wonder of the place, and, pulling aside a piece of sacking, began to examine one. 'They are stacked all around the walls. Perhaps they are more of Giovanni's poor efforts.'

Carl came at once to her side. And as he looked, hardly able contain his excitement, his hand closed upon hers in tight excitement, and his breathing quickened. 'My God, these are not amateur pictures.' He stripped off more covers. 'I am no expert, but this must be a Botticelli and could this be a lost da Vinci? It's incredible.' Carl bent down to examine another. 'This one is signed by Giotto di Bondone. He was one of the great painters who led the way to the Renaissance ideal. And here are some terracotta figures very like the ones by Donatello we saw in the museum.'

Abigail was smiling and Polly squealing with delight. 'I think you have found your fortune, Carl. Here it is. Your ancestor Prince Giovanni may not have been much of an artist himself, but was certainly a skilled collector, perhaps one of the earliest collectors of great works of art. There could be any number of important paintings here that no one even knew existed.'

'They were no doubt some of them his friends, since he was a man of culture himself.'

'And took lessons to improve his own modest skills.'

'Exactly.' Carl looked up at Abigail and laughed in open delight. 'What value now your photographs? Does this not convince you that art is the greater beauty?'

The mention of her photographs reminded Abigail of pictures she'd sooner forget. Her smile faded and she could do no more than nod, a bleakness creeping into her heart.

Carl had fixed his torch into a sconce upon the wall and the light from it now radiated about the small room, making the typical Renaissance colours glow with new life, revealing the beauty and intricate detail of each picture.

They were all three of them at once struck dumb by the overwhelming magnificence all around them.

'Now you can restore your *castello*,' Abigail said, and there was a sadness in her voice so that Carl glanced at her, his brows drawing quickly together in a frown.

'Are you not glad for me?'

She let her eyes drink in the beloved beauty of him, memorising each and every detail of his joyful face, for she would have long to remember it and time might make it fade. 'Of course. I am delighted. But now that you have your fortune, and Emilia is so well settled ── ' she hesitated, took a deep shivering breath and then boldly went on ' ─ you have no more need of us.'

His face closed as cold as the stone crypt that surrounded them. 'You intend to return to England?'

'I do.'

Polly let out a gasp of distress. 'You cannot mean it, Abby.'

But Abigail gave a little laugh as if it were all of no account. 'You did not imagine we were to stay here forever, child? This is not our home. We came here to do a job and it is done. There is no more reason for us to stay.'

'None at all?' Carl quietly asked.

Abigail was forced to swallow the huge lump that had gathered in her throat before she could answer. 'N-none at all.'

Even Polly was stunned into silence by this.

Before leaving the crypt they carefully covered the pictures up again. Having them all removed to the light would be a job that required great skill and care. But Carl had found his fortune, not in gold, but in something he prized far more — his beloved art — and for that reason alone he should be a contented man. Abigail was therefore surprised to see that all the excitement and pleasure had quite gone from his face.

'I shall not sell them all,' he said quietly to Emilia as they told and retold their tale that night over dinner. 'Only what is necessary to restore the *castello* and keep us until the vineyard begins to pay its way.'

'Well I never,' Emilia said, as she had uttered a dozen times during the celebration meal. They were enjoying *vitella al forno*, a deliciously tender roast veal, served with *insalata verde*, and to follow were *tartufo*, the delectable truffles. 'How clever of you, Polly. But how was it that you came to discover Mercury in the chapel when no one else had noticed him in all this time?'

Polly flushed bright red. 'Well, I have to be honest with you and admit that I had some help from Ida.'

'*Ida*?'

Polly nodded. 'You know how in Devon you had us all write lists?'

Emilia sighed. 'In preparation for my demise, I remember, but what have my depressing habits to do with Ida, or the figurine?'

'Ida has got so firmly into the habit she started a whole new set here, at the *castello*.'

'Well, bless me.'

'And it was on her lists, you see. I'd searched everywhere I could think of and was quite worn out, so I was having a drink of milk in the kitchen when I saw she had begun a new inventory, of the chapel and the outbuildings. There were pages and pages, so boring. Oh. . . I'm sorry.'

Emilia hid a smile. 'Go on.'

'I just read them for something to do, because I was tired and wanted to sit quietly for a while with my milk and biscuits. And then it occurred to me that it might help me to see if Ida had noticed anything that I hadn't. And of course she had.'

'Ida would,' Emilia agreed. 'Never misses a thing.'

'Well, she'd listed every pillowcase and sheet, every cup and plate, of course, and also all the flower vases and ornaments, pictures and sculptures. It was really very thorough. And in her list of the chapel she listed six silver urns, five coloured statuettes and one plain.' Polly beamed with pride. 'It didn't mean a thing to me at first but when I was in the chapel, with the Count, it came back to me like a shiver of realisation and so I

looked first for the five coloured ones since they were
easier to find. And there it was, the plain little statuette
standing so unobtrusively beside them all these years.
I was so thrilled I must have gasped, for the Count
found it too, probably after I'd run off to find Carl.'
Polly stopped and flushed furiously at this point.

Abigail's cheeks flared with equal embarrassment
but Carl merely poured himself more wine, an enig-
matic smile upon his face.

'Oh, dear, I never quite get it right, do I? But I did
lead you both back to it, didn't I?'

'Yes, of course you did. You were very clever to
spot it,' said Abigail, and everyone hugged and consoled her, for she really had been the one to solve the
entire mystery.

'But I should have known not to trust the Count
from the beginning. You all warned me but I refused
to listen.'

'Part of growing up, dear child,' mourned Emilia.
'Obedience will come soon enough, and how very dull
it is to be always correct. A little rebellion never hurt
anyone.'

'We might have remained in ignorance but for you,
Polly,' said Carl kindly. 'So don't be too hard on
yourself. It is remarkably easy to be taken in by
people.'

He glanced across at Abigail as he said this and her
heart plunged. He was saying that he still did not trust
her. How right she was to decide to leave. She guessed
he was telling her that, despite their obvious attraction
for each other, and though he might have forgiven her
for the lie she had told to protect Polly, and for her
apparent betrayal, he could not abandon his other,

secret mistress, whom she had discovered, seen with her own eyes.

He clearly thought she should love and stay with him despite the other woman's existence. The Italian side of his nature coming out, perhaps, Abigail thought miserably, with more of his father in him than he cared to admit. Abigail was sorry if it denied Carl still further the faith he wanted to find in the unselfishness of true love, but she could not help it. She was eaten up with jealousy and pain, and wanted only to run from him, as far as she could go.

She got to her feet, a deep sadness suddenly overwhelming her. 'It has been a long day and I am tired.' It hurt her deeply to recall that she had had little sleep the night before, and why. She doubted she would know such love ever again, no matter how long she lived. With a quiet goodnight, she left them, aware that Carl reached at once for the wine cask and did not even watch her go.

The pictures were brought out and stacked against the walls of the long gallery. The work took several men, for there were many.

'I'll dust them down for you,' Abigail said as they stood together in the long gallery after the men had gone. 'Then they will at least be free of cobwebs when you get your art experts to view them.'

But Carl was not looking at the paintings; he was staring at Abigail. 'Do you really intend to leave?'

'Yes.' There was no hesitation in her answer.

'Polly is distraught.'

'She will recover. She always recovers.'

'How hard you have grown. Will you recover?'

And now the pause was longer than she'd intended. 'I must.'

She heard his sharp indrawn breath of exasperation. 'Are you going to tell me what I have done?'

Abigail started. 'I don't know what you mean.'

'I think you do. I believe we were friends, Abigail. More than friends. Will you not tell me? Do I not at least deserve that much?'

He sounded deeply wounded and Abigail's heart swelled with love and shame and despair. 'What can I do? You do not believe anything I say. You have your life planned out and I cannot see myself fitting into it.'

'I see.'

'Do you?'

'I will try.' The dark eyes were hooded, keeping his feelings to himself. 'I am not a man to beg, Abigail, but I need you. You know that I need you.'

'Needing is not enough,' she said, chin lifted high. '*I* need more than that.'

'Meaning?'

'I need there to be no more secrets between us.'

He reached for her hands, but she twisted away from him, not wishing him to touch her, for then she would be lost. Again she had rejected him and once again pain flickered momentarily across· his face and his mouth tightened. 'Very well. No secrets. I will ask you one more time. Why do you leave? Say your piece; state your case. I will listen and then let it be done with. We will at least know where we stand.'

Fear burned deep in Abigail's breast. Now was the moment to withdraw from this course of action. Now was the moment to accept him, no matter how many secret mistresses he kept and made love to beside herself. No matter if he did steal away at every free

moment to the long gallery or the east wing to this
elusive beauty he kept so well hidden.

But she knew she could not. Her jealousy would
sour their love and kill it. She had to be the only
woman in his life, for all time. Nothing less would do.

Drawing in a long, shuddering breath, she turned to
face him. And it was in that moment that she saw her.
There she stood, as clear as day, the woman in the
pearl-grey gown. She stood right in the centre of the
long gallery and she was shaking her head. Abigail
stood frozen with shock as if someone had hit her. She
knew instinctively the message the woman was giving
her, though she heard not a sound.

Love is all. Jealousy kills.

Carl looked into her face then his arms closed about
her and he was murmuring against her ear. 'Is she here
now?'

Abigail started, but no words would come. Was he
admitting it at last?

'I too have seen her. Every time I thought of you
with the Count, I saw her. She chided me for my
jealousy, telling me silently, powerfully, that I must
think and believe only in you, that I must not allow
jealousy to spoil my growing love for you. She wanted
me to forget everything but you.'

And now Abigail did speak. She had to. She looked
at him in wonder. 'Growing love?'

Carl held her gently in his arms and smoothed her
pale cheek with one hand. 'She was not in the photographs; she is not here now. She exists on some
separate plane, in our hearts, our minds. She is a spirit,
a ghost from the past, or a part of ourselves, I know
not. And when you banish jealousy from your heart,

she will be gone too, for there will be nowhere left for her to live.'

Abigail found she was trembling. 'I understand that now. But she looks so familiar.'

'She *is* you,' murmured Carl.

Abigail jolted. 'What are you saying? That she is the shadow of my jealousy? What are you trying to tell me, Carl?' Abigail's voice was scarcely above a whisper.

He shook his head. 'I cannot answer all your questions, my dearest one; some things are beyond us. I can say that you have no need to be jealous of anyone. Not your pretty, scatter-brained sister, not a beautiful ghost who haunts this *castello* looking for her lost love, not any living, breathing woman on God's earth. I love and want only *you*, Abigail. It has taken me a long time to discover it, too long, perhaps, but it is true. I need you with me always because I love you. I want you to stay here at Falenza with me as my wife. Do you think we could manage to agree at least on that?'

'Oh, Carl. I have waited so long for you.' And as they kissed, the shimmering figure faded away upon a sweet sigh of satisfaction.

'She has gone,' said Abigail, giving a breathless little laugh. 'I do not understand. How can she be me if she is a ghost? Did you see her that night when we first. . . when I discovered you in the long gallery instead of seeing off the Count's man?'

'I followed the sound of her. I did not understand then what she was trying to tell me. And I did not know that you too could see her until you clearly wished me to recognise her in those photographs.'

'Why did you not say?'

Carl frowned. 'I did not have any answers then, so what was the point of alarming you?'

'I wonder why she chose to haunt us, and if she will come again?'

'She will not come again,' said Carl with certainty in his voice. 'For now I do understand. We have found what she wanted us to find, unselfish, abiding love that will last throughout time.'

Just hearing him say the word left her weak at the knees. He was cradling her in his arms, smoothing kisses over her face that were growing more urgent by the minute. Her breathing quickened.

'You are certain it is not all a dream?'

'Perhaps, perhaps not. Some things in life cannot be fully explained.'

'Like the magic of love?' asked Abigail, reaching up to seek his mouth, and his breathing grew ragged as he pressed her tightly to him with fresh ardour.

'Wicked woman, we must marry soon for I'll not wish to wait.'

Abigail chuckled softly, teasing his curls through her exploring fingers. 'I never said you should wait.' And after one more long, breathless kiss, Abigail made a token protest. 'Oh, but I did say I would dust the pictures.'

'Later,' he growled, nibbling at her earlobe. 'There are more important matters to attend to.' He took her hand and they both ran, laughing, from the room.

So they did not discover just then a faded and dusty portrait of a fifteenth-century woman who bore a remarkable resemblance to Abigail, nor one of a young man very like Carl. But Elisabetta and Giovanni could wait a while longer for that; they had waited four hundred years for this moment, after all.

The other exciting

MASQUERADE
Historical

available this month is:

A MOST EXCEPTIONAL QUEST

Sarah Westleigh

'John Smith' was something of an enigma. Plainly
gently born, he had been fighting in the Peninsular War,
and had apparently lost his memory. While widowed
Mrs Davinia Darling felt sorry for him, she saw no
reason why her family should take Mr Smith to their
bosom! Still less did she see why her own services were
needed to aid Mr Smith in his search for his identity.
That she was discomposed by his effect on her, and
found the undercurrent of laughter in his voice
intriguing, she would not allow to weigh with her – the
sooner he found his memory, the quicker she could
return to her safe mode of life!

MILLS & BOON

Our ever popular historical romance series—Masquerade—will be undergoing a transformation in October 1993. The mask will be removed to reveal...

LEGACY *of* LOVE

An exciting range of 4 historical romances from mediaeval settings to the turn of the 20th century.

Every month will feature 1 much loved Regency romance along with an increasing variety of romance with historical backgrounds such as the French Revolution and the Californian Gold Rush.

All your favourite Masquerade authors and some newcomers have been brought together in 'LEGACY OF LOVE'.

From October 1993, in a new longer length. Price £2.50